ELSEWHERE

ELSEWHERE

by
DORON RABINOVICI

translated by
TESS LEWIS

First published as *Andernorts* by Suhrkamp Verlag Berlin in 2010

Copyright © Suhrkamp Verlag Berlin 2010

First published in Great Britain in 2014 by Haus Publishing Ltd
70 Cadogan Place, London SW1X 9AH
www.hauspublishing.com

A CIP catalogue record for this book is available from the British Library

Print ISBN: 978-1-908323-49-1
Ebook ISBN: 978-1-908323-50-7

Typeset in Garamond by MacGuru Ltd
info@macguru.org.uk

Printed and bound by TJ International Ltd, Padstow, Cornwall

For Schoschana and
David Rabinovici

In memory of
Joseph Ortner
1956–2009

Beside the road there stands a tree, it stands and bows,
Not a single bird remains, they all have flown away,
Two to the east, three to the west, and the rest have all
    flown south,
And left the tree alone, unprotected against the storm.
I tell my mother to let me be,
Because I will turn into a bird, one, two, three,
I will sit in the tree and sing it to sleep,
All winter long, I will console it with lovely melodies.

Itzik Manger 1901 (Czernowitz, Austria-Hungary)
to 1969 (Gedera, Israel)

1

THEY TOOK OFF. He was pressed back into his seat. The plane rose steeply and banked. He looked out through his neighbour's window. Far below, the city surfaced, its flat chalk-white and pitch-black roofs sporting water tanks and solar panels that reflected the sun's glare. A thicket of antennae and power lines, the silhouettes of high-rises, the Diamond Exchange, the scallop-shaped Greek Synagogue, City Hall in Rabin Square, streets lined with trees and Bauhaus buildings, and in the middle of it all, the old city centre complete with minaret and clock-tower, a wedge of history jutting into the sea. Tel Aviv and Jaffa, the beach and then nothing but water; the child he once was craned his neck along with his adult self to peer down at the land his mother and father had pointed out to him back when he was a four-year-old and on his first flight out of Israel.

Homesickness or travel nerves – what was it that had overcome him? He felt light-headed; the boy he had been back then, sitting between his mother and father, still crouched deep inside Ethan Rosen, lecturer at the Vienna Institute for Social Research, and this little Ethanusch, Tushtush, Ethanni, as his mother called him, or Mr Finicky, as his father teased, was watching the stewardesses' pantomime: a ballet in case of emergency. The short skirts, the caps perched on their pinned-up hair, their dark stockings – and little Ethanni, eye-level with the swishing nylon pantyhose, watched the exotic temple dance performed to a woman's velvety monotone. The plane rose.

These days, there was no trace of the high priestesses' ceremony from his childhood, none of the precisely choreographed movements that must have come from some strange world beyond the clouds. Now a short film with security procedures was shown on screens that folded down from the ceiling. Cold, dry air blasted from the ventilation nozzles. He knew that the suntan he had built up over the past few days, more salmon-red than golden-brown, would peel off in layers. He would return looking as pasty as when he had left. His eyes itched. His lips burned. Nothing soothed the sociologist Ethan Rosen's migraine. The pain just grew; his skull felt too tight. He had been up until three in the morning writing an essay in German on 'Transculturality in Hebrew Literature' and then an op-ed piece in Hebrew for an Israeli newspaper, a polemic against any legitimisation of torture. Rosen wrote these newspaper articles in a cold fury. He fired them off like little packets of explosives or batteries of firecrackers: fifteen minutes for a thousand words. He composed his academic studies soberly, but seethed in his commentaries, spicing them with the emotion he denied himself in his research.

Rosen was renowned for being eloquent in German, Hebrew, English and French. More than a few people were impressed that he also understood Italian, Spanish and Arabic. Some of his colleagues murmured that his theses and theories were simply translations of the many concepts he picked up here and there. He was just a peddler of academic ideas who profited from floating between continents and continuities, between regions and religions. But he wasn't motivated by a benevolent interest in the world. His intuitions and inspirations were fed by fear. Ethan mistrusted civilizations and ideologies. He wrote along their fault lines.

It was no coincidence that he had been asked to write an obituary for Dov Zedek. First to ask was Katharina, the old man's forty-year-old girlfriend. Since Dov's death, she had cultivated a passion for him that Ethan had never seen in her while Dov was still alive. Then Fred Sammler, the editor of a Vienna newspaper, had called him in Tel Aviv. Since Ethan had already travelled to Israel for his old friend's funeral, surely he could put together a few words for an appreciation, Sammler thought, a farewell to Dov Zedek for his Austrian readers.

Ethan had declined. He had never wanted to be a funeral orator, and was not going to be one now. He had never even been willing to give a birthday toast. At the cemetery, he had hugged Katharina. Although surrounded by tear-stained faces, he felt nothing and did not shed a tear. In the middle of the cemetery, the group of mourners appeared to shrink under the glare of the midday sun. It seemed to him as if each of those gathered here were shrivelling up. This place bore no resemblance to Christian graveyards designed as shaded sites of contemplation. Here, there was no sense of solace. Unlike at Catholic funerals, there were no flowers or wreaths to offer comfort, no ensembles or musicians to listen to and no imposing family vault waiting to be visited.

The rabbi's chant sounded like a lament. The corpse was not hidden in a casket, but covered with a black cloth.

Beneath it, Dov's body, which had always seemed so powerful, was short and slim. For a moment, Ethan thought someone else was lying there.

He had only spent four days in Israel. He had driven straight from the airport to the funeral in Jerusalem, where Dov had lived for the past two decades: shiva in Dov's apartment. Ethan could not get the many discussions and arguments he'd had with Dov out of his mind. The following morning, he took the opportunity to look up a colleague at the Hebrew University and discuss a possible collaboration. It wasn't until the third day that he headed to Tel Aviv to see his parents. His mother had pulled him aside to talk, but his father intervened. He wanted to take Ethan straight to his favourite bar. As they were leaving, Ethan caught her laser-like gaze, still just as penetrating as it had been in his childhood. Father was scheduled for a thorough examination at the hospital the day after tomorrow.

On the return flight, Ethan wanted to read a dissertation. He was trembling with exhaustion and felt as if he were fading, dissolving with fatigue. Not only his body but his thoughts, too, were losing their consistency. On top of that, he had the impression that everyone could see how he was feeling, that they must see right through him, because he felt transparent. He had worked constantly through the last few days and had had less than three hours sleep the night before. Still, he was ashamed of these thoughts. He knew that everyone around him had to have been up in the middle of the night as well. Who here wasn't bleary-eyed? They were hanging over their seatbelts. Everything was in limbo, up in the air.

The passengers had all arrived at the airport hours before departure. Just two days earlier, there had been an attack in the city centre. He vaguely remembered the bar that had been hit. The emergency squad was filmed as they scraped bits of flesh from the walls and picked body parts up off the floor and put them in plastic bags.

To his left sat a woman in her mid-seventies, her waxen face covered with make-up; a lizard with a crocodile purse, her hair platinum-blonde. On her right hand was a diamond ring, and she had a matching pendant on her necklace. She wore a suit of crimson damask with dull gold buttons, garlands of flowers glowing in the weave of the silk. It reminded Ethan of the patterned Chinese wall hangings in Versailles. She could have been the Sun King, Louis XIV's secret Polish *Yiddishe mame*, the mother of all absolute rulers. When he briefly glanced in her direction, she caught his eye. She nodded to him as if she knew him.

On his right, a fat Orthodox Jew reached down for his bag, and pulled out a velvet case which held his prayer book and straps.

Why did he, of all people, have to sit next to this revenant, Ethan thought, next to this ruminant of the scriptures, who reminded him of a sheep with his sidelocks, his woolly hair, his long beard. These guys don't want to do anything but pray, and he's going to rock back and forth the entire flight. How was Ethan supposed to get any work done? The week before, on the way from Vienna to Tel Aviv, he had also been seated next to a devout Jew, but the rituals hadn't bothered him, quite the contrary. They had each been immersed in their own world. What made this believer different from the other? Then, Ethan had seen the original Jew, and had kept an eye on him, ready to defend him from any disapproving stares, to confront anyone who might look down their nose at his black kaftan and broad-brimmed hat. Now, in the opposite direction, from East to West, Ethan noticed the sickly-sweet fusty odour of the man, who was dressed too warmly, and the smell reminded him of the cemetery, of the rabbi and cantor he had seen at Dov's grave and of the prayers and laments they'd intoned. Now Ethan was the one looking with disapproval at the man praying, watching him bind the greasy straps to his left arm and his forehead and leaf through the book, as he droned on and on and tried to rock back and forth, to seesaw. But there was no room. His body seemed encased in fat and made Ethan think of an enormous caterpillar that did not want to emerge from its chrysalis, did not want to turn into a butterfly until the Messiah appeared.

The left armrest was occupied by the woman, the right by the believer. Rosen sat hunched, a four-year-old between mother and father. The signal sounded, the seat-belt light went off, clasps clicked open and a number of the passengers stood up as if on command. He knew this ritual among his people, as if they were following an unspoken order, a law of their nature, an instinct of eternal restless-ness. His devout neighbour was already asking to be let out, which meant that Rosen and the older woman next to him had to stand up to let him pass. The pious man stood by the curtain that divided business class from the rest of the plane and, holding his compendium in one hand and bracing himself on the side of the cabin with the other, he started to rock back and forth as if he wanted to increase the plane's momentum and reach his destination more quickly. The prayer box on his head added to the sense of wildness; it looked like a horn springing from his forehead, a vestige of earlier eras. Ethan knew the Jewish mystics. He had studied Hasidim in different countries but had never yet met a man who dived into the scriptures with such fervour. He seemed to be shaking this world to get behind its façade.

Ethan grabbed his laptop and turned it on, then opened the dissertation file and started reading – an analysis of representations of immigrants in Austrian film.

The woman to Ethan's left suddenly announced that she knew him – she knew him well. He was little Danni, that's what they used to call him as a boy, and Ethan agreed, since many people had shortened his mother's nickname for him, Ethanni, to Danni, because it sounded better in German. She'd been a close friend of his parents. When he assured her that from the start he'd had the feeling they had met before, she waved him off. 'Spare me, please.' She reached into her purse and took out a medicine dispenser in which the various pills, tablets and capsules for each day were divided into their own compartments. This was her breakfast. She spread out a white silk handkerchief and arranged her medication on it like pieces on a board game. Was she suffering from some medical condition? 'No, several.' She looked around. Not even in a plane, she remarked, could the members of their tribe, those masochistic cosmopolitans, sit still for a moment. Even in the air, they behave like nomads. The men are always restless; maybe it begins with circumcision. It's as if they have a twitch in their legs, a flight reflex that had probably been helpful in the shtetl.

From the row ahead of him, he could hear a Viennese accent. Scraps of conversation penetrated the motors' vibration. Someone was talking about diving in the Red Sea: rays, sharks, moray eels. The other, a pilgrim, talked in falsetto about the Via Dolorosa, the Church of the Holy Sepulchre, Capernaum.

The Orthodox Jew whipped back and forth, bobbed up and down, then started head-banging like he was in a hard rock band, though his bouncing sidelocks looked more like a Rastafarian's dreadlocks. Then he started chanting, like someone wearing headphones who doesn't realise he is singing along to the music. The passengers around him gaped. If two lovers had carried on in the aisle, they could not have attracted more attention. The stewardess asked him not to block the access to business class. He only wanted to finish his prayers, he told her. He held onto the drapery tightly, as if it were the curtain of a Torah Ark, as if he were standing before the Aron Kodesh. He had to pray here.

A second stewardess came up from behind with a trolley. Would he just sit down, Ethan's neighbour called. Why was she butting in, the Orthodox Jew asked. Had she prayed yet today? And what about him, he pointed to Ethan, had he laid on his tefillin yet and fulfilled his obligations? Perhaps he wasn't a Jew?

He definitely was, and no less a Jew than someone who wore black clothes and a Polish fur hat, Ethan Rosen retorted, and he hadn't laid on his prayer boxes this morning, just as he hadn't laid them on yesterday morning, and he wouldn't be laying any on in the next few days either. He wasn't into leather.

Couldn't they give it a rest, the diver asked from the row in front of them, he'd like to drink his beer in peace. His neighbour, the pilgrim, nodded. The devout Jew did not even look at the two of them, but lifted his hand, and both Viennese passengers as well as the stewardesses fell silent. He looked at Ethan as if he'd begun the entire ritual just to provoke him; as if, from the beginning of time, everything had been leading up to saving this Jewish soul. 'What if,' he asked, 'right here, right now, our father Abraham came out of business class and asked you, "Tell me, have you laid on your tefillin yet today?"'

The stewardess behind him said, 'It makes no difference if your father is sitting in business class. You have an economy ticket! So please take your seat.'

A bald man sitting right in front of the partition stood up. They could switch. He didn't feel like sitting there anymore with someone's backside swaying in front of his nose. The rabbi could swing whatever he wanted up there all by himself.

The man sat down next to Ethan. He was an Israeli in his early thirties, in jeans, with a grey jacket over a white T-shirt. A barcode tattoo decorated the nape of his neck below his clean-shaven head. On one wrist he wore a gold bracelet and on the other a stainless steel sports watch with a large face and three smaller dials. He's going to bring the whole plane down if he keeps swaying back and forth like that, he said to Ethan in English. Besides, it looks obscene, as if he wanted to get it on with the entire plane. These people's *geschojkel* had already got on his nerves in Israel: half the country rocks back and forth as if Israel were an asylum, and every obsessive-compulsive believer, every fetishist of tribal rituals carries on likes he's suffering from hospitalism.

Ethan acted as if he couldn't hear and kept his eyes on his computer screen. The stewardess offered refreshments. Water, the elderly woman said, and put the first pill, a small, raspberry-red sphere, into her mouth. Ethan ordered tomato juice. His neighbour wanted a beer and put his glass and bottle right up against the laptop. Was Ethan happy with that computer?

The plane began to shake. The pilot made an announcement requesting that passengers fasten their seatbelts. The woman spilled a bit of water on her damask suit. Two pills rolled and dropped between her legs. The man held on tight to his bottle and glass. Ethan, tomato juice in one hand, snapped his computer shut and put it away.

Was he here on business?

Ethan explained that he was Israeli. His neighbour stretched a little, and peeled off his shoes and socks as if throwing caution to the wind. Well then, he said, they could speak Hebrew. Why hadn't Ethan said so from the beginning? Why had Ethan let him go on like that, twisting his tongue out of shape with English?

Was he going to Vienna for a holiday? No, Ethan answered, he worked in Vienna, at an institute, had done for three years now.

The airplane dropped briefly and some of the passengers exchanged nervous looks. Did he still feel like an Israeli?

'I'm a citizen. Do you want to see my passport? What do you mean "feel like an Israeli"?'

The man smiled and nodded knowingly. 'That's a typical Jewish, a typical Viennese-Jewish question.' He took a swig of beer. 'I'm supposed to move there. To Vienna. My company wants me to.' He was falling prey to that old fear of being a *yored*, an emigrant. As if they were back in the pioneer days.

'I don't want to stay there. Two years at the most,' he said. Ethan swallowed the comment that the road to the Diaspora is paved with Zionist intentions. He took off his jacket, grabbed a sweater from his bag, stood up, and asked the woman to let him out so that he could go to the toilet.

He pushed his way through a cluster of stocky Bukhari Jews talking animatedly in Russian, and squeezed into one of the rows as the stewardess pushed the trolley past him and kept moving forward. An acquaintance he'd met once at an event in Vienna's Jewish community centre greeted him. He'd already spotted the man when they were boarding. At that point, the man had still been wearing a kippah, but now it had disappeared.

There were quite a few people queuing for the toilet. He waited, feeling like he was falling asleep on his feet. A boy pushed passed him and said in Hebrew that he couldn't wait because he was still little.

In the cabinet, Ethan thought his sunburned face looked suddenly pale. In Israel, he always resembled those tourists who baked themselves in the sun until they were burnt to a crisp. He was careful, but his skin was practically allergic. His hair, golden-brown just a few hours ago, now looked dirt-brown in contrast with his pallor. This change could not be due only to the neon light that drained the colour from everything in the small washroom. Was it his imagination? He let the water run over his hands and splashed a bit on his face. He dampened his curls and smoothed them back, away from his forehead. He noticed that this changed his face even more. It looked smaller and his features more severe. On top of everything, he had got his watch wet. He took it off and rubbed it dry with a paper towel.

He didn't want to return to his seat and, after leaving the toilet, was standing in the aisle as a stewardess approached with her trolley. He spotted a free seat and slipped into it. Before he knew it, a tray was put in front of him. He was going to decline it, noticed the woman next to him, and nodded to her. She smiled and said reassuringly in English with a Hebrew accent that he could sit there and eat if he wanted; her neighbour had disappeared at the beginning of the flight. Ethan unwrapped the food. In the seat pocket he found the Vienna newspaper that had asked him to write an article on Dov. He opened it and saw the obituary. Apparently someone else had taken on the task of honouring his friend. The author began with an account of Dov's life in Vienna without any mention of persecution or flight, only of emigration. Dov Zedek was known around the world as a champion of peace and understanding. All those who'd heard Zedek's German speeches, his Jewish jokes and his double-edged Viennese charm could not conceive of him as anything but an opponent of every kind of nationalism. And yet, it must be said that the kibbutz he had co-founded stood on Arab soil. Although Zedek always presented himself as open to dialogue, in his heart of hearts, he lived by his vision of an exclusively Jewish state in the Holy Land. Some voices in Israel had already criticised his campaign for commemoration, in particular the organisation Zedek had founded to bring Jewish adolescents to tour Auschwitz. Perhaps it would be suitable to outline here the heated debate currently raging among Jews. At this point the author of the obituary quoted from an article in a Hebrew newspaper, in which a well-known intellectual lambasted the organised trips of Israeli adolescents to Auschwitz. Birkenau is not a youth camp and the incinerators' chimneys are no place for campfire romanticism. The kids with their constantly ringing mobile phones and iPods should stay away from the crematoria. All they will learn from these trips is that the entire world is enemy territory. A few of them might be interested, some even receptive, but collectively they become an ignorant, biased mob always ready to unite against the other, against Poles, Germans, non-Jews. It would be better to take them a few kilometres west, to the occupied territories, to show them what is happening around them.

Ethan put the paper aside and looked at the woman next to him. In English he asked if he had taken her newspaper.

She shook her head and offered him a copy of *Ha'aretz*. Did he know Hebrew?

Ethan did not want to revisit the question of origin and identity, to have to justify where he had chosen to live yet again on this flight. He said that he didn't know a word of Hebrew and had gone to Israel on vacation, scubadiving in Eilat.

She told him she lived in Vienna, but was originally from Jerusalem. She had moved to Austria years ago, for love. But she'd been separated for a long time now. She worked as a freelance graphic designer, taking commissions from clients all over the world. She created typefaces and logos, redesigned newspapers and also helped launch new websites, but at the moment she was showing her own work in an art gallery. She told him the name – a prominent gallery in the centre of Vienna. As she spoke, her hands drew sketches in the air. Her name was Noa, Noa Levy.

'Johann Rossauer,' he said.

The better they got to know each other, the more fundamental the misunderstanding he'd caused with his lie became, and with each sentence the gap widened between the person he was and the person he was pretending to be. When she explained that she came from a family that had always lived in Israel, residing in Hebron up until the pogrom of 1929, he pretended to be surprised to hear that there were Jews who had never left the country. He played the part of the clueless Austrian perfectly, so his eagerness to know more about her and her background did not come off as flirting, but as a discussion untainted by prejudice. Every glance at her *décolleté* was a contribution to cross-cultural dialogue. Every look deep into her eyes a step towards coming to terms with the past.

A short, stocky man with frizzy chest hair spilling out of his open collar interrupted their conversation. This was his seat. Ethan nodded goodbye. She smiled at him. He didn't dare ask if he could see her again.

To get back to his seat, Ethan had to wake the woman

in the damask suit. He nudged her and asked her to let him in, but, half-asleep and confused, she started and said, 'Absolutely not. There's already someone here.'

'But don't you recognise me? I'm the one who was sitting there. That's my jacket and my laptop.'

'Nonsense.' She turned to the bald Israeli. 'Would you please tell him someone else is sitting here?'

The man hesitated and looked at Ethan closely. Suddenly, Ethan remembered how pale he had looked in the bathroom mirror, that he had combed his hair, now damp and brown, back over his head and put on a turtleneck sweater. He might as well have been in disguise, with new clothes and a different hairstyle.

'Excuse me,' the stewardess interjected, 'Are you Herr Rossauer?'

He wanted to deny it, but thought of Noa. 'Yes.'

'You forgot your watch.'

He glanced towards the rear of the cabin as the bald Israeli said, 'Rossauer. Rossauer? You're right. He's not our neighbour.' And the woman answered, '*Nu*, that's what I say.' The stewardess asked Ethan for his ticket and when he bent forward to fish his documents out of his jacket pocket, his neighbour objected. 'That's not your jacket. It belongs to Danni Löwenthal.'

'You're confusing me with someone else. You did from the start. I'm Ethan Rosen.'

'Don't give me that nonsense. I know who was sitting next to me. Danni Löwenthal. I've known his parents and him since he was a child. Danni Löwenthal.'

He would have liked to shout at the woman in the

damask suit that she was meshugge and that instead of pills for her heart, she should be taking something for her head. He wanted to yell at the Israeli, but suddenly felt worn out. He was dizzy with exhaustion and closed his eyes, afraid he would collapse in the aisle. At the same time he realised that his silence spoke against him, that he had to say something so as not to appear completely suspicious.

He whispered hoarsely, 'Listen. I am Ethan Rosen and that is my seat. Maybe I do look like your Danni Löwenthal and maybe I went by Johann Rossauer just then, but my name was and is Ethan Rosen. Understand? I, Ethan Rosen, work in Vienna. I was in Jerusalem for my friend Dov Zedek's funeral. He died. Do you understand? He is dead.' And as he said these last words, he noticed that, although he had been completely unmoved during the burial, his eyes filled with tears.

'Excuse me, please.' Ethan heard a voice behind him. It was the Orthodox Jew who had got up to sway back and forth. 'I don't know if this man's name is Rosen, Rossauer or Löwenthal, but he did not lay on his tefillin today. And do you know why?' He grinned and looked around triumphantly. 'He's not into leather!'

Suddenly no one had any doubts about who he was, not the woman in damask, not the bald Israeli and not the stewardess either. They remembered him and it seemed as if the three of them had elected the Orthodox Jew as a higher authority, one who would not be deceived by external appearances and who for all time would be able to recognise Ethan among thousands.

2

AFTER LANDING IN VIENNA, Ethan drove to the small apartment the Institute had put at his disposal. He unpacked his bags, turned on his computer and checked his e-mails. Then he listened to his answering machine. His mother, whom he'd seen just the day before in Tel Aviv, asked him to call her back. Her tone of voice reminded him a bit of a police siren. Then Esther Kantor. She invited him to an open house that weekend, a party for no particular reason. Everyone had to come. She talked about the food she was going to serve, hummus with tahini, pita and babaganoush, special hams and fine cheeses, cholent and tsimmes – you name it, we've got it – but also matzoh and matzoh brei in case there's anyone who doesn't have unleavened bread coming out of their ears from Passover. She'll do the cooking. Ray will grill the sausages. Oh, and they won't forget the American steaks.

Ethan could not reach his mother. He called the Institute to let his secretary know he was back and headed out, dissertation, pen and keys in hand, slamming the door behind him. He sat in a café. It took him hours to read it all. Then he looked for the Viennese newspaper that had published the piece on Dov Zedek. He read the obituary again, but this time the article struck him differently than it had in the plane.

Back at home he called Fred Sammler and told him he

wanted to write a response to the article. 'But I did ask you for the obituary first. After all, you knew Dov Zedek very well.'

Ethan was silent. He couldn't stand funeral talks or commemorative speeches. He felt physically ill when he was forced to listen to honorary talks. He didn't send personal letters either. Even the women he'd been in love with had only ever received sociological analyses or op-ed pieces from him.

'I don't want to write an obituary of Dov Zedek, but a response to Klausinger.'

'If you can finish it today, I'll run it the day after tomorrow.'

Ethan sat at his computer. Fifteen minutes of fury; he wrote in the heat of the moment. It is particularly fitting, he typed, for this writer to trot out, in the Führer's native country, an unnamed Israeli's arguments when the fundamental question is one of glossing over a nation's amnesia. Ethan wrote about the imperatives of memory and of tendencies, whether in Budapest or in Tehran, to deny the Shoah. He was writing against weariness, raging against exhaustion. Having read over his piece, he sent it off and sat motionless. Still far too agitated to relax, he wrote an evaluation of the dissertation.

That night, Ethan dreamed he was caught in a crossfire of memory shrapnel. He saw Udi once again, his belly torn open and bleeding, but Udi laughed and suddenly turned into Dov Zedek and roared, 'I'm dying.' He yelled, 'I'm dying, Ethan, I'm dying laughing.' Dov's laughter, his infamous pipe organ, was drowned out by applause, by thousands of salvos of laughter flying in from all sides and exploding.

Ethan spent the next day in the Institute and at the university. He missed his mother's call again. He should just call back already, was the message she had left on the answering machine, it's about Father. The results of the medical exam at the hospital were not good.

Just as Ethan was reaching for the telephone receiver the next morning, Fred Sammler called. The reaction to his article was strong.

'Is it really that bad?'

No, it's good, Fred told him. A real debate had sprung up. Ethan had written his way right into the middle of a fray and seemed to have landed half way between the two sides.

'Klausinger claims that the citation he worked into his article came straight from the horse's mouth.'

'What?'

'Yes. He says the Israeli intellectual he quoted is you.'

Ethan Rosen felt a wave of heat wash over him. It occurred to him that he'd been arguing in Hebrew for a long time against tour groups to Auschwitz. Not denouncing them completely, but issuing clear statements against the idea within longer articles. The memory of a recurring nightmare flickered briefly in his mind. In it, he was convicted of a long forgotten murder, his guilt seemed to stem from another life.

'I can't believe it either. Klausinger said that he didn't write who you were because until now, your name didn't mean anything to him. He didn't know that you lived in Austria too.'

'Where did he find the quote?'

Sammler mentioned an Israeli newspaper that had an English version on the internet. Ethan started stammering and stuttering. Even though it sounded crazy, he thought it might be possible, in fact, he was almost certain that five years earlier he had written something along those lines in that liberal Tel Aviv paper. So Ethan couldn't rule out the possibility that he was, in fact, the intellectual Klausinger had quoted.

Fred Sammler took a deep breath. 'OK, hang on a minute. Just so we're clear. Five years ago you wrote against these youth tour groups, in other words against your friend Dov Zedek's project, got worked up about – how did you put it, "campfire romanticism in the shadow of the ovens", and now you're charging Klausinger with anti-Semitism when he writes the same thing?'

'Anti-Semitism? No. I explicitly did not do that.'

'Right, but by so explicitly *not* doing it, you implied it.'

'What? You think I should have charged him explicitly, so that I would implicitly *not* be doing it?'

'Who cares what I think? I just gather other peoples' opinions. Would you like to comment on the contradictions between your two articles?'

'I actually don't see any contradiction,' Ethan whispered.

So much the better, the editor replied. Ethan should explain his position more clearly in an additional article. In the next few days, he would like to publish the other viewpoint, and then, early next week, Ethan would have another opportunity to state his point of view.

After their conversation, Ethan was overcome with

shame. He fled to the Institute. He bought the newspaper. The tram juddered up to the stop. There was a drunk on board. The voice over the loudspeaker announcing the next stop was distorted. He opened the paper, looked for his article, saw the headline and leader and was appalled. *Tradition of Alpine Ignorance*. He had used each of those words in his response, but not in that combination.

'So, what have you got against your colleague Klausinger?' asked Professor Wilhelm Marker, head of the Institute, philosopher and media theoretician. He greeted Ethan with the question. Ethan answered that he didn't know Klausinger, and Marker grinned, as if impressed by his colleague's brazen lie.

'You don't need to put on an act. You can tell me.' Klausinger had given a lecture at the Institute a few months earlier. He had talked about the cultural geography of Berlin. Didn't Ethan remember? Klausinger had argued with Henri Lefebvre. You know what that's about: no space is innocent.

'I know Lefebvre, but not Klausinger. No space is innocent, but *I* am since I didn't go to the lecture.'

'Yes, of course,' Marker agreed. He understood Ethan's point of view. Klausinger overshot the mark in his article and should have expressed himself on the matter with greater sensitivity. Still, he had to contradict Ethan on one point: Marker could vouch that Klausinger was no anti-Semite.

'But I explicitly made sure I didn't claim he was one.'

Certainly, Marker offered, precisely that formulation

was excellent, because a phrase that doesn't state anything explicitly says it all implicitly, and who, if not Ethan, could impute suspect motives to an Austrian on this highly sensitive topic. He can trade off his identity, he can enjoy the advantages of, how should he say it, being able to play the Jew card, yes, the Jew card.

'But I specifically wrote that I didn't want to question Klausinger's motives.'

Exactly, Marker chuckled. He glanced around and said that Klausinger was one of the applicants for the professorship at the Institute. Of course, he doesn't stand a chance, but still, he's now Ethan's competitor. After these words, Marker patted him on the back and turned away.

Several people mentioned the article to him, so Ethan wasn't surprised when Esther Kantor called to invite him once again to her open house and to assure him that she supported his position against Klausinger and that Israeli he quoted. Ethan had forgotten his mother in all the commotion and was again unable to reach her at home. That evening, he finally dialled her mobile phone number. She answered in a whisper. She was visiting friends. They were doing well. Father was sitting next to her. 'Did you need something?' Ethan asked. She said she would call him the following day.

Ethan read Klausinger's reply in a café the next morning. The headline read 'Two Different Rosens'. Klausinger didn't just reveal who it was he had quoted in his obituary of Dov Zedek. Since he had not been quite certain if the author of the article in Hebrew was the same Ethan Rosen as the sociologist in Vienna, and since he and Ethan Rosen had both applied for the same academic position, Klausinger had deemed it more correct not to name the man who was now his rival, so as not to bring personal matters into the discussion. But now he felt he had no choice but to break his silence. Rosen held a different opinion in one country than he did in the other. Perhaps for him, it's not a question of opinions or views, but a matter of disposing of his competition. In conclusion, Klausinger again cited Ethan, who had warned in the Israeli paper against bringing up the accusation of anti-Semitism too hastily or too often. It would be good for Ethan Rosen, Klausinger wrote, to follow his own advice.

At the Institute, Ethan saw Wilhelm Marker disappear into his office. Later, as he was looking for a book in the library, Ethan felt he was being watched by an assistant and a colleague who were sitting between the shelves. That afternoon, he called Sammler. The general commotion had surprised even the editor. A huge number of comments and letters were pouring in. A professor of German studies pointed out that Klausinger was employing the traditional terminology of Jew hatred. In a whole range of responses, readers argued for the importance of memory and com-memoration, but most reproached Ethan for using the anti-Semitism cudgel against Klausinger, against Austria, against Islamists, against the entire world. One reader asked if Ethan were not simply talking about Austria's history to avoid talking about Palestine's present.

Ethan left the Institute earlier than usual. An early summer rain had set in. People hurried past him, pressed up against the walls and sought shelter in doorways or under arcades. He trudged through the drizzle. In a corner protected by scaffolding, an Eastern European woman sat in a loose, shabby dress, her feet bare and legs swollen. Her mumbling reached Ethan as an incomprehensible whine. The damp had reached her dress and was leaching up through the fabric.

The chair at the Institute was tailor-made for him; the job description was a summary of his qualifications. His appointment had never been in doubt. But now everything seemed to have changed. How on earth had he gambled away his chances with a single article? No one had paid any attention to Klausinger before the controversy. It was Ethan who had drawn attention to him. After all, Klausinger had quoted Ethan without citing his name. So why was Ethan now suspected of having drawn his rival applicant into a trap? Klausinger had mentioned the Institute, he hadn't. Why were all the reproaches aimed at him and not Klausinger?

Before, in the Sixties, as a small boy in this city, he had occasionally been greeted with a peculiar friendliness. Some, who seemed to hold his parents in contempt, respected him because he wasn't a 'ghetto Jew' but a young Sabra, born after the state of Israel was founded, one of those Israelis who refused to put up with anything anymore. But that mood had changed a long time ago. He remembered a radio programme he'd heard a few weeks earlier. A well-known historian had spoken about the extermination. The listeners could call in and speak. One woman had said, 'Professor, what you're describing, what the Nazis did, is horrible, of course. But what the Jews are doing to the Israelites is not acceptable either.' The scholar had corrected her, 'You must mean what the Israelis are doing to the Palestinians?' The woman then answered, 'Oh, whatever they're called over there – I really can't keep track.'

Once home, he sat down at his desk to answer Klausinger. He waited for the tension that always flooded him, and yet, although he was full of rage, hatred even, he could not focus his thoughts. He had to keep starting again.

'Run him over,' his mother had always said during their first years in Vienna, whenever his father would brake for an elderly man at a crosswalk. '*Dros oto*' was her motto, and he, as a boy, had always joined in enthusiastically: '*Dros oto*! Run him over! He's old enough. Look at him. That's the way they used to look at you. Run him over.' And his father, who'd escaped the camps, who'd lost his entire family, just laughed. He would smile at the pedestrian, gesture with the palm of his hand that he was free to cross, and say, 'Next time, darling, next time.'

After fifteen minutes, Ethan deleted everything he had written so far. What he had written in Vienna must sound false in Tel Aviv and vice versa. Nothing seemed to make sense anymore. Klausinger would be proved right in any case. He closed his laptop.

When Esther called to remind him of her open house, he decided to put his work aside. He showered, dressed and went to his car. The engine spluttered three times before catching. At that moment, his mobile phone rang. His mother had finally reached him.

'What can I tell you, Ethan? My kidney, I mean, his kidney, in any case the one he got from me, isn't working any more. Papa is back on dialysis. I'm scared.' She fell silent.

'Why didn't you tell me sooner?'

'The best thing would be to get a new kidney,' she answered.

Esther lived on the other side of the river, not far from the Old Danube, in a development of detached family homes just outside the city. Her daughter, Sandra, opened the door. 'Hey, Ethan.' He hugged the seventeen-year-old, and was peeling off his jacket as Esther came out of the kitchen carrying a full tray of fruit. 'Ethan, how nice you could come,' she said, as if she hadn't just telephoned him thirty minutes before. She passed the fruit plate to Sandra. 'Here, take this in, please.' The kiss she gave Ethan's cheek was as fruity as the peaches and plums on the tray. Her face retained some of that same firm ripeness. The way she beamed at him made him think of lines from a Yiddish folk song, *beckelach wie kleine pomeranzen, fisselech was beten sich zum tanzen* (Cheeks like little pomegranates, tiny feet that beg to dance).

It was the same as ever. The house was full of people drinking red wine out of plastic cups and eating salad and dip from paper plates. He knew most of the guests, who were talking animatedly, telling each other the latest variations of old jokes or whispering about new developments in intimate relationships. In the dining room, he happened on a couple of Israelis sardonically deriding their government. The kitchen was busy with collective cooking: Middle-Eastern salads, babaganoush and hummus. Amos Stein was in a corner, chopping a tomato. 'Hello, Ethan.' Ethan's presence was causing a stir. At the foot of the stairs, two men and a woman were discussing in Hebrew a production at the Vienna Opera. Michael, a psychologist from Haifa who ran a jazz music store and sold insurance policies on the side, greeted Ethan with a smile. He was speaking with a fashion designer whose words flowed as smoothly as her dress, her voice silkier than the outfits she created. In the living room, two women lounged on the sofa, giggling. One glanced around and said to the other, 'Don't worry, he's in the kitchen.'

Mickey Scheffler squatted in front of the bare stone fireplace. His parents had been Jews of the Communist persuasion. He had rebelled against them in their communes and cadres, but since the New Left had begun to look so old, he longed for origins that not even his great-grandparents would have wanted anything to do with. Ethan retreated to the foyer. The historian, Sonia Winkler, called out, 'Hello, how are you? Now we can read you twice – for and against.'

'That Klausnitzer's a Nazi,' announced Peppi Golden, a retired ornamental metalworker who, as a small child, had survived the persecution hidden in a cellar. His non-Jewish mother had given him life twice, him and his twin with whom he had hidden for months in a small bed behind a false wall but for several years now had refused to see. He hated his alcoholic brother, that high-proof waste of space, as he called him, even though they'd escaped extermination together and fought side by side in the Six Day War. They were battling in court over their grandparents' inheritance, over possession of those houses that had once been stolen from the family and only restored to the brothers in recent years. He no longer knew exactly why, but if they were in the same room for more than five minutes, they always started shouting and sometimes came to blows.

'His name is Klausinger.'

'He has no right to write about Dov that way. It's good that you answered him. It was just stupid to call him an anti-Semite.'

'I didn't.'

'I know. Calm down. I agree with you regardless.'

Lydia Frank asked Peppi which of Ethan's articles he agreed with.

'Both,' Michael interrupted. 'I don't see any contradiction. What if the articles are just two sides of the same coin? What if I feel at home in that discrepancy? What if we all come here tonight precisely because we all live in that abyss?'

'Nonsense,' Lydia said. She didn't live in any abyss, but in an apartment in Währing. They couldn't forbid Klausinger to view Dov just as critically as they did themselves.

'He's a Nazi!' Peppi Golden yelled.

'What shit. He didn't deport Dov.'

'He would have!'

Ethan wanted to watch, to listen without joining in. They were talking about him, about things that had been tormenting him for days, and now that others were arguing about him as if he weren't even there, he was no longer upset about the situation he'd got himself into.

'Why is it,' Lydia was asking, 'that when an Israeli expresses a certain opinion he's considered a Leftist, but an Austrian's a Nazi when he says the same thing?'

Sonia picked a few sunflower seeds out of a bowl,

cracking the shells between her teeth as she stole over to Ethan. Would Ethan explain to her why he had gone after someone who had quoted his own article? Had he really not recognised his own words? Could he explain that to her?

Ethan smiled and shrugged. Michael maintained that every word sounds different in Hebrew and in Israel than it does in German and in Austria. Ethan hadn't recognised his own lines because they weren't his anymore. The different context had changed their meaning into the opposite. Besides, he didn't understand at all where the mistrust of their common friend was coming from. Did anyone there believe that Ethan had intentionally lied?

'He's a liar.' A woman's voice came from the dark. Only now did Ethan notice the woman sitting in a wing chair, facing slightly away from the group. Only her calves were visible, tanned and slender. They dangled over the armrest. The timbre of her voice reminded him of someone, but he couldn't remember who until the stranger peeled herself off the chair and he recognised Noa Levy from the aeroplane. He felt a curious delight at seeing her again.

'He lives off changing identities. I'd believe anyone else saying they hadn't recognised their own words. But Ethan? Not Ethan. Culture gaps – that's his profession, his field. He's a specialist in the art of jumping from one context to another. Isn't that what he's always going on about? About – what's the term he uses? – perception. The reciprocal translation of ideas and theses, that's his subject. Everyone says that he always knows what has been said and argued here and there and everywhere. And he's the one who's meant to have lost sight of the big picture? He's a liar.'

The others contradicted her, but so faintly that they seemed actually to agree with her. Lydia claimed she was exaggerating. Ethan wasn't a fraud, at least not intentionally.

Michael took a stand for Ethan. How did Noa come to think she knew Ethan so well? Why is she so sure he's a liar?

'Because he already introduced himself to me with a false name and fake biography. He disowned himself. He wanted to fool me.' She spoke very loudly. Others noticed and started to gather around the little group. Esther and her husband were among them.

'That's not how it was. It was completely different,' Ethan said.

'He said his name was Rossauer. Adolf Rossauer.'

'Oh please, it wasn't really Adolf, it was Johann. Johann Rossauer.'

'So it's true, then,' Michael said.

'Johann Rossauer? You couldn't come up with anything better than that?' Peppi Golden asked.

'Johann Rossauer, an Austrian who wanted me to tell him all about Israel and Judaism.'

They all seemed taken aback, except for Lydia. 'I wouldn't have expected something like that from you,' she smirked.

Noa told Lydia that she might find cons like that amusing, but not for a minute should she imagine that Ethan didn't recognise his own quote. The whole farce about Cohen and context, yidden and identity is ridiculous. It was malice, pure and simple, to brand Klausinger as an anti-Semite.

'Show me exactly where I did that. And why? I don't even know him.'

'Exactly. You don't even know him. You don't even need to know this Klausinger to go after him, because you think you already know all the Klausingers. I sat next to Ethan when he read the article in the plane, while he was pretending to be one of these Klausingers or Rossauers. He let me go on and on about Israel, as if he had no idea. It was clear to me then that he already knew more than he wanted to about both sides. His 'understanding' of any given other side is, in fact, nothing but contempt.'

Ethan didn't answer. The others were silent until Michael finally said, 'You know, you should have just written Dov's obituary.'

Ethan turned and went into the library. He was hungry and thirsty, but didn't want to join everyone in the kitchen or at the buffet. He sidled along the shelves. He was alone and thinking of Dov, and growing more and more concerned about his father.

When Noa came into the library, neither spoke. She came up to him, her arms behind her back, and stood before him. He was in the corner and did not try to slip past her. They stared at each other fixedly until he whispered, 'Dov Zedek is dead. What do you want from me now?'

'Just be Johann for me,' she answered. 'What if we're Noa and Johann again? Leave the dead in peace. From now on, just be Johann.'

He paused and smiled faintly. 'Who else would I be?'

'Good. I brought you an Israeli specialty. You must be hungry. Burekas. That's what we eat in Israel, Johann. From street vendors. Try one.'

Before he could object, she stuffed his mouth with a small, filled pocket of dough. 'That one is cheese, this one's potato, and this one eggplant. They should be eaten warm.' And she kissed him.

They left the party together, a bottle of wine under his jacket. He drove her home and as Noa unlocked her front door, she asked with a grin, 'Do you know how to yodel, Johann Rossauer?'

'A point of honour.' But when he tried to start crowing, he could only snicker and she burst into laughter along with him. He didn't know why, but he couldn't get a hold of himself. He was being swept along with her and she with him, plunging from a great height, and he let himself fall. Head over heels, he suddenly realised what was rushing up towards him from below, what lay far beneath him and deep within. He saw himself with Dov and then at the cemetery. Then, as if on a bungie cord, he threw himself into the depths as the cord stretched, tightened and pulled him back upwards, up to the apex of the arc, and he sank once more, rose again and fell. He was just a yo-yo, rising and falling. Everything welled up again inside him and his eyes filled with tears.

And so he told Noa, over the next few hours, about Dov and the funeral, and about his father and his father's kidney disease. And she admitted that she had recognised him right away, even on the plane. He hadn't fooled her, since she'd heard one of his lectures a few months earlier. They listened to each other and afterwards fell asleep until she kissed him awake the next morning, at which point some things fell into place.

3

I DON'T NEED ANYONE to say Kaddish for me. You hear, Ethan? Katharina's still sleeping. I'm in my study. I'm tired and I can't sleep. Outside I can hear the first buses driving through Jerusalem. I've got my tape recorder in front of me, the one you always found so amusing, for some reason. Listen to me, Ethan.

I don't need anyone to say Kaddish for me, no prayers or eulogies on my account. They'll write obituaries and mount a plaque or maybe name some bus-stop shelter after me. Everywhere we look, we're told who paid for this park bench or for that seat in the cinema or for some flowerbed somewhere. Pretty soon every single pissoir in Jerusalem will honor some Moische Pischer from New York. Urinals against forgetting. Public conveniences of commemoration. Powder rooms to prevent silence.

But still: you were out of line with your article five years ago, the one against school trips to Auschwitz. I was there. Thousands of teenagers, not just from Israel, but from all over Europe, from the United Shtetls of America, religious, leftist, rightist, apolitical ... And at the centre of it all, the survivors. Some turn pale every year when they enter the gate. Some come alive as soon as they find themselves back there with other survivors. When I visit them in Tel Aviv, Los Angeles or Buenos Aires, they seem lost, afraid they might wake up one day back in the barracks; but the minute they're back in the camps, they look like they've been liberated, like they've come home.

Some wander around, going over the same old story, cling-
ing to the familiar sentences. They hold on tight. They were
branded and have themselves become the chronicles, like living
versions of those audio-guides you get in museums. Type in the
numbers on the sign and you get the story. They were written
off, and now they're superfluous. They show their number …
their tattoo always ready to hand.

And the kids are all around them. Are you listening, Ethan?
Everything revolves around the survivors. They stagger from
one station of the Cross to the next. They circle around their
sorrow. Those of us who are still here put on a show. Toys for
adolescents – each of us is a skip-jack and all together, we're
just a carousel.

You wrote about a 'Disneyland of extermination' in your
article, and asked if teenagers could deal with these experi-
ences, if they wouldn't just confuse history with a horror film.
I remember your words. As boys we went to the Prater amuse-
ment park. Step right up, Ladies and Gentlemen! Take a
seat in the ghost train! Back then we still paid money to be
frightened. These girls and boys who come to the camps in
groups are the same age we were then. They stand in forma-
tion. They raise their flags. History as a scavenger hunt. The
extermination camp as vacation resort. What can I tell you?
On one of these visits some kid was running around wearing
earphones, listening to music as he made his way through the
barracks. 'Turn it off right now!' another of them yelled, barely
older than the first. 'Put that thing away! Otherwise you can't
come with us into the gas chamber.' It sounded like they were
talking about a Javanese temple complex, some sacred place,
some inner sanctum. Then the first one said, 'You're going to

stop me going into the gas chamber, you Nazi?' Those were his words. 'You're going to stop me, you Nazi?'

Are you listening, Ethan? They were still just kids, standing before mounds of suitcases and piles of eyeglasses. And they brought their ringtones into the crematorium, the latest hits, part of a movie soundtrack or a TV show theme song. Once, right in the middle of a moment of silence, all of a sudden Wagner's 'Ride of the Valkyries' rang out, the first syncopation soft, the next louder, and then some poor schlemiel ran to his backpack and emptied all the pockets, sending the contents flying, trying to find his mobile phone as the ringtone stormed on in full gallop, and when he'd finally got hold of the thing, Gerhilde and Helmwige's Hojotoho resounded through that bleak room.

You were wrong with your criticism. I'm sitting here. Do you hear me? I'm sitting here and talking to you from Jerusalem. I've known you since you were a child. I visited your family in Vienna, with Malka, my girlfriend at the time, the gym teacher – do you remember? Your father, as usual, was elsewhere, on a business trip. Your mother insisted we take their bed. She moved to the sofa. Early in the morning, I felt something crawling up my leg, something creeping up along my body, then the covers were thrown back and you – you were four then – suddenly appeared. 'Are you my Papa?' And I told you no, but you snuggled up to me anyway.

I'm not going to pretend your article didn't hurt. But I wasn't angry when I read it, over and over again. In fact, I was proud of the boy who had lain on my stomach back then.

Years later, your family moved to Paris, London and New York. But no matter where you were, you were the Israeli; only *in Israel were you Viennese, a* Yekke, *French or American. Even as a seven year old, you were as comfortable speaking in Hebrew as you were in German. You didn't have the slightest accent, and that's exactly why you never felt like a native anywhere, and you still don't. No matter where you are, you're always a little detached.*

I remember one time when your parents dressed you up as a little forester, in lederhosen. I can still hear the undertone in your voice when you told us that in Austria, kids your age still believed in Santa Claus. They didn't recognise the kindergarten teacher behind the fake beard. 'Are they blind?' you asked. A few summers later, I saw you in Tel Aviv. You were watching the kids next door, and you said – again, not without a touch of mockery – 'They think that in Vienna I'm persecuted for being a Jew.'

You're a mishmash from Tel Aviv and a mélange from Vienna, Ethan. I visited you again when you were a student. Your parents told me how you'd announced in high school that you didn't want to learn Latin. No one needs it in Israel. The teacher advised you that it's useful to study a classical language and you apparently told him, 'Unlike you, Sir, I can speak Hebrew, which is older and more classical than all your Roman antiquity.' Do you remember?

Don't you remember? At some point you read about that rumour that Hitler had survived. For an entire year, you ran around the city, trying to ferret out the Führer. 'Dov,' you once asked me, 'if Hitler isn't dead, could he be living on our street?' Remember? You suspected a certain man. You wrote him letters. Your mother was terrified when she found some of your drafts and read what you'd written to this high ministry official. You threatened to expose his past. You blackmailed him. 'And if he sues us?' your mother asked. She wanted to go and apologise the next day, but the morning papers reported that he had stepped down unexpectedly, for health reasons. He's a reverse chameleon, your father always said about you, he never fits into any environment, but always stands a little bit apart.

And what will happen when we're gone? When they come from Dresden, Tehran and Tennessee, from Vienna or Vilnius and not one of us will rise from the dead, no one will bear witness to what we went through. No, for me it's not about my own death. I don't need anyone to say Kaddish for me.

Ethan turned off the tape recorder. Somewhere a dog barked. The light of a cloudy afternoon shone dimly into the room. The tape recorder's tiny lights glowed like small red, blue and green jewels. He and Noa sat on large, mud-coloured beanbag chairs, next to a table with a teapot on a warmer lit with candles.

She said, 'He recorded the sections separately and recorded over others. You can hear the click when he turned it back on.' Noa was curled up on her beanbag, her chin on her knees and her arms hugging her shins.

'He always had this ancient tape recorder with him. He even brought it to conferences. He'd bring the thing out and keep pushing the buttons until no one could follow the speaker any more. Even he was too busy trying to record everything so that he could listen to it afterwards, to follow what the speaker was saying. But he never played the tapes back later. They just gathered dust on his shelves.

And the truth is, he didn't need to. He knew perfectly well who said what. He even knew what everyone was going to say, before they said it. He could tell you what you were planning on saying in the next minute. And the worst part is, he was never wrong. He'd take me to task, saying something like, "As for the question you're about to ask me," and then would go on about some topic that caught my interest the minute he started talking about it – "Take it from me, Ethan." That's how it was. On the other hand, he never taped his own lectures. He never recorded himself on any subject. He gave a speech titled, "Never Forget!" and threw it out as soon as the last word faded away. He demanded that memory be preserved, but covered all his tracks. So why did he make these recordings? Why did he suddenly break with his habits?' Ethan opened the cassette compartment. 'Besides, there's no date on the label. He never gives the day or the month. I hear his voice as if he were standing next to me. Just this week, I shovelled dirt onto him and now … Greetings from the crypt. And why the talk about Kaddish and my article from years ago?' The barking dog began to howl.

'His voice sounds so intimate, so close. One of those old guys – in Tel Aviv or Netanya,' said Noa.

'Jerusalem,' he said.

'Jerusalem, then. There aren't many of them left.'

'There was no one like Dov,' Ethan said, 'no one.'

Noa told him she'd been thinking about that country. She was thinking about going back.

Ethan didn't look at her. From the very beginning, he'd suspected that everything that had happened over the last few days was too good to be true. She never would have noticed someone like him back when she'd been in Israel. He told her, 'I wouldn't have stood a chance in Israel.'

'No, not you, but Johann Rossauer would.' She drew her foot along his shin and he felt as if she had struck a chord deep within him and the two of them were in tune.

Later, his doubts returned. It wasn't that he didn't trust her, but he worried she might be mistaken about him. The more he was attracted to her, the more his self-confidence wavered. He didn't understand the first thing about her work or her profession. Her drawings amazed him. She'd designed a wall covering for a high-rise that was going to be built in Barcelona. A Berlin newspaper was planning a relaunch and had commissioned Noa to design a new typeface. What did that have to do with him, with his lectures and seminars or his research? Or with the papers he corrected, the exams he set, the references he had to write? Nothing. Or all the departmental intrigues and committee meetings in the universities? Her life seemed so unencumbered and free in comparison.

One day she asked if he wanted to come with her to a bar where she would be DJing at midnight. Years earlier, she'd had a regular gig as DJ Bat Schlemiel. These days, she DJed only rarely, when friends of hers in the music scene asked her. Ethan was surprised by her dexterity. She mixed retro-pop, deep soul, funk and fusion, but threw in some electric oriental and Balkan rhythms as well. She didn't just play singles one after the other, she ruled the turntable, turned one record back then let a second one loose, spun the first, then the second again until a new rhythm was set, letting each number flow seamlessly into the next. Ethan watched her dance all the while as if what she was doing were the easiest thing in the world, and again, he felt close to her and distant at the same time because he had no idea what this woman, who seemed to have come from another universe, saw in him.

When he saw her move to the beat, he believed he understood how she had let herself be charmed by her ex-husband back then. She and a man from the Tirol had joined in a pact to rebel against the curse of family lineage and against the past and to escape the confines of the countries they'd been born in.

But Vienna and Austria were not exactly epitomes of openness to the wider world. Their attempt to lighten the burden of history and heritage here in Vienna of all places was doomed to failure from the start. What was she seeking now in him? He had a suspicion that she wasn't so much in love with him as with their shared identity. That's all he could think about when she said of Dov, even though she knew nothing of Ethan's dead friend besides his recorded voice, that she recognised in him all the other old Jews from Tel Aviv up to Netanya and over to Jerusalem. It was the longing for a homeland that drew her to him and that made him wary. In Israel, he would be just one among many, but here he suddenly mutated into a Sabra, a soldier in a Zionist outpost. This woman only liked him because of his birthplace. Was she really in love with him? Or was she just putting up with him because in this country of alpine cowherds he was one of the few representatives of the Chosen People, and on top of that an Israeli citizen?

When you truly love someone, it's not a matter of choice, you simply know for certain. He, however, was merely the negation of her earlier marriage. She wanted to return and he was a ticket to her own personal 'Old New Land'. She dreamt of family, of her old family and of a new one. In short: nothing but childishness. And was he at all suitable, he who could barely stand family ties, to be the head of an eastern tribe, a clan, a *khamulla*? When she now spoke of going home, she meant going native with him. That's how people talk when they long for a sense of home, an idea of home much cosier than it ever was in reality and much more harmonious than they could ever stand. But maybe he just couldn't imagine being the one, not for someone like her. He didn't dare believe his good fortune. He couldn't remember ever having felt this way before. When they were together, he never had to explain anything. Her voice soothed him. Everything about her was outrageous and familiar at the same time: her comments, her intonation, her sense of humour.

He was convinced that he just had to see her knee, her ankles, her thumbs, and he could pick her out of a crowd of thousands. She smelt of resin. Even when he wasn't touching her, he knew how she felt, her skin's silky tautness. With his eyes shut, by touch alone, he would know her hand from all the rest.

They called each other at exactly the same time. He answered before the phone even rang. When he wanted to text her, an alert would already be sounding from his phone. He was afraid she would leave him, and just as afraid that he wouldn't measure up in her eyes. When she was gone there was a void and when she came into the room it was almost more than he could stand. He said, 'It's better if we don't see too much of each other or you'll get tired of me.' She didn't push him. She didn't take his anxieties as an insult or a rejection. On the contrary, she found his shyness touching. She wasn't surprised that he didn't want to talk about her 'Old New Land' dream, and only asked her, 'There must be a stamp on the envelope Dov sent the recording in. When was it mailed?'

Noa said, 'Don't you know Israeli mail, Johannes Rossauer? You can die of old age before a letter is delivered.'

Everything about that country kills you, he replied. He had no idea what was drawing her back there.

She'd come to Austria because of her ex-husband. Now she no longer had a reason to stay. Was he always going to play the Wandering Jew, the mongrel of social sciences, the specialist of hybrid life forms?

He searched for the envelope. 'The letter was sent after the burial. It's as if Dov were still alive.'

She looked at him. 'You're not a ten-year-old anymore. Hitler is dead and so is Dov.'

I don't need anyone to say Kaddish for me. I've been one of the undead for a long time. Some days I look at myself in the mirror, Ethan, and I see how decrepit I am. It's like looking at the face of a corpse – the pallor of my skin scares me, I can smell the stink of decay that comes from my mouth and it reminds me: there's poison brewing inside. Trust me, Ethan, my heart is so full of this poison, just a taste would kill you. You hear me? My expiration date is long past. I'm a remnant

– I've survived my parents, my brother and sister along with my brother-in-law, my nephews and nieces, aunts and uncles, as well as the murderers and their crimes, and what's more, I've even outlived myself.

Before I couldn't feel what was eating away at me from the inside. I didn't consider myself a victim or an exile. I conquered a world. I helped found a state, helped build a new society. Adolf Gerechter didn't exist anymore – I, Dov Zedek, had overcome and extinguished him. I murdered him.

It was my last day in Vienna. I wandered into a men's clothier in the inner city. 'I'm going on a long trip. I'd like a completely new wardrobe. Please show me what you have to offer. Up-to-date, but dignified. Five shirts, three ties, two suits, a hat, and an overcoat.' Yes, I told them, 'I'm going on a long journey.' The manager himself took care of me. 'But of course, sir! My pleasure!' I let him show me everything. I tried to be discerning. I held the trousers out at arm's length. I draped the jacket over my shoulders and looked in the mirror. I wanted to see the overcoat in natural light and was almost halfway out the door when I saw a neighbour passing, a Nazi of the first vintage. I quickly turned around, disappeared into the dressing room, pulled the curtain closed behind me, and took a deep breath. In the shop, all was still.

So I kept trying on clothes, one thing after another. The trick is not to let anything show, you understand. I sent back whatever didn't fit. Whatever I liked, I asked them to take up to the counter. Finally, I finished. I went up to the cash register. A sales assistant wrapped everything in blue tissue paper. I pulled out my wallet and asked, as if in passing, 'Just one last question. You do only serve Aryans here?' The owner smiled and *gestured gracefully at the shelves and the sign reading* We do not sell to Jews! *'Not to worry. This is a purely German store.'*

I put the money back in my wallet. 'Well in that case ... There's nothing to be done,' I said, leaving the owner dumbstruck. You should have seen it. His smile melted and I left without deigning to give him a second glance. I was the one who left – and not out of fear but defiance. You understand?

I took off the next day. An illegal journey. To Palestine without a visa. The British had blocked all Jewish immigrants for some time by then. At home, I said goodbye to my parents and no one said a word about seeing each other again. There was a Jewish roll call at the train station, right in front of soldiers and civilians, the Gestapo, too; strapping young Jews standing to attention. You should have seen the looks we got. In the middle of Nazi Vienna, our commands were in Hebrew. The short leader's brief speech. About how on this journey we were not fleeing, but returning home. Then there was silence and suddenly a girl started singing the anthem, the Hatikva, *in a thin but pretty voice; the song of eternal longing for Zion, of hope for our own state, and, surrounded by SS soldiers in full uniform and civilian policemen, others joined in and the melody spread until the chorus echoed through the hall.*

We ran right into the trap. The ship, paid to smuggle us across the sea, did not make port. We waited. For weeks. Our papers became invalid and we knew the murderers were getting closer. I decided to act, to trade for my own account. I set out. Under a false name.

Then came the rumour of my death. It reached Vienna, which means my father, the former editor-in-chief Heinrich Gerechter, wandered like a ghost through the streets of the city with torn garments and a blank stare. He was looking for me, his son. He asked everyone he met if they'd seen me. My mother, too – previously she'd invited artists, writers and intellectuals to our home for concerts, readings or discussions, but from then on she refused to leave the room in which my parents lived, crowded together with my siblings, and she never spoke to anyone again.

My brother, my sister – the whole family spent those days searching for Adolf Gerechter. But I'd long since changed my name. They say my father was picked up in the November Pogrom, a confused elderly man. In the midst of all the murder, he asked everyone about his son. He was beaten down and hauled in and then sent to Dachau. Even in the train, he mentioned my name. Asked if anyone knew what had happened to me.

Who, tell me, who will ever weep for me more desperately than my father? No, Ethan, I don't need anyone to say Kaddish for me.

He had just collapsed. In the end, it wasn't clear what had happened. Ethan's mother said, 'Maybe it wasn't my, I mean, his kidney, at least not the one he got from me.'

'So what does he need then?'

She simply sighed, and then said: 'I don't know what I'm supposed to think of these doctors.' She explained that Felix had been in hospital since yesterday. His body was bursting, his circulation running riot and his breathing was light and shallow as if he had run a long distance race, not just lain in bed. 'When he stands up, he gets dizzy. If he wants to go to the toilet, he needs my help.'

'Why are you dragging him to the toilet? They should just stick a pot under his behind.'

'Stick a pot under your own. Your *tuches* is far away. What do you know? You sit there, all cosy, and bellow at your mother.'

'Please, I'm being quiet.'

'Do you think I'm running an obstacle race through intensive care with him? What planet are you on? Abba is writhing in pain. He says it's breaking his back in two.'

Felix Rosen was known for not letting anything get him down. He had survived hunger and the camps, and even in the middle of dialysis had remained so polite and calm that many of the nurses had raved about the good-humoured, older gentleman. He submitted gratefully to every procedure and treatment. His old friends still talked about how Ethan's father kept fighting in the War of Liberation even after he was wounded, and how he'd comforted the less seriously injured soldier next to him and bandaged up his own leg after it was riddled with shrapnel. Felix Rosen held their position until both could be relieved and taken to the military hospital. Felix's son should be proud. A hero, a warrior, and now he was whimpering as if he were in labour.

Ethan's mother said, 'You can't help with anything here. It's better if you don't come for now. Abba would think he was at death's door. A phone call is enough.'

After he hung up, Noa asked how his father was doing and as she pulled the covers up and snuggled against him, he told her about the pain and the elevated blood pressure. As she pressed herself more closely, he elaborated the patient's story with a few lurid details.

He absolutely had to go to Tel Aviv, she decided. Immediately. There was no time to lose.

His mother had advised him not to, he explained to Noa, so as not to upset his father.

'Nonsense. So she advised against. It's still your decision. Nothing is more important than standing by your parents in these situations. You have to go. I'll come with you.'

He drew back. 'Are you planning our return to the homeland? What is it you have in mind? I've applied for a position here. I can't possibly leave.'

I don't need anyone to say Kaddish for me. You hear me, Ethan? Not only because my father already wept for me. And not even because I don't have a single family member left who could bury me.

In the last few years, I've already been mourned endlessly. I was invited here and there to play the survivor. I performed in my role as contemporary witness. I'm the last of the Mohicans. They look at me like the last remaining specimen of an extinct species. Whispering spreads around me, because something like me shouldn't exist. Then comes the request that I say a few sentences, and each of my words sounds like my last, like a farewell, yes, like a message from the netherworld. I can't resist these presentations, rituals and class trips. I talk and children turn into adults, adults into children. I tell stories. Once upon a time, there lived many Jews, and when they didn't die, they were murdered.

I talk about the feeling of shame that overcomes me. I give my account. I rush from one event to the next as if my life

depended on it. What the murderers didn't accomplish with
their hatred, their children and their children's children do
with their benevolence. It's a curse. I'm on the run again, the
dead at my heels. I'm damned to play the Eternal Jew.

Back in the Seventies, I travelled to Segovia with some
friends. One afternoon, we went strolling through the old city.
We asked the locals if anyone there knew anything about the
Jews who lived in these very streets half a century ago. One girl
called for her abuela until a wrinkled figure hobbled down
the stairs, and this figure said, 'I never saw any myself. It's
easy to spot Jews with their clubfeet and tails.' We let her talk.
And to the others' delight, I shouted in her ear, 'In that case, I,
fortunately, can't possibly be one of those Jews.' At that point,
she looked closely at my feet and backside and finally shook her
head emphatically.

I, Dov Zedek, the Israeli, couldn't care less about the bab-
blings of some granny in Spain. Grandfather and Grandmother Gerechter would surely have nervously checked to
make sure they hadn't grown any clubfeet. We laughed when
we heard we had long appendages on our asses. 'No, Madam,
not back there,' we joked.

But for some time now, I've felt that something is cling-
ing to me. Some people come into this world with gills, others
with the remains of a tail, an extended coccyx. The traces of
something that seemed to have been overcome are resurfacing
in me, too. The adolescent I once was looks at me from the
mirror as a corpse every morning. I can feel how he suddenly
takes possession of me. I can see how, in the eyes of others, I'm
no longer Dov Zedek, pioneer and warrior, but a refugee. I'm
not the hero but the victim; and gradually Adolf Gerechter, the

strapping young Jew from Vienna, resurfaces from deep within me. After spending decades in the desert under date palms, as a kibbutznik *and in Israeli politics, he's worming his way in, the displaced person I never wanted to be – and he's taking over.*

I put myself on display before the children of those who once wanted me dead. They look at my feet and my ass – and you know what? – they see the clubfoot, and they spot the tail and the devil's horns on my head. They point, but unlike their forefathers, they're not disgusted and they don't incite against me. Instead, they murmur respectfully. They call out for Adolf Gerechter, not for murder. They bow low before me as if they wanted to kiss the clump at the end of my leg.

These spawn of the Christian faith revere me as a martyr. In their eyes, I'm not cursed to be an Ahasver and a travelling salesman of memory, but a wonder. They celebrate my transformation as the central ritual of a mass. My suffering is not a disgrace, but a Passion. I wish I could escape them. But Adolf Gerechter cannot refuse when he is asked to commemorate. He's the one who makes me attend every play, every reading, every film on this topic. He's the one who's got me running from one classroom to the next and accompanying children to Auschwitz. He is stronger than I am, stronger than Dov Zedek. If I could, I'd make Adolf Gerechter disappear again, before there's no trace of Dov Zedek left. Murdering myself to save myself, that would be the solution.

Listen to me, Ethan: sometimes I resolve to pretend to die, so that I can enjoy my final years under a third name on some foreign continent. I dream of letting Dov Zedek and Adolf Gerechter drown while swimming, or throwing them overboard on some cruise. I would disappear and resurface elsewhere. Understand? Just to survive. A silent farewell with no funeral. There's no need for a grave or a eulogy, not for my sake. I don't need anyone to say Kaddish for me.

'It'll all die out,' said Wilhelm Marker. The head of the Institute had asked Ethan to see him in his office. It had nothing to do with Ethan's qualifications. No one doubted his competence, but a few objections had suddenly been voiced. Since that editorial appeared there'd been discussion about his requirements – his expected salary, which was markedly higher than the average salaries paid by the Institute. It was no use pointing out what everyone already knew, that he could earn even more at other universities. The consensus had shifted. All of a sudden, the general opinion was that the professorship in Tel Aviv was not very compatible with a position here in Vienna.

'But I only give one independent seminar there.'

'The objections are ridiculous. The attacks aren't really meant personally. Ultimately it's about my position as director of the Institute.' Marker leant forward. 'Make peace with Klausinger, Ethan! Put an end to all this! You understand? Otherwise we'll never get rid of him. Publish an open letter. Explain that you had, in fact, recognised your quotation, but wanted to force him to identify you by name. Everyone will understand.' He whispered, 'You've got to embrace someone like this, take him gently by the neck, then squeeze hard. You've got to break his back. That's true scholarship. That's deconstruction.'

Marker told Ethan he had also invited Klausinger to the

meeting, and before he had finished his sentence, there was a knock on the door and the acting Chair, Professor Karin Furner, walked in. A man followed her, casually dressed in a light jacket and square rimless glasses. He seemed pleasant, unostentatious, just as Ethan had imagined him from others' accounts. Karin Furner said, 'May introduce you: Ethan Rosen – Rudi Klausinger.'

The two men nodded and Wilhelm Marker remarked how agreeable it would be if the accusations on both sides could be put to rest. Would both of them please sit. To which Klausinger objected that he hadn't accused anyone of anti-Semitism.

Ethan said that he, too, had explicitly not said anything about it. He had simply come to the defense of a dead friend.

Well, he himself had already been accused of resentment, even though all he'd done was quote Ethan Rosen's own words, Klausinger explained.

Wilhelm Marker tapped his fountain pen on the table. Was Klausinger not aware that the exact same sentences can have a completely different effect when spoken by someone else, he demanded. Had he never heard of context? Especially with such a delicate topic.

Nevertheless, Karin Furner said, Klausinger had taught in Jerusalem and Beer Sheva. If his article lacked distance, it was only because he was familiar with the debates in Israel. Klausinger, she felt it necessary to point out, was a phenomenon.

'Yes, well,' Klausinger said.

It's true, Karin Furner insisted, she had heard him speak

at international conferences, in London, in Paris, in Rome. Everywhere he went, he had immersed himself in that city's particular way of life, and he'd not only spoken each language without any accent, but immediately adopted the local inflections. Even his outward appearance had taken on some of the host country's characteristics. He was a quick-change artist. As far as the related prejudices were concerned, Klausinger was, after all, a specialist in Jewish studies; he had studied Modern Hebrew, understood the Ladino of the Sephardim and spoke Yiddish better than all but a few. He had written important papers on modern works in the language. It was entirely conceivable that Klausinger had studied Judaism in greater depth than Rosen had.

'And?' Ethan asked. That was, in fact, not his area of speciality. Why was this field of study suddenly under debate?

'So everything that I, an Austrian, write stems from resentment, while any statement my Israeli colleague makes is attributed to tenacity and talent? What if I, myself, were Jewish? Would my obituary suddenly be legitimate? And what if I wasn't Jewish, but my father was? No, don't wave dismissively. Listen to me. What if I were the illegitimate son of a survivor? A bastard. Then what? What if I'd been searching since my childhood for my mother's lover? If, when I wrote dozens of references for Viennese emigrants, I always had the thought at the back of my mind that this could be my father? Maybe otherwise I never would have gone into Jewish Studies, learnt Hebrew and studied Yiddish.'

Klausinger made a face as if he had just revealed some intimate secret, and Ethan was reminded of guests on some talk show, who, inflamed by the audience's applause, confessed their sexual proclivities, shocked by their own courage. The way Klausinger presented his parentage, a simple biological fact, was fervent and sanctimonious, Ethan thought, and resembled the bigoted revelation of a secret that was only rumoured to be immoral.

Karin Furner smiled. Now she understood.

'What next?' Marker asked.

The son of a Jew could hardly be anti-Semitic.

That sounds like a new race theory, Ethan said. Our colleague Professor Furner seems to believe that anti-racism is genetically transmitted? By Jewish fathers, perhaps?

Marker looked at Klausinger and asked if he'd ever met his father.

No, Klausinger answered, and added that his father was an Israeli, that much he'd been able to discover, a businessman from Vienna, active with companies around the world, who now lived in Tel Aviv. As he spoke, Klausinger watched Ethan closely, looking at him as if he were addressing only Ethan in a secret code that just the two of them could understand. He was not going to let anyone censor him on any topic, not even, say, on the mass destruction of the Palestinians' olive trees! He was, however, willing to issue a joint statement that would put this dispute to rest and remove the Institute from the public debate. An explanation in which it would be put on record that neither party was engaging in any personal attack. No prejudice, no disingenuousness.

Marker nodded to Furner as Klausinger pulled a piece of paper from his jacket pocket and unfolded it. He'd already drafted the statement, he said. All were silent. Marker read through the lines. He handed it to Ethan, who laid it on the table without a glance.

The others looked at him questioningly, but Ethan Rosen stood up and simply said, 'It won't work. I withdraw my application.'

'But that's ridiculous!' Marker exclaimed.

Furner agreed. 'Please stay.'

And Klausinger: 'Don't you at least want to read my statement?'

'There's no point,' Ethan said. 'I'm sorry.'

Pink plexiglas Buddhas. Lentils on square plates. They met in the Indian restaurant in the skyscraper and sat on either side of the corner at the table, sharing the dishes and serving each other. Carmen McRae sang *Black Coffee* in the background, and as Ethan talked, Noa scooted closer.

Klausinger had then asked the group what it all meant. He'd kept up his side of the bargain, after all. And what about the research project he'd been promised?

Noa laughed and shook her head, but Ethan waved his hand. For him, it wasn't at all about Klausinger. Nor had the prepared statement changed his mind, even though this twin-pack communiqué could not have been more false. Marker had immediately claimed that no one was insisting on a joint statement. It had merely been a suggestion in order to contain the dispute. The head of the Institute, his friend, had caved; he'd evoked their years of solidarity and begged Ethan not to behave rashly. Even Karen Furner had suddenly reversed her position and assured him that there had never been any intention of reducing his chances of getting the professorship. Still, nothing they said had changed his mind. He was done. Klausinger's revelations about his origins were obscene. He did not want to work anywhere where ancestry was considered an underlying proof of quality, where merely being a so-called 'half-Jew' was qualification enough. On top of that there was the look on Klausinger's face, his whispered confession of having a Jewish father, as if the two of them were related, as if Klausinger were his illegitimate brother.

In truth, Ethan added quietly, even that wasn't the real reason he'd withdrawn his application. In truth, he couldn't help but think of his father when Klausinger had mentioned an Israeli businessman, of the laughter when Felix Rosen returned home, when he greeted Ethan, his son, when he hugged his wife and brought her head to his, like a fruit, and covered her mouth with kisses. Dozens of kisses. A hug like a vice. Ethan wanted to be there for this man who now lay sick in hospital. It might be his last chance to be with him – he who had always been travelling, always elsewhere.

In truth, Ethan admitted, he'd caught her desire to return to Israel together. No, it wasn't her arguments that had convinced him. But he'd rather make a mistake with her than be right without her, he said, and she answered him by smiling and nodding very slowly as if she were moving through thick liquid.

They're going to say Kaddish for me. You hear me? Outside the city is boiling, a jackhammer pounding, an excavator

*screeching over the asphalt, metal and stone grinding against
each other. Jerusalem – city of gold and copper and light, city
of sanctity, metropolis of urgency, the fundament of all funda-
mentalists – is expanding. Katharina is awake. I can hear her
in the kitchen. She's turned on the water and is letting it run.*

*Today, once again, I'm taking eighteen-year-olds to Aus-
chwitz. I've been going to their school over the past few weeks
to prepare them for the trip. Yes, maybe also to ensure that the
kind of thing you warned against in your article doesn't take
place. But maybe I'm not at all afraid of what you fear. What's
wrong with children understanding which orders they have to
disobey to keep from becoming criminals? And isn't it good for
them to learn what it means to stand there without their own
country, their own army, without power? After all, I am willing
to become Adolf Gerechter again so that no Jewish child ever
has to be an Adolf Gerechter. They should understand what
happened there. A few youngsters will pull out a piece of paper
filled with names that their grandmother or grandfather has
given them, so they can read aloud the names of their ancestors who were murdered there. Some will break down when
they realise where Grandma and Grandpa come from. They're
going to hang on me, on their foster-grandpa, and I can't help
but see in them all the nephews, nieces, grandchildren and
great-grandchildren that I never had. The fonder I become of
these children with names like Halbwachs, Süsskind, Jacobson
and Kleinman, the more I hate myself for it. I, Dov Zedek,
am being destroyed as Adolf Gerechter grows stronger inside
me and justifiably calls for revenge, because he constantly asks
me, in the name of all my relatives, why I'm still alive – and
the only answer I can give him and the others is that I'll soon*

be dead as well. This assurance should also appease those who don't want to hear another word about the Jews and their suffering, those who grumble that it's enough already. Be patient — it won't go on much longer. And even for you, Ethan, I can't come up with any other justification than that I, myself, am gradually becoming nothing more than memory and forgetfulness, so please bear with me. This cassette will reach you when I'm gone. Then you'll mourn me even though you'd do better to remember those who were murdered, because there's no need for prayers on my account. You hear me, Ethan? I don't need anyone to say Kaddish for me.

4

THE CITY EMERGED from the sea of nocturnal darkness. The lights of Tel Aviv shone below them. Noa said that she didn't care for Jerusalem, but she did like that city down there. *Ha-buah*, the Bubble: Tel Aviv's teasing nickname was actually an honorary title. The city floated like ethereal foam above war and conflict, beyond religion and regionalism, shimmering and multifaceted. Here there was air enough to breathe.

'Sooner or later, bubbles burst,' Ethan said, and asked if she'd like to drink a glass of champagne with him – because drinks were free on this flight.

'I'll have tomato juice.'

'With salt and pepper?' he wanted to know, but the seat-belt sign lit up. The plane began its descent.

Before the plane had even come to a stop, mobile phones were turned on all over the plane. He couldn't stand the commotion. Everyone behaved as if they had to get out as quickly as possible to escape being hauled back whence they'd just come. He remembered how before everyone used to clap when the plane touched down. Israeli pilots earned extra applause, he'd been told as a little boy, because they were the best pilots anywhere, all trained in the military. In the Seventies, immigrants from the Soviet Union had broken out in cheers as soon as the wheels touched the ground and then sung *Hava Nagila* or *Hevenu Schalom*

Aleichem. One of the newcomers had asked Ethan's father if there was any demand in Israel for eyeteeth specialists.

Just before disembarking he was overcome with agitation, as if he were a new immigrant who was leaving one existence behind and burning all his bridges. And yet everything was much easier than in earlier times when even a holiday trip to Tel Aviv could only be arranged with careful planning. Back then you had to bring along certain pastries which acquaintances in the Middle East remembered with longing. To be treated as a favoured guest, you only had to hand over a few Mozart Balls. *Mannerschnitten* chocolate wafer bars from Austria caused raptures, as if they were made of solid gold. And travelling in the opposite direction was no easier. When Ethan's parents flew to Vienna, their suitcases were filled with pita, falafel, hummus, tahini, gherkins, nuts, books in Hebrew and Israeli magazines. These days, there were Middle Eastern stores in Vienna in which Ethan could choose between Iraqi, Turkish, Georgian or Lebanese flatbread. In Austria, he read his favorite Israeli newspapers on the internet. When he turned on the television he could watch what was broadcast in Israel over satellite. He barely had to bring any gifts now. The same things were available everywhere and he could always book a cheap flight to the Middle East.

He hadn't planned on bringing much. He had sent three boxes on ahead. He asked his mother to store them temporarily in his old bedroom. That was it. Still, he grew more and more nervous as the day of his flight approached. His birthday was a week before his departure. Noa woke him with breakfast and champagne in bed, but while he was kissing her, anxiety seized him again. He had never been able to stand it in Israel for very long. It was the feeling that everyone was constantly reminding him of his duties or trying to co-opt him that he couldn't stand. This time, too, he dreaded their expectations. He could picture family celebrations, banquets and a wedding reception coming at him.

Later they strolled through Vienna's City Park. There were some teenagers sitting on the edge of the canal passing a joint. One of them was strumming a guitar, and Ethan would have liked to sit with them – even better, to step out of his life as if stepping off a bus. At that point, Noa said, 'I know I'm the one who wanted to leave, but I've got a sinking feeling in the pit of my stomach.' He nodded as soon as the words were out of her mouth and they smiled at each other as if she'd just given him a gift.

They sat down in a café to reassure each other that it would probably be better to stay. 'Let's not worry about it.' – 'Yes, we'll just stay.'

An elderly man sitting near them tried to grab his wife's purse. 'She robbed me,' he yelled. 'Help! Police!'

The waiters gathered around the table and whispered.

The man's wife said, 'This has been going on since yesterday. He doesn't recognise me. Let go of the bag. It's mine!'

'I have no idea who this is. She robs me blind. All the time!'

One of the waiters spoke soothingly to him. 'But Mr Brauner, she's your wife. The two of you have been coming here together for decades.'

Another waiter came to their table to take their order,

but Noa and Ethan just giggled like the teenagers in the park. The waiter grinned. 'You haven't even ordered anything and you're already happy?'

'Two glasses of champagne!' Noa called out.

As soon as they were back in their apartment, they were on each other, head over heels, holding each other tight, until Ethan asked if they should buy the suitcases together.

While the other passengers were already up and pulling their hand luggage out of the overhead compartments, Ethan turned on his mobile phone to call his mother. She wanted to know if he'd listened to her message. She'd been trying to reach him for an hour. Father had taken a sudden turn for the worse.

Ethan told her he would come to the hospital as soon as he could.

As they stepped off the plane, the heat wrapped itself around them. Everyone sprinted to passport control. Then the wait at baggage claim. It was a free-for-all. There was no doubt: they'd arrived.

Noa's mother and one of her brothers met them at the airport. Ethan tried to back away, but Noa held his arm tightly and whispered, 'They're taking us to our apartment, after all.'

Her mother immediately asked why they didn't want to stay with her. Noa gave her a kiss and smiled. Her brother Aron looked at Ethan condescendingly and said to Noa, 'You shouldn't wear high heels.'

Together they loaded the suitcases into the car. A small Subaru. Noa's mother asked, 'How long have you lived in

Vienna?' And: 'Where do your parents live?' And: 'In which university do you teach?' And: 'Why did your parents leave back then?' And: 'Where do they come from?' And: 'Where were they during the war?' A battery of questions, but his answers were so terse, taciturn and unfriendly that she turned away abruptly, as was the local custom, and did not speak another word to him for the rest of the trip. He knew he was home, but felt so strongly that he was both one of them and a foreigner that he was overcome with the urge to leave the country immediately.

They drove to southern Tel Aviv and stopped not far from Shenkin Street. Noa had found an attic flat in the neighbourhood. A friend of hers who was spending a few weeks abroad was letting her use it. They didn't have to pay rent, just water the plants and feed the cat and the budgies.

'Feed both birds to the cat and you've got two fewer problems,' Noa's brother suggested. A neighbour gave Noa the keys while Ethan and Aron carried the suitcases upstairs.

Noa's mother was so impressed with the apartment that she offered to cook them dinner and invited Noa's siblings and their families. 'Great idea,' Ethan said, and toyed with the thought of booking a return flight on the spot. He walked back and forth to figure out where he should set up his laptop.

Noa's brother hugged his sister. 'If you need anything, Noale ...' Then he raced off down the stairs.

Her mother asked what they had planned and if they'd like to come over for dinner? 'Impossible,' Noa said. 'We have to get settled. There's such a lot to do. Ethan has to leave right now, anyway. His father is in hospital. That's actually why we're here.'

Noa's mother put her hands to her mouth. She looked at him with distress as if she'd known Felix Rosen for many years. Yes, Ethan said, unfortunately he had to leave right away for the clinic. He'd have liked to spend more time with her. No, no, she shouldn't drive him there. He'd rather take a taxi.

Ethan's father lay in a private room. Without his glasses he looked like a stranger. He looked at the ceiling, his gaze unfocussed, his face swollen with edema. His skin was shiny and sallow. All in all, he looked pallid and puffy. His breathing was fitful. The space around him seemed to groan with him. But when he saw Ethan, he beamed. 'Tushtush? You're so pale.' Ethan bent over the patient, kissed his forehead, and Felix Rosen made an effort to raise himself towards Ethan, but could barely move his head. Ethan's mother stood on the other side of the bed.

When Ethan asked Felix if he was in pain, the sick man raised his eyebrows as if surprised by the suggestion that he, who lay there groaning, might have anything wrong with him. Ethan should have seen him at noon, his mother said, this was nothing compared to then. Felix Rosen, the old warrior, looked at him, not as if he were hanging on an IV drip, but as if he were lying in a foxhole. The hand-towels aren't clean, we need fresh ones, Ethan's mother said, and left them alone. She was barely out of the door when his father whispered, as if revealing a secret, 'Hell doesn't come after you die, it starts before that.' He lay crookedly on the bed, his left leg elevated, his right shoulder propped up. This position helped, he explained. He was dressed in a green nightshirt, or some kind of gown, and when the cover slipped, his bottom flashed.

Weren't they giving him any medication, Ethan asked. His father smiled. The pain was too much, too much for his body. It was an alien creature tearing his insides apart. He grinned as he spoke, then gasped again. He couldn't tolerate certain medicines because of his kidneys. What an amusing merry-go-round, a dog biting its own tail. His irony masked his uncertainty, a weakness that grew out of fear and a fear of weakness, because here lay Felix Rosen, a patriarch whose power and wealth extended well beyond his immediate family, now vulnerable and defenseless. Still, he let nothing show, but caressed his son's hand and talked, not answering any questions put to him and giving answers no one had asked for. When the nurse came in, he said in a strained voice that this was Frida, the Soul of Nephrology, who took care of everything associated with his kidneys. With his one kidney, at least, which also didn't work anymore, he added, and Frida assured Ethan in a heavy Russian accent that he didn't know how lucky he was to have such a father. Felix waved the compliment aside. She should stop exaggerating and tell him when his next examination was scheduled. He was meant to get an X-ray and an ultrasound. Could she find out when the neurologist was coming? The pain specialist wanted him to make an appointment and the physical therapist had called as well, and after that the cardiologist wanted to see him, only out of friendship, actually, but it had to be coordinated with the internist. Once Felix had given the nurse all the instructions and she had scurried off, he whispered to Ethan that there was nothing but chaos in this hospital – even though the doctors were distinguished specialists, the professor was a medical luminary and the nursing staff worked very hard, the whole business was a Moloch and if Mother didn't keep an eye on everything or if he didn't take charge himself, nothing would happen. 'For the transplant, Ethan, I'll have to cut myself open!'

Twenty years earlier, a tumour had been removed from his stomach. Ethan's father had rushed through the clinic, planned his own treatment, carried his files from one ward to the next, found himself a private room, making business calls all the while, and no doubt would have donned a white coat and tagged along on the rounds if he hadn't been forced to lie in bed and have his stomach and chest shaved before being wheeled into surgery. While the surgeons operated on Felix, Ethan and his mother sat in the waiting room and it seemed as if Dina Rosen was disintegrating, as if her insides were being cut open, not her husband's. 'What are they doing in there? Why is it taking so long? Doctor, do you know if anything happened during my husband's operation?' She rubbed her neck. She rushed into the corridor as soon as she saw a doctor passing and wanted to know when her husband's procedure would be finished and when she would finally be able to see him. The more worked up she became, the calmer Ethan was. He'd have liked to have told the entire staff that he didn't know her. You see that woman, that fussbudget, how much would you like to bet she's going to start in on her husband, her Felix, with whom she's ready to share everything she has. She doesn't want to be parted from him, not even for a second – she even misses him terribly when she's on the toilet, so much so that she's completely beside herself and dying to interrupt the operation to make sure her husband is alright. You see that cardio-chambermaid, the one with the big hair – how she runs back and forth bursting with nervous energy – that one there, yes, there … You see her? I never met her before in my life. I have nothing to do with her!

But it was the same old thing. What he found acutely embarrassing enchanted everyone else. No one could resist his parents' charm. 'Pay no attention to your son, Mrs Rosen. I don't mind at all when you ask after your husband.' The senior physician waved them over. For Mrs Rosen, he was happy to make an exception. He would allow her into the recovery ward, a room of absolute quiet where visitors were otherwise forbidden.

Ethan's father was hooked up to tubes and machines, and an oxygen mask covered his face. His mother caressed Felix until he woke. Ethan stood at the foot of the bed, reached for his father's left foot with its crooked toes and gently massaged the instep, rubbing his heavily veined skin. Rosen blinked at the light, dazed by the anesthesia. In the background a patient whimpered and Dina said, 'Don't get upset, but – they took off your wedding ring.'

His eyes shot open. Utter horror. Dina didn't mention that they'd just cut out a quarter of his stomach. She was only worried about the ring. He, too, acted as if that were his only problem, as if it nothing was more important.

'They were worried about the risk of thrombosis,' she explained. 'But don't worry, I'll bring your ring first thing tomorrow.'

Rosen smiled weakly and whispered into his mask, 'Then for one night I'm relieved of all conjugal duties.'

His wit was never quicker than in situations that left everyone else speechless. He could find his way out of any dead end. He knew adversity; it was his home turf. Dina said that she first went on a date with him when he got tickets to a concert that was completely sold-out. She married him because he always managed to get seats in over-crowded cinemas and jam-packed buses and to find rooms in overbooked hotels. Even when every ticket had been sold, he always managed to find someone who, because of a trip or a professional obligation, couldn't use the tickets he'd bought and was willing to give them up. Felix would search these people out, in their offices, on military bases, in the ministry. Ethan's father loved finding a solution at the very last minute when everyone else had given up. To please his wife, no trouble was too great. He took care of Ethan in the same way. He ran to the teachers, importuned them for his son, implored them to take the boy into their classes, since the family had moved to Paris or New York in the middle of the year and now had to get Ethan into a school in the new city. The boy just had to learn the language first. 'Unfortunately, Professor, we can't speak French or English much better than our son.' Felix loved to bend over backwards for his own.

For his thirteenth birthday, Ethan had his heart set on one particular cassette recorder. He had studied the brochures for months. He had delved into magazines, talked shop with friends. Ethan knew exactly what he wanted. His father took him to the store to look at the trendy gadget and asked the salesman if he had any better ones in stock. Indeed, the salesman replied, there's a more expensive, premium-quality model in the back. For specialists. Ethan's father wanted to buy the apple of his eye a special machine. Was his son not his treasure? Nothing was too expensive for Ethan, Felix's one compensation for all his lost relatives, the one thing for which Felix lived and for which he had fought so hard to survive; a battle he continued to wage in this store, at the concert and theatre box offices, at the cinema ticket booth and on parent-teacher conference days. And so Ethan had no chance of contradicting his father. He was given something he did not want because he was so deeply loved. His parents wanted so much for him to be happy that they paid no attention to his wishes. Ethan was small, but their devotion was enormous. The tape recorder was so complicated that he never managed to figure it out. His classmates shook their heads. They couldn't decide if they should be jealous of Ethan or feel sorry for him.

But who could reproach Felix Rosen for mothering his son so mercilessly? Everyone saw how he beleaguered his family with his love. They were all deeply moved by his paternal self-sacrifice. Ethan was not coddled by one *Yiddishe mame*, but by two of them.

Outside the house, Felix was simply a businessman with a reputation for being able to dig up the most impossible things and then find buyers for them. Owls to Athens?

Tea to Beijing? Watches to Switzerland? Such tasks were easy for him. Back then, in the 1960s, you had to call an operator to place an overseas call. The Eastern Bloc past the Iron Curtain was not far from Vienna and Greece, and Spain and Portugal were run by their militaries. Import taxes were levied at all the borders within Europe and every little country had its own currency. Whoever wanted to send an urgent message went to the telegraph office. At the time there were no faxes, no internet and no mobile phones. There was just Felix Rosen. And if someone didn't know what to do with surplus underwear from Bulgaria, or how to get stockings to the women of Lagos, or who needed East German licorice, or where to send a load of shoes from Prague, Felix Rosen stepped in, got to work, made connections right and left across the entire world. He then shipped sewing machines from Hong Kong to Prague, and from there he shipped toys to London. With the proceeds he bought bananas from Panama and traded them for Soviet nickel, which he sent to a Japanese corporation that in turn paid him enough to cover the cost of the appliances from Hong Kong with which the profit-carousel had begun. This merry-go-round was his favourite sport and he often had several inscrutable transactions going on simultaneously. For Felix Rosen there was no such thing as difficulty communicating. He understood every word in every language, he just didn't know what they meant. But that wasn't necessary since he understood what his counterpart meant before anything was said. No one could get the better of him. He banked on trust and built up reserves of trust, even though he'd never reveal where the goods originated. Even when he pushed negotiations to the limit, strong-armed his partners and bargained hard on prices, he was esteemed and respected. His partners loved doing business with him even though it was evident that he had skimmed a little off the top, because he never went too far, showed sympathy for their difficulties and was ready to help them when they were in need.

So it was no surprise when his hospital room turned into a kind of encampment, as if he were the commander-in-chief in the war against disease, a general who spurred the doctors on to battle like fellow warriors, a Napoleon who knew the entire regiment by their first names: Felix Rosen, Hero of the Medical Battalion.

'This time, it's different.' Ethan's father lay there, twenty years after the operation on his stomach, fifteen years after he received his wife's kidney in transplant. He was convulsed with pain. Felix groaned. And then he moaned again, 'This time, it's different.' He begged for painkillers. Ethan went for help. A doctor asked him to describe the pain and to show him exactly where it hurt, but Felix Rosen didn't answer any questions. Instead, he talked about his dialysis, mumbled something about his bloodwork and his lack of appetite. He, Vienna-born and bred, whispered the names of typically Austrian dishes like the *Powidltatschkerln*, *Zwetschkenknödel*, *Brandteigkrapferl*, *Esterhazyschnitten*, *Guglhupf*, *Topfengolatsche* and *Mohnnudeln*.* He had never given these up completely, despite his doctors' warnings.

---

* Damson plum pockets, plum dumplings, cream puffs, almond meringue and butter-cream torte, bundt cake, cheese kolaches, and poppy seed noodles.

And yet, a few days earlier, he hadn't even looked at his wife's *Milchrahmstrudel*!* The merest glance at it had made him nauseous. *Milchrahmstrudel*! He'd once been able to polish off innumerable slices in a single sitting.

Ethan noticed the old man was talking past the doctor. He interrupted his father, asking him to just answer the question, but the doctor said, 'What? Why are you butting in? Felix is the one lying here in pain. It's his right to talk about how he's doing and what's bothering him. You should be proud of your father. What an amazing man!' The internist called his patient Felix, as if they'd known each other for decades, as if they'd fought side by side in the War of Liberation. 'If the pain becomes too much, ask the nurse to give him an infusion. But watch out for side-effects.' Dina promised she wouldn't let Felix out of her sight and would raise an alarm if necessary.

The two of them were inseparable allies and always had been. Together they suffered and celebrated profusely. They were a couple from the day they met. For a long time now, they had no longer been able to manage without each other. When they were apart, they felt lonely even surrounded by friends. They could only live in symbiosis. The Rosens had a reputation for hosting dinner parties that went on until there was not a guest left standing, until they were all under the table. Their dinners opened with hors d'oeuvres, soup, then a meat dish, followed by fish and after that two kinds of torte. And whoever was unlucky enough to have the good fortune of being invited to dinner at the

---

* Cream strudel.

Rosens had to taste some fruit compote before the cheese was served. Felix did the shopping while Dina spent days working in the kitchen. He ranged through the markets and sought out shops where he was a treasured customer. The merchants knew which kinds of fish he preferred, how he wanted the different cuts of meat prepared. In these shops he knew they would give him only the best.

No one savoured every joy and sorrow more deeply than they did. Occasionally they would spend an entire night huddled against each other, sobbing loud enough to wake their son, whose bed was directly on the other side of their bedroom wall. But just as often they might start to sing and would not stop because it reminded them of all they had been through together. They were the refutation of the proverb 'a shared sorrow is half a sorrow', because with the two of them, everything – good or bad – was doubled.

The kidney donation had not weakened their bond but had made it stronger, as if they had become a single organism or grown together like Siamese twins. Still, the balance of power had shifted slightly. Ethan's mother seemed calmer, perhaps even unburdened, but definitely relieved. She had offered him a piece of herself and it had become a pledge of her freedom and sovereignty. It has always seemed to Ethan that she was in his father's debt. Ethan had often tried to work out why that was, and after the transplant she appeared to him to have been freed, to have redeemed what she owed. Only now that he spent hour after hour at Felix's side did Ethan ask, 'Isn't it difficult, having to live with Ima's kidney of all people's?'

His father shrugged. 'At first, I was against it. I was

afraid. Over the years, when you spend so much time in hospitals for dialysis, you get to know the stories of people in the same situation. One woman gave her husband a kidney and then left him. Right after the operation. She got up from the hospital bed and got a divorce. With another couple, it was the reverse. The man who received his wife's kidney felt pressured. He told me he could no longer love her without feeling obligated. He left her – the entire family was outraged – as soon as he recovered from the operation. Yes, I was afraid. What if the kidney didn't work properly? What if my body rejected it? I heard about the recriminations that fly in those cases. One donor felt rejected completely. He was ready to sacrifice a part of himself and she, according to him, simply wouldn't accept it. Her lack of love and her lack of trust were to blame. The man said to his wife: you've never accepted me for who I am, you've always shut me out, even when we were having sex. It's no wonder you don't like my kidney. Yes, he meant that literally, she didn't like his kidney. He acted as if it was a question of affection between his kidney and her liver. It's crazy: suddenly people have an allergic reaction to each other. He becomes one of her antibodies and she turns into one of his … It wasn't just me. Dina heard about these cases too, but she wasn't at all frightened. She was just afraid to watch me die. Only one story made her worry. One husband donated his wife a kidney that wasn't healthy. They'd overlooked a growth and after the operation it turned out to be cancerous. He'd given his wife an organ filled with malignant cells. They both died in this hospital. First she died, then he did.'

Before the transplant, the Rosens seemed from the outside to have grown callous, but now none of that hardness was visible. Felix and Dina were very pleased with themselves. By dividing her kidneys, he had become her better half and she his.

Ethan said he would come back the following morning. He wanted to be there every day to take care of his father.

'What about your lectures, your symposia and seminars?' Felix Rosen asked.

'Don't worry about my work. Right now you need to get better.'

Dina objected, 'You have to work. I'm here with Felix.'

'So am I, Ima. I'll be back early tomorrow morning.'

'He's dying,' Ethan said. He didn't get home until late. He could see it in his father, he told Noa. Felix's look was vague. His eyes were sunken and his cheekbones stuck out. His face was turning into a mask.

Noa didn't believe him. She told Ethan that Felix was a fighter. You can't write him off that easily.

He wanted to cry, but couldn't for some reason, Ethan said. It was like breaking a leg. Shock dulls the pain. Actually, no one had been able to explain what was wrong with Felix. Renal failure doesn't cause those symptoms.

'Maybe it's just a harmless infection. A swelling that's pressing against the lumbar vertebrae. Something like that can be extremely painful,' she said.

He rinsed out the cat's bowl and filled it with fresh cat food. The cat ran out from under the sofa and jumped up at him. He tried to duck. Then he poured birdseed into the feeder. The olive-green budgie hopped towards it, the cobalt blue one kept sleeping.

Ethan had spent the entire day at the hospital and had paid no attention to his work. He still had a few articles and references to finish. His calendar was full for the next few weeks: a lecture in New York, a seminar in Rome, a talk in Budapest, a presentation in Antwerp, then a conference in a French chateau. He had no desire to leave Tel Aviv and his father now. On top of it all, in two of the event schedules, he read that Rudi Klausinger would be appearing as well.

Noa had been out. She'd stopped by a friend's gallery and a colleague's studio. She'd begun looking for an apartment. The city had become even more expensive.

'For you, I can offer a special price,' the estate agent had said. 'But if you're going to move in with your friend … Wouldn't it be better to look for something larger right away? Aren't you staying in this country? What about marriage? Don't you want children? Why not? You make enough money. Don't you want to invest in property? We have a few wonderful things in Jaffa. An old Arab house. Gorgeous walls. But don't worry: it's all newly renovated. Latest construction techniques. The entire street is being rebuilt. Before, the area was run down. Now the neighborhood is 'in'. A lot of young families from Tel Aviv are moving in.'

The man smelt like a mixture of perfume and semen. He pushed his business card on Noa. She took it with the tips of her fingers. Outside, she called a friend. She was back in the country and was looking for a place to live.

Ethan had sublet his studio on Basel Street to an English chemist. They could only stay four weeks in the attic flat that Nurith had left them while she was travelling in America. Noa had declined to move in with Ethan's mother, even though Dina Rosen insisted there was enough room for her and Ethan. No problem! Two bathrooms, two bedrooms, and along with the kitchen, living room and breakfast nook, there was an office that Noa wouldn't have to share with anyone beside Ethan.

Noa turned down her offer. She wanted to be alone with Ethan. Her family was always imposing on her. The last thing she needed was demands from his *mishpoche.* It was hard enough to keep her own at arm's length. Every visit from her mother left Noa exhausted, she told Ethan. She always felt like she was being swallowed whole. Her mother's cooking was delicious, but as everyone knows, portion size can be toxic. It wasn't just the abundance of food, but the excessive love, too, that turned every tasty bite to slops. Noa's father, on the other hand, long divorced from her mother, only met her now and then in a café or a shop. He was always in a hurry, as if he were running away from something.

When she spent extended periods of time with family, she always had to diet for weeks afterwards. Her oriental relatives– unlike Ethan's – were not survivors, but they were no less attentive. Here, every return home was met with an orgiastic welcome, a *mulatschak.* His extended family included many dead – the murdered, who looked over his shoulder with every bite he took. Her great-aunts and great-uncles from Hebron and Marrakesh were deceased of another sort, they lingered among the living but had definitely passed on. Her grandfather, descendant of the Jewish-Palestinian branch, had not felt at home in the land of his birth since it had become the land of Israel. He no longer recognised his homeland, but the more lost he felt, the more bitterly he hated any enemies of the state.

The old man had been outraged when Noa told him she was moving to Vienna. The Levys had stayed in Zion for centuries. Why join the Diaspora now? Had her elders stuck it out so that the younger generation, the children of Israel, could run away once they'd finally become rulers in their own land? Her family denounced her love as a betrayal of the entire people of Israel and a personal insult to Ben Gurion and King David. But she had rebelled. Why, she'd asked at the time, couldn't the Jews here finally have a nation like every other? Do Finns, Italians or Turks have to justify themselves if they decide to move to Vienna? She found it suffocating. And she hadn't gone to Vienna back then, ten years ago, just to be stuck in her childhood room again.

Noa and Ethan barely saw each other. He had to take care of his father and they both had to deal with professional transitions. They were very busy. Neither reproached the other. They spent their days alone. At night they were together. Maybe it was the way she saw another person in him. Maybe it was the way she looked at him, the way she lifted her head when she did. He didn't know what it was about her that took his breath away and what didn't. In the dark she called him Johann or Rossauer. He could let himself go when he was with her. Afterwards he never knew how much time had passed. It always took a few heartbeats before he figured out where he was. The red tabby avoided their bedroom.

The doctors didn't know what was causing the pain, Ethan told her. It wasn't clear if kidney failure was the cause or if other ailments had caused the organ to fail. Symptoms like his could be caused by a combination of afflictions that are unremarkable on their own but together can bring about a collapse of the whole organism. The doctors went after Felix Rosen with electronic devices and put his blood through chemical analyses, but they could not determine the cause of his pain.

Ethan spent the entire day at the hospital. His father asked him repeatedly why he had come to Tel Aviv. Did things look that bad for him already? 'Tell me, Ethan. I want to know if I'm going to die soon. It's my right.'

'I reassured him,' Ethan recounted to Noa. 'Even though I felt I shouldn't. I told him about Dov's obituary, about my response … I just wanted to distract him … I told him about you, too … to distract him from his worries. But he didn't even seem to be listening. He only showed the slightest interest when I told him about Klausinger's article. But then he wanted to know why I'd given up my position in Vienna. I told him about us. He wasn't convinced. I wasn't either. We both lived in Austria. We're two Israelis who preferred to live on the banks of the Danube. We wanted to get away from this country and could have lived anywhere else in the world. Neither of us had to move. Neither of us is forced to work here. On the contrary, you're independent and have an international network. You can find and fulfill contracts in any major city. My situation is more complicated. I need a university, a research centre, and I can find better offers and opportunities elsewhere. Why come to Tel Aviv together? Why take on such an uphill struggle? Twin-pack migration … Father wanted to know what you do. As soon as I told him, I no longer understood why we returned here either. We could work in a lot of countries, but in very few of them would the conditions be as difficult as they are here. Yes, Tel Aviv is a wonderful city, but only to visit. The sun. The sea. But living here? Tell me: aren't there cheaper, more peaceful, safer places to live? And my father, who always wanted me to come here, who only ever talked about Zion and told me how painful it was for him to see that I had inherited his roving spirit, he looked at me as if he were worried about me. "These are difficult times," he said. As if things were so easy here otherwise. I didn't contradict him. I've only been in this country a short time and I already want to leave. It's like an allergy. As soon as I walk out of the airport and see the whole *mishpoche*, the assembled tribe, that mishmash of God and ghetto, kitsch and *kishkes,* and on top of that, the entire apparatus for which extraordinary measures have become the only reality, the security personnel, the soldiers, I have trouble breathing. Because this haste, the tension engulfs everyone immediately. Where else do you have the feeling that everyone's racing for their lives even if they're only hurrying to the car park or going to withdraw some cash? Every move is made as if in a state of emergency. They all grasp and grab as going for a ripcord. They think they're in free fall. Always. Not that people here are more conformist than anywhere else. Just the opposite; every single one of them is convinced that he or she is the only one who has the right solution. Each of them will tell you that all the others are mistaken and are racing headlong into the abyss. No, conformity isn't the order of the day, paranoia is. It's a disease that's both endemic and epidemic, a disease brought here from every corner of the earth, one that grew out of what people suffered on their native soil, then takes root and spreads here, too. Not without reason; this is the Middle East, after all, but the persecution complex that was our Diaspora folklore and was essential for our survival has reached a critical mass here. In Vienna, I always forget how suffocated I feel here. Not only that, when I come across someone there with the same mindset, someone who tells me that in this corner of the Middle East there are just too many of us in one spot, then I start in on him until his eyes glaze over. When that happens, I forget that I have the same reaction as soon as I step foot in Israel. Still, when Abba wanted to know why I'd come back to this country, I couldn't come up with any of the answers I'd have given if an Austrian had asked me the same question. I looked at my feet and shrugged. Then I squeezed his hand and said, "But I've only got one father." He just looked at me, wide-eyed.'

The next morning, Ethan cancelled all his appointments. He wrote to New York to say that he was now unable to come for the lecture. He excused himself to his colleagues in Rome, he would no longer able to teach the seminar there. Family reasons. He also declined the weekend in the French chateau. He withdrew from the conference in Antwerp, begged off the symposium in Berlin. He could not travel to Budapest for the talk. He was terribly sorry, but he was not at liberty to come to Wroclaw. He called everything off. He felt like he was the one lying on his deathbed, rather than his father. He issued a professional death notice. He didn't even call the university to inform the Tel Aviv Institute that he was back in the country. He didn't have the time or the presence of mind.

Four days after his arrival, for the first time in his life, he sent an email explaining that he was not in a position to write the article he had promised. Due to illness. Once he had put this unpleasant duty behind him, he felt such relief that he immediately sent the same message to all the other newspaper editors and publishers to whom he owed articles over the next few weeks.

Ethan also wrote an official letter to Wilhelm Marker reiterating his decision to withdraw his candidacy for the position in the Vienna Institute, not because of the flap with Rudi Klausinger, but in order to be with his father. After he'd printed the document, he shut his laptop. To the post office, he told Noa when she asked where he was headed.

He joined the queue. Only two windows were open and the queue was long. An old woman pushed her way forward: 'Let me through. I'm sending this express.'

'And?' someone asked. 'You think I can fly because I'm sending this airmail? Go to the end of the queue. Express means the letter goes faster, not you.'

Another joined in. 'Relax. It's just mail, not survival.'

The first one retorted, 'What do you think I am, a *Freier*?' In Hebrew, that German word referred to someone who was generous and open-handed to a fault, and for several decades now, in Israel, no one wanted to be one. *Kibbutzniks* were probably once *Freiers*. The *chalutzim*, the pioneers, who sacrificed themselves for their ideas, had no doubt once been *Freiers*, but they were now considered unreliable either because they were too ignorant or because they were following hidden agendas.

After leaving the post office, Ethan bought some pickles at the grocer across the street. The shopkeeper said, 'Just look at this lettuce. It's grown right here in our wonderful land. Isn't that marvellous? What a wonderful country. Here, feel it. Would you like a taste? When you take a bite, you know God exists, that the Messiah is coming. Don't you believe that the Messiah is coming?'

'Will my answer change the price of your pickles?'

'Of course not!'

'There you have it!'

The shopkeeper asked if he lived in the neighbourhood, where he worked, and then turned to serve another customer.

Noa sent him a text message: 'Want sushi?'

'No time. Going to see Father,' he wrote back.

He took a taxi to the clinic. When Ethan named his destination, the driver immediately wanted to know if he was sick, and if not, why exactly he was going there. A deluge of questions, and every answer brought another query. Then the driver told Ethan about his own ailments because of which he'd had to give up his earlier business, a kiosk.

He asked Ethan about his work, and when he heard where Ethan had lived for the past few months, exclaimed, 'How can you live there? Supposedly they're all anti-Semites. Don't Jews there have to fear for their lives?' The conversation stalled after Ethan reassured him that these days in Austria not a hair on any Jew's head was being harmed. The man looked at Ethan as suspiciously as if he'd just declared that Nazis were extremely amiable people and the whole story of the persecution was simply a misunderstanding.

Ethan was reminded of the cabbie in Vienna who had driven Noa and him to Schwechater airport a few days earlier. 'To Israel? Is it safe enough there? I mean … because of the attacks.'

'Driving a taxi is more dangerous,' Noa had responded.

Ethan's father's condition had worsened. He lay there utterly drained of strength. The slightest movement was too much for him. He wheezed. His body was occupied territory. Pain laid siege to him, had taken over his limbs. Father and pain: each stalked the other. Nonetheless, Felix wanted to speak. He didn't give up but looked sadly at his son, as if he wanted to apologise for his demeanor, as if it pained him to know that because of him, his child had to witness suffering.

'You shouldn't have started an argument over the obituary.'

'It doesn't matter now.'

'You should have written something about Dov, not a polemic against others. An homage. That's what he deserved.'

'I couldn't.'

'But don't you see? A commemoration would have been a better response ... Without mentioning the other one. What's it to you if Klausinger thinks that's the way to honour Dov, the displaced ... Let him. Why make it your problem?'

'You even remembered his name? Abba, let it go. Why don't you eat the yoghurt? And you need to drink your water.'

Felix waved the glass away and struggled to speak: 'No one would have held it against you. Your commemoration of Dov ... On the contrary ... But now he's a controversial figure. His corpse, his biography is a battleground. And you're to blame.'

'Should I have kept silent? Must we let others spit on us and claim it's raining?'

'You should have written about Dov.'

'Here's your yoghurt.'

'Let me be, I can't eat any more ... It's not too late. Sit down and write.'

'I don't want to. I'm fed up with the whole debate.'

They looked past each other. Ethan picked up the bowl and a teaspoon. The patient turned his face away. 'Dov was no racist. It was a matter of survival. We were fleeing for our lives.'

Ethan spooned the food into his father's mouth.

But after the second mouthful, Felix gasped, 'Do you think we had a choice? There was no way out. Where should we have gone instead? To Auschwitz? Should I have stayed in the camp?'

'This is not about Auschwitz. Klausinger wrote about Israel, about Dov, about the kibbutz. About the land of our former Arab neighbours ...'

'They had fled. We didn't start the war.'

'This is not about Auschwitz,' Ethan repeated.

'I had a feeling. You secretly believe they're in the right. I know you. A son I coddled and raised … My own flesh and blood …'

Ethan shook his head but said nothing.

From his hospital bed, Felix Rosen looked up at his son, bending over him and looking down at him. Felix Rosen saw his end. Soon he would be no more. The poison was spreading inside him, flooding his body. He not only had the feeling that he would no longer exist, but that he was watching as everything he had been was extinguished. Even his past was being retrospectively falsified and obliterated. He had not come to this land as a Zionist, but simply with his last ounce of strength. Many of those interned in the Displaced Persons Camp had carried on all day long about the promise of a Jewish state. All he was concerned about was how to keep from collapsing. Before fleeing to Palestine on an illegal ship, he had tried to get a visa to the United States. In vain.

Back then, being a victim, a survivor, was nothing special. The disgrace of persecution clung to him. He stank of death and fear. No one wanted to hear what he'd been through. No one wanted to know how he'd escaped the murderers. No one dared ask him why he hadn't been killed and cremated, and he felt suspect just for being alive.

Hardly anyone at the time had taken any interest in someone like him, the young Felix Rosen. Neither the Americans, nor the Russians. But Dov Zedek certainly had. He had searched for him, found him and got him released from the DP camp.

'You don't know a thing,' Felix Rosen groaned as Ethan bent over him, yoghurt in hand.

'He acts as if I had no idea. I know the story. I know who it was who ferreted him out among the other survivors and how. I've heard it dozens of times – from both of them. Does he really believe I accused Dov of being a racist? I visit him, hold his hand, support him when he has to go to the toilet, I bring him the newspapers and read to him out loud. I don't want him to thank me. I do it because it just wouldn't do otherwise. I'm not doing him a favour. It's something I have to do. I'm his son. That's all. Done. But I can't put up with any more of his attacks.'

Noa listened. For a week she'd watched Ethan as he put his life on hold and did nothing but spend the days with his father. At their feet sat the red tabby, Tshuptshik.

Ethan cooked as he told her about his father. He began to roll out dough for a strudel and recounted how he'd shouted at the doctor, because there had to be some cause for the pain. He chopped the salad and complained that his father wasn't eating enough. Only when he served Noa dinner did he tell her, 'Father wants to meet you.' She took a sip of water. Tshuptshik stood up, stretched and slipped out of the kitchen. There was flapping from the budgies. How did the topic come up, she wanted to know. He's bound to forget soon that he wanted to meet her.

'Do you know the difference between a Rottweiler and my father? Sometimes a Rottweiler will let go.'

'That's what they say about *Yiddishe mames*.'

'Exactly. My father is the mother of all *Yiddishe mames*. My mother, on the other hand, is not. She's an Israeli tank commander.'

A few days later, Ethan's father felt a little better. 'Bring her with you,' he shouted into the phone. 'I need variety. I think you're afraid to introduce her to me. You're worried she might like me too much. Does she have a weakness for invalids?' Not much later, he called again, 'The sight of you bores me to death, my son. Show me your girlfriend and everything will be better.'

Noa and Ethan drove to the hospital with Dina. The two women got along so well that Ethan was tempted to get right out of the car. He drove his father's car as Noa and Dina gossiped and laughed together in the back seat. In the passenger seat lay a bouquet Noa had bought. Ethan's mother told Noa that he'd been an absent-minded professor even as a young child, the opposite of Felix. Both of them, however, were fundamentally faithful souls – a declaration that unleashed the women's laughter in stereo.

They drove past a plateau-shaped mound, a garbage pile covered with earth, an artificial elevation made of rubbish. He looked up at the bare hill. In the distance, cactus plants stretched across the fields, boundary markers of the earlier Arab owners. The roads were lined with deep green. There wasn't a house or garden without flowerbeds or fruit trees. Here bougainvillea poured over the fence, there a eucalyptus rose in the shade of a wall. Sprinklers sprayed everywhere. The entire country was kept shipshape. An endless battle.

Life here seemed sustainable only with extraordinary

exertion. In Vienna, everything came easily. Now he couldn't muster the strength to write a text or even to visit the Institute. The argument with Rudi Klausinger no longer mattered to him, the dispute was barely worth mentioning. His father was right. Why hadn't he written an homage to Dov Zedek instead of a polemic against Klausinger? Why hadn't he evaded the attacks? As he turned into the hospital parking lot, he thought for a moment he glimpsed a southern twin of Klausinger, a phenomenon he knew from his many travels, whether in Mumbai, Colombo, Hong Kong, in New York, Sofia or Marrakesh. Everywhere – on the street, in a restaurant, in the airport – he saw someone who seemed a lighter or darker double of a familiar face in another country. Even as a child, Ethan had had such visions. He had once been convinced that the doorman in a hotel in Delhi was the waiter in his father's favourite Parisian café. And why did no one else see that the electrician in New York was really the tobacconist in Vienna?

Felix Rosen received them with his hair combed, his face washed and in clean clothes. This time he was wearing wire-rim glasses, a gold-coloured model from the Eighties, but the lenses had become dull over the years. The room had been aired and the sheets changed. He sat upright, slightly tense and still puffy and pale. The position was obviously painful, but he refused to let his pain show. Noa offered him the bouquet. Felix smiled at her and took her hand. He'd heard so much about her.

Ethan asked him in German if the night nurse had been friendly. 'Speak Hebrew,' Felix interrupted, 'we have no secrets from Noa.'

Noa told him she spoke German. She'd lived in Vienna for years, after all. Her sentences – flawless but with a guttural accent, the sibilants deeper and the vowels darker – caused an almost hysterical euphoria. 'Can you believe it? She speaks German!' Had they come upon Martians singing Viennese songs or dancing a waltz, they would not have acted more surprised.

For Ethan's parents, speaking German was a distinction. For years, their kind, Jews from Austria, were scorned for speaking the language of the murderers. And yet Felix had despised their former neighbour on Ben-Jehuda Street, because although this man had lived in Israel for decades, much longer than Felix and Dina had, he still couldn't speak Hebrew. Ben-Jehuda was the centre for German-speaking immigrants in Tel Aviv. This was where they had lived. This was where Ethan had taken his first steps. It wasn't enough for the inhabitants to put *Rechov,* the Hebrew word for street before the name. Ben-Jehuda was framed with both Hebrew and German. The Berliner Hermann Steiger used to say he lived in the Rechov-Ben-Jehuda-Strasse and that choice of words made him a Prussian Judean, a Zionist Prussian, a *Piefkinese* from Tel Aviv.

'We're not *Yekkes.* We're Jews from Austria,' Felix explained to Mr Steiger. 'We're not *Yekkes,* we're from Austria, from Vienna,' he repeated to his business partners, to the grocer and the barber. But what about those who came from Iraq or Yemen or Morocco, what did they know? *Nebbish* – nothing. For them he was a *Yekke* and would always be one. Even the Poles, the Czechs and the Romanians couldn't tell the difference. The Viennese themselves called Ben Jehuda *Kanton Ivrit,* because you won't hear a syllable of Hebrew there, 'Kan Ton' echoing Viennese German for 'not a sound'.

In the corner bookstore, you could find the works of Goethe, Schiller and Heine. They only sold Herzl and Freud in the original. Next door was a dentist's office with a sign reading 'All languages spoken here!' One day Felix ventured the question: 'Do you speak every language, Doctor Kohn?' The dentist bent over him and said, 'I don't, but my patients do.'

Felix and Dina asked about Noa's parents and grandparents. Ethan knew the ritual. They loved to pretend that all the Jews around the globe were in one family business. Abba asked about her last name and both of them, Felix and Dina, looked at each other meaningfully. Dina claimed she knew Noa's relatives. Ethan looked at the ceiling and sighed, but Dina would not be dissuaded. Where did Noa's parents live? What did they do professionally? Noa told them about the divorce, told them about her grandfather, his bakery, the candy store in Jerusalem, and about her father who had owned a store for photographic and optical equipment with his friend Menashe Salman.

'Salman? The photographer? We know him well!'

'Really? But he's not a photographer.'

'What are you talking about, Felix?' Dina cried. 'Since when was Salman a photographer?'

'Yes, today he's stuck in a print shop! Before, he used to run around with a camera.'

'What do you mean, a print shop,' Ethan objected. 'It's a chain that sells optical and electronic appliances. They have stores in Haifa, Tel Aviv, Beersheba and Eilat. Do you think there's only one Salman in Jerusalem?'

'Who asked you? What's your problem? You don't even know Salman. He's the bald one …'

'He hasn't got much hair left, that's true,' Noa admitted.

'Like I said. An old friend. A belly like this.'

'Well, he's not really that fat.'

'Look at her, sticking up for him,' Dina laughed.

But Felix was concerned. 'He's lost weight. How's his leg?'

'He does Nordic Walking.'

Dina said, 'That's wonderful! No wonder he's not overweight anymore. You hear, Felix. His leg is healed. His hair has even grown back a little. That's him – our Salman!'

Felix grew quiet. His lower jaw jutted out. His eyes narrowed. He propped up his body with his arm. The effort it took to hide his pain was obvious. Dina had brought him soup, but Felix wasn't able to eat a single spoonful. Noa poured water into the feeding cup he could drink from without sitting up. He thanked her with a nod. He was completely silent.

The doctors arrived on their rounds and asked them to leave Felix's room. They stood in the hallway, and when the doctors were finished the attending physician came up to Dina and Ethan. Noa retreated a step and said she'd bring them all coffee.

The physician said they still didn't know exactly what was causing Felix's pain. It wasn't kidney failure. It must be a local infection or a pinched nerve. Felix had screamed so loudly that night that he'd woken the other patients.

When they returned to his room, Felix waved Ethan over. He sat close to the bed. Felix whispered, 'She's special. Gorgeous and smart.'

'You know our son. You'd be better off telling him you don't like Noa,' Dina butted in.

'Please leave me alone.'

'You see? Everywhere and always contrary. In Paris you work on colonial films, in Jerusalem on a study of Palestinians in literature. In Tel Aviv, you give talks on those Muslim ruins. You lecture Austrians about anti-Semitism and in Chicago, you insist on bringing up Communism. And when Father took you along to East Germany, you had to pack literature critical of the Soviet Union.'

'And the research fellowship in Tirnovo,' Felix added, 'he'd barely arrived before he gave a paper on the state of the Roma in Bulgaria.'

'Was I wrong?'

'You're a know-it-all! Mr Smarty-pants. You start lecturing everyone around you before you've even unpacked your bags.'

He was used to this mockery. They had raised him to be a little genius and reproached him for it at the same time. His mother had chided him when he was in elementary school, 'You're a real wonder-child. The wonder will pass and the child will remain.'

In the middle of the argument, Ethan's father groaned. He had to go to the toilet right away. He breathed heavily, but couldn't get up. The pain flattened him. Ethan tried to help him. Felix started whimpering as soon as Ethan grabbed him, so Ethan let go and his father yelled at him for dropping him. When Felix was finally upright, he panted as if he'd just climbed a hill. He moaned with every step, but the worst came when he tried to sit down. He wasn't able to bend his right leg. He could barely crouch, and when he was done he cried out that he couldn't stand up again. They had to lift and support him while he washed his hands.

Then the return trip. As he lay down he panted, 'Slowly. Very slowly! You hear me? Get me Frida. I can't take it any more. An IV! Quick!'

Ethan found Noa at the coffee machine.

'Didn't you notice? How he tried to hide how bad it is … How he pulled himself together in front of me? Don't you see?'

They returned to Felix's room together. Nurse Frida had come and gone. Felix lay under the IV bottle; the painkillers were working. His eyes were dull, a little glassy. The tension had drained from his face. Dina stood at his side and caressed him. She whispered to Felix that she was going to drive into the city. He smiled, exhausted.

'Yes, please. Go home. All three of you. I need sleep. You should relax. Go, Ethan. Don't worry about me. Take Dina and Noa home. And take that veil off your face.' And then, as they looked at each other, he waved at Noa, 'Hello, Doctor.'

'But Father, this is Noa.'

He looked at her as if he were peering through fog. Was it the painkillers? Or another one of his jokes? Felix's eyes closed and he snored softly. They went to the lift, took it down to the lobby and trotted to the parking lot.

Ethan reached into his pocket; 'I forgot my mobile phone.'

Dina told him it didn't matter, he'd be back again the next day, but Ethan handed Noa the car key without a word and called back as he ran, 'Go ahead without me. I'll take a taxi home. I'll be there soon.'

And there he stood, no double, no mistake. It was him, Ethan's adversary. Next to his father's bed. Suntanned, as if he'd spent a year on the beach, without his glasses and dressed completely differently than when they'd met a few days earlier in Vienna. Felix Rosen was no longer snoring. Quite the opposite. He was alert and smiling.

Ethan stared at him. He looked from Klausinger to his father and back again. He went up to the former. Hoarse and with a tremor in his voice, Ethan asked, 'What are you doing here?'

Klausinger looked at the floor and took a step back. 'I'd better go.'

'It would have been even better if you hadn't come in the first place.' Ethan forced him to retreat further.

'I wanted to be alone with Felix.'

'What for?'

'Stop it, Ethan,' Felix said.

'Do you know who this is, Abba? Leave my father in peace. He's critically ill.'

'Rudi, Rudi Klausinger,' Felix said, and these words stunned Ethan into silence. Had the old man arranged everything? Were his attacks of pain, his hallucinations, his dozing off all an act? Is this why he had sent them home? Was it all just so he could keep an appointment with Klausinger? And what did that man want from his father?

Klausinger stood there, silent, stone-faced. He looked at
Felix as if waiting for an explanation. Ethan gaped at him.
An Israeli businessman, a survivor, was how Klausinger had
described his mother's lover. He couldn't possibly believe
that man was Felix Rosen of all people?

'What is he doing here, Abba?'

The patient looked at Ethan defiantly. He was obviously
not reluctant to confront his son. Felix said, 'He wants to
rewrite Dov's obituary. And he will. Isn't that right, Rudi?'

It seemed to dawn on Klausinger only gradually that
Felix had spoken to him. He nodded doggedly, turned
down the corners of his mouth and frowned fiercely.

'Where did he get that idea, Abba?'

Felix grinned. 'Why does it matter?' With that, everything was said. Once again Felix Rosen had commandeered
someone to his cause. He'd used one of his tricks and they
were more effective if no one asked how they worked.
'Why does it matter?' The same old story. Felix was in his
element; he had negotiated a deal. Klausinger, this much
was clear, would rewrite the tribute to Felix's dead friend.
What price had he paid for this? That was his secret and
would remain so, but Felix had mobilised all his forces to
find a solution, as if he were arranging concert tickets for
Dina or an internship for Ethan, as if finding a job for his
father and sister to prevent them from being deported, or
as if planning his escape from a detention camp just as
he had back in the autumn of 1941 when he convinced
an SS officer that he had only come to the camp to bring
his brother a certificate, but one paper was missing and he
needed to go get it.

'And?'

'But if I leave the camp now, they won't let me back in.'

So the SS officer said to the guard at the gate, 'You see this one? When he comes back, let him in.' One more escape for Felix Rosen before he was arrested and deported a few months later.

Ethan asked, 'Why is this man in your room, Abba?'

'Since when do I have to ask you who can visit?'

Ethan shouted at Klausinger, 'Why are you stalking me? How did you even know that my father was in hospital?'

Klausinger said nothing, but Felix said calmly, 'Why do you need to know? The only thing that matters is that he's going to write an op-ed that will correct everything that struck you as false.'

'Me?' Ethan shook his head. His father had cut a deal with his adversary behind his back. He was sick with rage. He gripped the foot of the bed frame tightly.

'Children, stop arguing.'

A nurse came into the room. She checked the IV, changed the towels, asked the patient if there was anything he wanted and cleared away the food tray. A cleaning woman entered the room at the same time. She mopped the floor and went into the bathroom to clean the sink and the toilet. The three men were silent while the two women worked around them. They didn't meet each other's eyes.

As soon as both women had gone, Ethan asked, 'I just want to know one thing. When did you first get in contact with my father?'

'Let it go, Ethan … You don't have to answer, Rudi.'

'I wrote Felix a letter weeks ago.'

'Why does it matter?' Ethan's father sighed.

'So, even before the obituary?'

Klausinger was silent, and Felix shouted, 'Please, that's enough!'

'No doubt also before you applied for the position in Vienna,' Ethan continued calmly.

'What does that have to do with it?' Felix groaned. He suddenly looked worn out. 'Take that veil off your face, Rudi. You too, Ethan. Look at each other.'

Felix wheezed. His moans alternated with whimpers. Klausinger took a cup from the nightstand and ran to the sink to fill it for the patient. Felix bellowed, 'I can't take any more, Ethan! Don't you understand? … I need Frida. Get her. It's unbearable!' The pain flared up, flooded through him. He screamed, and both Rudi and Ethan finally ran to get help, finally went to get Nurse Frida.

5

FELIX LAY BETWEEN THE SHEETS, exhausted. The IV hung above him. It seemed to hover far above him, a balloon pulling him upwards. He floated. The pain had not disappeared, but it no longer crushed him. He felt weightless. Warmth flowed through his body, and his face glowed. His head lolled to one side. He didn't want to talk anymore. Ethan and Rudi, Rudi and Ethan. He wouldn't look at them. The mere sight of them was taxing. His eyelids were heavy and he couldn't open them. He heard himself say. 'That's enough, children.' His voice sounded muffled. Someone covered him with a blanket.

Ethan stared at Rudi as he bent over Felix and stroked the sick man's forehead, his attention completely focused on Ethan's father. Ethan's adversary didn't deign to look at him. Ethan said, 'Listen, my father needs to rest now.'

Dusk was filling the room. It was late. Noa telephoned. He saw her name on the display and stepped out of the room. A patient was strolling down the hallway, his family creeping along behind him. He held tight to the IV stand. The sick man advanced like a bishop, the metal crosier in his hand. A procession.

Noa asked, 'What's taking you so long? You obviously found your mobile phone. Are you still with Felix?'

Ethan whispered. She'd never guess who was here … No, no one in the family, no, not a close friend. No.

Rudi Klausinger. Rudi Klausinger! Klausinger … That one, exactly … The guy is standing, right now, at Father's bedside, stroking his forehead … But that's what he's telling her … They've pumped Father full of medication. Ethan described Felix's attack of pain, the episode … Klausinger is going to write a new obituary. That's what Father decided. A kind of reparation.

He hissed with rage into his mobile phone. 'It's as if he followed us here … I think he's stalking me. First he applies for the same position. Then the article. It's as if he's obsessed with me.' And then there's Father's idea, Ethan went on, that this snot-nosed upstart should write a second article on Dov. Bullshit! In the last few years, Dov had become Ethan's close friend. If anyone should write about Dov, it was Ethan. He'd spent many evenings with Dov, accompanied him to events and discussions. Felix hadn't seen Dov alone for a long time – they'd only met in large gatherings.

Noa tried to calm Ethan down. 'Come home. There's no point in yelling at each other across a hospital bed.'

'First, I've got to throw the guy out of Abba's room. I'm not leaving Felix alone with him.' Ethan hung up.

Rudi had waited the entire day to be alone with Felix. Under no circumstances did he want to cause a stir. On the contrary. His plan had been to avoid Ethan and Dina and to only stop in to see Felix after they'd gone. When the others had left the room, he and Felix were together undisturbed, but not for long. There had been no time to talk. Only a few seconds. Just enough time to say hello. After exchanging letters for months, and a lengthy telephone conversation, Rudi was finally standing before the man he believed was his mother's secret lover and his father. Felix remained distant.

'You knew my mother, Mr Rosen?'

'Call me Felix.'

'Did you … Were you … with my mother?'

The invalid had looked at him wearily. Exhausted. He smiled vaguely, a gleam in his eyes. A sick man on a drip. But then Ethan burst into the room and Felix suddenly woke from his fog. He was anything but dazed. Not a single word had been said about a new obituary before this. Dov Zedek hadn't been mentioned in any of the letters or in the telephone conversation. Out of nowhere, Felix claimed that Rudi had agreed to write a new article. How could he contradict Felix in such a situation? The old fox had put one over on him before he was overcome with pain.

Now Ethan was outside, talking on the phone. Felix was unconscious. The infusion seemed very strong. Felix whimpered in his sleep, whispering to himself now and again. Fragments of sentences, a gasp, a grunt, as if an animal were speaking. A few words were vaguely intelligible. Did he just say Ethan? And Dina and brother? Rudi tried to free his hand from the man's grip, gently, without waking him, but each time he tried to pull his hand from Felix's, he felt the latter's fingers tighten. Strangely, he didn't feel so much constrained as used and trapped in the sick man's claws.

He was still fighting against the old man's stubborn strength when he heard Ethan reenter the room. 'Kindly leave my father in peace. What are you doing?'

Rudi finally manage to loosen Felix's grip and at that same moment, the old man opened his eyes.

'Naked,' Felix said. He stared at the ceiling as if watching a film. 'Look … There … Look at that. A jungle. Legs … Bums, arms and breasts … A fresco … They're getting it on. They're shagging. Don't you see? Can't you hear? The screams of pleasure!'

A nurse entered the room. She turned on the light and set down his dinner. Felix didn't even look at her. She asked if she should clear the teapot. Ethan nodded. When she'd gone, Felix said, 'Lucky she didn't notice anything. Still, you can't miss it …'

'There's nothing there, Abba,' Ethan told him.

But Felix looked past him, up at the ceiling and murmured, 'What do you know?'

'It will all be fine.'

'You have no idea.'

'Don't be afraid. It's nothing serious.'

'It's perverse. An orgy.' Felix looked at him, looked through him. 'You think I'm seeing something that isn't there. But you see nothing. Nothing. Do you understand? Nothing.'

He closed his eyes and whispered, 'You're brothers. You hear me? Brothers. Tell the nurse you need an infusion. Then you won't feel any pain and you'll see everything.'

Outside, darkness had fallen. The streetlamps lit up. Felix fell asleep. He snored. Ethan went to the door, and Rudi followed him out after turning off the light.

'He's hallucinating,' Ethan said. They went to the lift together. 'You understand, Klausinger?'

'Call me Rudi.'

They waited for a lift. A bell rang when one arrived, but it was too full. Another ring, another lift. This one was also packed, but they squeezed in. It stopped at each floor. On the ground floor they got out and continued their argument. Ethan was formal, Rudi very familiar. The Sabra was distant, the Austrian completely informal. Klausinger switched to Hebrew, which he spoke fluently. In Ivrit there were no formal terms of address, so Ethan called him Mr Klausinger.

'He's not himself, Mr Klausinger.'

'He's my father and we're brothers, Ethan.'

'Did you get too strong a dose, too?'

'I found some letters in the papers my mother left.'

'That's the way it is with inheritances.'

'Love letters.'

'Oedipal issues?'

'The man signed the letters *Motek*. He called her *Gingi*. How many Austrians back then knew that meant sweetheart and redhead? He writes that he wants to meet her on Seilerstätte.'

'And?'

'You know, that's where Felix's office was.'

'That doesn't prove anything. My father would never have abandoned his child. Never! He's not a coward.'

'He didn't know about me. That's just it. He had no idea. That was my mother's revenge.'

They arrived at the taxi stand. Rudi asked, 'Shall we share a cab?'

Ethan got in the first taxi and drove away.

Avi Levy would stand in his bakery, spreading the flour, kneading the dough, sweating and groaning over it, shoving the loaves in the oven, swinging the paddle like an oar, dusting the bread and humming a tune, always brimming with passion, as if it were the only thing he cared about. The women customers could watch him from the front room as he leaned his muscular torso – clad only in a sleeveless undershirt – into his work, as he stoked the fire until sparks flew and pressed and massaged the dough.

Whether buns or flatbread, rolls or pita, each piece, according to Saba Avi, Noa's grandfather, tasted a little bit of him, and in private he would explain how important it was for a baker to smell good. As a young girl, Noa had seen how her grandfather welcomed his female customers, how solicitous he was and how he followed them with his eyes. Avi Levy was a master when it came to turning up the heat and he lit a flame in all women who came to visit.

Noa remembered. She could see her grandfather in the bakery now, see how Mrs Efron would sniff the bread and say, 'What a wonderful smell,' looking deep into Grandfather's eyes until he smiled at her and the ceiling fan whirled a little faster and the air was so charged that little Noa held her breath. Her breath still caught when she thought of it.

Her parents were divorced and in new relationships. Why didn't Ethan believe his father capable of straying? Why did he refuse to entertain the idea? There weren't all that many Rosens left. He'd shown her a photo album. A tiny group of Ashkenazi aunts and cousins. All these *Yiddishe mames* who had pinched his cheeks when he was a boy. That was the typical gauntlet he'd had to run as a child because the excessive love in his family was not meted out in small doses, their affection was ruthless. Why not share some with Rudi Klausinger? Wouldn't a half-brother from Vienna's Favoriten district be an asset? Wouldn't someone like that help loosen the family ties a bit?

Ethan complained incessantly about his constricting kin. And now, when a Viennese crossbreed had finally come along and exploded their Jewish version of the Holy Trinity, elbowing his way in between Ethan, Dina and Felix as the *corpus delicti* of marital infidelity and forcing the faithful husband to a confession, how did the renowned cultural anthropologist, the expert deconstructor of all myths, the master of all social relativity theories react? What did the great breaker of taboos do? He declared that his *abba*, his daddy, could never have had an affair. Even if Abba himself admitted it.

They lay in bed. Umm Kulthum sobbed a song. The violins played. The mood shifted. He kissed Noa and the telephone rang.

Ethan should at least take a look at the letters, Rudi suggested. Then he could make up his own mind. Maybe he would recognise the handwriting. Did he have no interest at all in the truth?

Ethan replied, 'What do such letters prove? Even if they were in love, was Felix Rosen the only man in her life?'

'Are you scared to look at them? Are you afraid you might have to admit Felix wrote them?'

Ethan watched Noa disappear into the bathroom. Tshuptshik the cat hopped down from the wardrobe and ran after her.

Ethan and Rudi agreed on a café in Shenkin.

An hour later, the three of them sat on the café terrace. Noa was surprised at how much they resembled each other. Rudi was a southern, more conventionally handsome version of Ethan. The waitress, a petite woman with dreadlocks under her turban, brought their drinks. She carefully arranged them around the letters and documents. A cappuccino for Ethan, Campari and soda for Noa and a bottle of Israeli beer, Goldstar, for Rudi. At the next table, a group of young people talked, a pit bull at their feet. At another, a young couple flirted. At a third, three men sat in silence, watching women walk by and letting their eyes speak for them. A ragged street musician sat on the ground some distance off and played the fiddle. Isolated notes floated towards the cafe. Russian folksongs.

Ethan looked through the letters. His father couldn't have written them, he said. This wasn't his handwriting. And Felix expressed himself differently, more clearly, not as coyly as whoever wrote these.

Noa objected. 'These aren't business letters, they're love letters. Besides, Felix is bound to have been more romantic forty years ago than he is now on dialysis.'

Rudi nodded. His brother, he said, yes, he did say his brother, would refuse to admit anything until he had seen a picture or, even better, a film that showed what Karin Klausinger had got up to with Felix Rosen, and how his mother had then become pregnant and brought him into this world. Only when the two of them could look into the camera and confirm that Ethan and Rudi are half-brothers, only then would he – perhaps – accept the truth. But even then, it was more likely that he'd claim the scenes were re-enactments. In truth, though, Ethan knew just how untenable his position was. 'You're lying to yourself.' Rudi called the waiter over and ordered another Goldstar.

'You accuse me of lying? You, of all people?' Maybe it was a coincidence that Rudi had applied for the same job, written Dov's obituary and on top of that quoted Ethan in it? How high is the probability of someone ending up competing with his half-brother for the exact same position while having a public disagreement with him at the same time? And that wasn't all. Hadn't Rudi been in contact with Felix recently? It was about Rudi going after Ethan's position, there was nothing else to it. Yes, *Ethan's,* because the position was tailor-made for him. Ethan said, 'You didn't write the obituary for Dov, but against me.'

'What should I have done? Are you paranoid?'

'I'm your *idée fixe.*'

Rudi acted as if he weren't listening. 'Don't turn this into a mystery play. What's so strange about me writing an obituary for a survivor from Vienna? I write them often. And aren't you a famous Israeli intellectual? Why shouldn't I quote you? Is it forbidden?'

Noa gave a silky smile. 'No,' she said, 'of course, you're allowed to quote your own half-brother without giving his name. It's just significant.'

Ethan shouted, 'You knew who I was. The whole production, the debate in the newspaper, it's all a lie. It was from the beginning. That's why I don't believe you. You're not my brother, you're just some bastard with an ulterior motive.

Right, a bastard, Rudi sneered. Of course. That's what he'd always been, from the beginning. And that's exactly why Ethan was refusing to acknowledge him. He 'd known it all along.

'What on earth are you thinking? You can't reproach him for being a bastard.' Noa turned on Ethan. Her voice had turned throaty. 'You two deserve each other.'

'I don't give a shit about your sympathy. At least Ethan gets to the point. I'm a bastard. A love-child. It doesn't end with childhood, it follows you your whole life.' He pushed back his chair.

The pit bull under the next table jumped up, growled and barked at him. Rudi flinched. The owner pulled the dog's leash and forced the animal down. With a sharp '*Scheket!*' he ordered the dog to calm down. It was an enormous, pitch-black animal with broad jaws. 'Sit, Nebbish,' the man said. The dog sighed and laid its snout on its paws.

Ethan said, 'Would it be too much to ask you to muzzle your dog?'

'Nebbish is completely harmless.'

'So we've seen! I don't understand what a fighting dog is doing in a café.'

'Nebbish is not a fighting dog. He doesn't do anything. I've got him under control. As long as you don't step on his paws.'

Another customer said, 'It's a Jewish fighting dog. It belongs in a café.'

'Jewish? Is it a fear-biter?' Noa retorted.

Rudi scooted his chair back close to the table. He spoke softly. At first he hadn't been at all sure that he had stumbled on his father. Suspicion alone wasn't enough for him. That was why he'd done his research. Why he'd visited Felix in hospital. He knew about the letters and had written to Felix a while ago, but until now the old man had remained vague. He hadn't denied anything, but had voiced some doubt about his paternity. Yes, it was true, he was a bastard, a mutt. For gentiles, he was a Jew and for Jews, he was a goy. He was used to infiltrating and adapting himself to other groups in every culture and every country. Whoever thought that ended with childhood didn't understand a thing.

Rudi's voice had risen again. The pit bull terrier raised its ears and drew back its lip. The neighbouring tables had been discreetly eavesdropping on the discussion for a while. The waitress patrolled the aisles. Rudi ordered another bottle of Goldstar. He didn't see what was objectionable. He had applied for a position for which he was qualified. He had written an article because an editor had assigned it to him. He had quoted Ethan without identifying him. Alright, fine. That wasn't in good taste, but it was hardly a crime. How could he have foreseen it would cause a scandal?

A child trundled by on a plastic tractor. The waitress brought his drink and Rudi lifted the bottle and let the beer flow down his throat. 'The hell with it.' It was more belched than spoken. And then, 'Who needs you as a brother anyway?'

Rudi stood up. Someone at the next table declared that the two were definitely related, only family members argued like that. Rudi sat back down.

Ethan looked through the letters. They were all short,

hastily written. 'In principle, of course, I don't deny the possibility. Naturally, we could be brothers. This is not about disrupting the family order.' He grimaced with disgust as he said the words 'disrupting the family order.' 'You can't choose your siblings. If Felix claims he's your father, who am I to contradict him.'

Rudi straightened up and leaned towards Ethan, his arms outstretched to hug Ethan, but the pit bull, which had been following their argument with twitching lips and bared teeth, sprang up with a snarl and snapped at Rudi's rear end. Rudi screamed with pain. Ethan yelled at the owner, 'I'll kill you for this, not the dog, you!'

'Everything's fine. Calm down,' the man replied. 'Nothing happened.'

'What's that supposed to mean? What if it has rabies?' Rudi yelled.

'Nebbish,' the man said. It wasn't clear if he was talking about Rudi or calling his dog.

That was it. The owner of the café appeared and cleared the tables. He banned the beast from the premises and told the whole clan, brothers or not, to get lost. This minute. Forget the bill. Out.

They all wanted to go home anyway. The dog bite had hardly left a trace, but Rudi wanted to lie down. Ethan and Noa also went home. That night, Ethan clung to her. They held onto each other tightly as if the bed were tilted. In the dark, Ethan felt the cat padding over his feet.

They ate breakfast together the next morning. Afterwards, Ethan read three seminar papers that had been sent to him by email. He had to respond to several inquiries.

He declined an invitation to a conference with thanks. A bureaucratic communiqué reached him from Tel Aviv. He deleted it. Wilhelm Marker asked him to reconsider applying for the position.

Letters had begun to pile up on his desk. He opened the envelopes. Bills, event announcements and advertisements. He left them all unread and listened to his voicemail. A Rabbi Yeshayahu Berkowitsch asked Ethan to return his call. The name sounded familiar, but Ethan couldn't remember where he'd heard it. He sketched out a few ideas for an essay on suicide attacks and drove to the university at noon.

He climbed the stairs to the main entrance and opened his bag for the security control. His office building was across from the library. Students greeted him, and when he entered the office, a young assistant asked him about the professorship in Vienna. She was astonished that he wanted to reject the appointment and return to Tel Aviv. She looked at him as if he were suffering from a terminal disease. A lecturer in German History asked him if he would consider teaching a joint course.

Ethan knocked on Yael Steiner's door. She had been appointed Head of Department six months earlier. She was just on her way to the dining hall and asked him to accompany her.

They missed him at the Institute, she said. He had good news on that front, Ethan told her. He would probably decline the chair in Vienna. He would, however, have earnt more there and so wanted to renegotiate his contract.

She gave him a tired smile.

He could expect to earn more anywhere else, but here at home, so to speak, he would not receive what he was worth elsewhere. A foreigner teaching the same curriculum would surely be better compensated.

She nodded and said hello to a colleague from the East Asian Department. She could recommend the lunch menu today. A stir-fry, she said, and without even pausing, asked Ethan if he was the one who had given up his office here. Then she took a sip of coffee, rummaged in her bag for a cigarette and stuck it between her lips, though she did not light it since smoking was forbidden in the building. 'In Vienna you didn't want to be treated like a foreigner, but now you claim you'd be better treated as one here?'

Who had told her about his issues in Austria, Ethan wanted to know. He guessed the answer before he'd even finished the question.

'A colleague. An Austrian. Rudi Klausinger, I met him years ago at a conference in Beer Sheva. He's teaching here this semester … What's wrong, Ethan? You look so odd all of a sudden.'

He dialed Dov's number. The answering machine turned on and he heard Dov Zedek's voice. 'This will definitely be a one-sided conversation, but I'll call everyone back who leaves a message.'

'This is Ethan. Katharina, I'm trying to reach you. When you get this message, please call me back. My number is …'

At that moment, he heard a click, then Katharina's voice. 'Ethan? Are you in the country?'

'Father's in hospital.'

'What? Felix? Is it his kidneys?'

'They don't know.'

'Will you come by when you're in Jerusalem?'

'Are you free in an hour?'

'I'll wait for you.'

He picked up his father's car from the garage. Forty minutes later, he reached the switchbacks leading up to Jerusalem. Dov's apartment was in Mahane Yehuda. He wound through the streets but couldn't find a parking space. Finally, thirty minutes late, Ethan rang the doorbell. Katharina greeted him over the speaker. When she opened the door, he was surprised at how good she looked. She'd never looked more beautiful. She smiled at him. Only when he asked her how she was doing did he see her slump.

'Getting by,' she answered. The rooms were unchanged. Full of clutter. The walls were invisible behind shelves and built-in cabinets. Books and magazines were piled everywhere. Dov's desk seemed untouched. The last book he'd been reading lay open on the couch.

Dov had furnished one room with rare antiquarian books. Ethan entered the room. It smelt of wood and old paper, with the sweetish scent of leather and maybe a faint smell of glue, as well, but that could have been his imagination.

'Come, Ethan, I'll show you my collection,' Dov had once enticed the young boy, three decades earlier. 'People always ask: if you were going to a desert island, what would you take with you? Look, Ethan, this is what they brought with them to save themselves.' It was the books of earlier immigrants that interested Dov. He owned several editions of Freud's *Interpretation of Dreams.* Ethan remembered how Dov had stood with him in front of the bookshelves, pulled out a volume and said, 'Here, look. *The Interpretation of Dreams.* The second, augmented edition of 1909. A scientific revolution that still first appeared as a book rather than in a journal.'

Ethan was the one who later found a first edition for Dov on his eightieth birthday. He found it in the library of a New York colleague, who – terminally ill – had preserved his treasures for decades and now wanted to see them in the right hands. Ethan immediately thought of his old friend in Jerusalem and Dov, slapping Ethan lightly, said, 'You're going to make me cry, you stupid boy.'

'I arrived in Palestine with Freud's *Interpretation of Dreams* and Herzl's *Old New Land*'. Dov owned *Old New Land* in German and in Hebrew, but also in a Yiddish translation from 1915. He pointed at a copy of *Interpretation of Dreams* and one of *Old New Land*. 'Those were the two volumes I packed. What do you think? Which one is ultimately a book about dreams and which one helps us become independent people?'

On another occasion, Dov asked, 'What if Herzl had knocked on Freud's door one day and said, "Doctor, I have a dream?"'

On the left side of the room, Ethan saw the works of Arthur Szyk, of Bialik and Tchernichovsky. Not a thing had been changed and Ethan felt as though Dov could walk through the door any minute. Ethan took a newspaper off the shelf. *Die Stimme,* the old Austrian Zionist publication. Dov had never thrown away the issue from July 6, 1934. Bialik, it reported, had just died in Vienna. Ethan leafed through it. He read about the lack of visas to Palestine, then an article on the condition of Jews in Germany, Poland and the Soviet Union. A classified ad caught his eye. 'Are you a discerning man with a heavy beard, sensitive skin and no time to spare? Only a Schwing will give you the gentle close shave you expect.' On another page he found an announcement posted by the spa committee of Bad Gastein.

In one corner was a collection of Marxist publications in a wide variety of languages. Next to them stood the works of Heine and the plays of Büchner. Katharina entered the library, which had also been Dov's office. 'I haven't had the heart to come in here since he's gone,' she said. Ethan wanted to hug her, but she was holding a tray with cups and saucers, coffee and cakes. He took it from her and they went to sit in the living room.

Katharina claimed she knew nothing of the cassettes that Dov had recorded for Ethan. But he didn't quite believe her. 'On one tape he says you're in the next room, in the bedroom while he's in the kitchen. At the end of the tape he says you've woken up. And you never noticed anything connected to his recordings? Or his plan to send them to me after his death?'

'You know how Dov is.' She corrected herself, 'How he was. He worked on his own. There's a lot I never knew about.'

Ethan couldn't disagree. When Dov was alive, she had never been very close to him. As his widow, however, she was blossoming. Was it conceivable that he had kept these preparations for his death secret from her? He'd kept many things from her, after all. And he hadn't been faithful either. Even as an old man, he'd cultivated romantic relationships – not passionate affairs, but intimate friendships. Dov had never lied to her. After all, she knew he wasn't one to commit. He'd never promised her exclusivity. But even that had changed since she'd buried him. Now she was the one and only, even if it was only because she had met him late in his life and put up with him long enough.

Perhaps Dov had simply not wanted to burden her with thoughts about his death. He had recorded the tapes behind her back. At night, when she was asleep. Maybe that's what had happened. Ethan was ready to talk to Katharina about Felix and maybe even a little about Noa, but to his surprise, she brought up Rudi Klausinger. She'd heard about the obituary in the *Wiener Zeitung*. 'How despicable,' she said. 'That man must be a pig. An anti-Semite. A Nazi.'

'You're exaggerating, Katharina.'

'I know what this is about, my dear. I know my kind. I've got this type in my own family. I'm glad you wrote a response. It's good that you pointed out what a racist he is.'

'But I didn't write that at all.'

'Of course not. But everyone understood.' She lit a cigarette and inhaled deeply. 'Doesn't matter. Just forget it. He's not worth your time.'

'I saw him yesterday in Tel Aviv.'

She couldn't believe it. Klausinger as Felix's illegitimate son? Ethan's half-brother? He speaks Hebrew? But she soon pulled herself together. 'I know the type. In Vienna he attacks Dov in an article and here he wants to be part of the *mishpoche*. And that story with Felix! Your father, a Don Juan? Please. I could stretch out in front of him stark naked and he'd say, "Excuse me, Sir," and act as if he didn't recognise me. With Felix, not a chance! This Rudi Klausinger is just taking advantage of his condition.'

'Katharina, this Rudi Klausinger is absolutely convinced he's related to us. And Felix was completely clear. He confirmed it.'

'Are you protecting him because he's meant to be your brother? Before, Jews pretended to be Aryan to survive. Now the children of former Nazis are searching for ancestors who were persecuted as Sarah or as Israel so that they can instantly become kosher. Rudi Klausinger has found himself his Felix Rosen.'

'There are naked women up there. Men, too.' Positions he'd never seen before. A constant moaning and sighing. Pure porn. He groaned the words and lay there, utterly done in. Before the dialysis, he'd felt like a dead fish, swollen and rotting. Now he felt empty. He smiled an agonised smile. 'And here, on the other side of the bed, I sometimes see a man standing. And a very elegant man at that, I must say. He holds a walking stick with a brass knob for a handle. Extremely friendly. He gives me a nod and when he stands at the foot of the bed, his features blur as if he were standing behind wavy glass. Here he appears thin, there fat. Like someone in a fun house.' Felix waved at the empty air. On his arm, the hemodialysis was not far from his camp tattoo.

'He's floating back and forth. Right in front of me. As

clear as day … I know it's just my imagination. My brain tells me not to trust my eyes. You know? My mind is completely clear. It's an optical illusion, but I see through it. And you'll never guess who visited me yesterday. One of our mutual friends. Old Dov Zedek. As alive as you are. He stood there and told me to be brave.'

Ethan pricked up his ears. 'Could it be that Dov isn't really dead?' he murmured.

'Ethan, am I the patient here or are you? Which of us is on morphine, me or you? Who's hallucinating, me or you? Dov Zedek is dead and buried. He's dead! Accept it, boy. He passed away. What I see are delusions, but I'm conscious of it. My mind is crystal clear, Ethan. I could cut a business deal with you right here, right now. Dov is dead. But now what? What's left?'

Ethan knew the story that was coming. An old friend, who supplied steel, had called Felix a year ago. He had gone to the bank one day. He had learnt from the teller that his son, an authorised signatory, had withdrawn all the cash from the company account. The metal dealer was beside himself. He telephoned his son and asked the boy why he had transferred the funds. The money was now in a savings account, the son answered calmly. But what for? Why had he done something like that? He was a beneficiary of his father's will, after all. He'd have inherited everything after his father's death. He could wait that long, at least. But the snot-nosed brat answered that he had his own plans. He needed money to invest immediately. Why, the old man wanted to know, hadn't he just asked? How could he take such liberties? Did he not owe his parents any respect?

And besides, the capital in question was not private property but belonged to the firm. The old man's partners had trusted him with the money and now he owed them their share. He had to honour the debts he owed his clients. In the end, the father threatened to engage a lawyer. If his son didn't see reason, then he would have to bring him, his own son, to court. 'If you want,' the son replied. 'But then I'll report everything to the tax authorities. You'll lose a lot more then. There won't be anything left.'

Felix loved stories like these, about old men who had devoted their lives and created a state solely for the sake of their offspring, the *jeunesse dorée* of the small nation. These elderly men had escaped the camps and fled to this land to find peace, and what had come of it all?

Ethan's mobile phone rang. He left the room and stood in the corridor. 'Professor Rosen? This is Rav Yeshayahu Berkowitsch.'

'Yes?'

'I'm sorry if I'm disturbing you, Professor, but I must tell you a secret.'

'Must you?'

'Did I not say so? You can help me and not just me, but all Jews, all mankind, in fact.'

'I'm afraid you've got the wrong number, Rav. I won't give you anything.'

'Who's talking about money? On the contrary. It's about a legacy.'

'An inheritance?'

'A bequest, really.'

'Tradition? You want to bring me back to the faith?'

"Esteemed Professor, I've been told I don't stand a chance with you. You haven't laid on your tefillin today, you didn't yesterday and you won't lay any on tomorrow either. And you know what? I know why you won't.'

And before another word reached his ear, Ethan pictured the fat rear-end again, remembered the man rocking back and forth on the plane. He thought of the Orthodox Jew who had thrown himself into his praying, whipping back and forth as if he were trying to bring down the plane, and he heard the cleric say, 'You're not into leather!'

'Are you the observant man who sat next to me on the plane?'

'No, I've already told you, I'm Rav Berkowitsch.'

At that moment, Ethan realised whom he was speaking with and remembered having read about this Rabbi Berkowitsch in the newspaper. A spiritual authority. An ultra-Orthodox leader who operated behind the scenes in certain religious factions.

'The Hasid who was on your flight works for me. I've made enquiries about you, Professor. I need to speak with you about a very important matter. It has to do with your family. Your distant relatives. I can reveal a secret that no one else knows and that concerns you and your ancestors.'

'A secret?'

'More than that, a puzzle that not even your parents have any idea about.'

'What do my mother and father have to do with this? Can't you leave the two of them out of all this?'

'But I'm telling you: we must see each other,' the rabbi told him, and Ethan wasn't at all surprised when the religious man suggested they meet at the main entrance of the same hospital where Ethan was visiting his father.

There was a commotion in Felix's room. The family crowded around the hospital bed: Ethan's uncle Yossef, Dina's brother, and behind him Rachel, his wife, who pushed her husband aside and screamed with delight, as if she were not at the side of a sick man, as if there was no one there who needed peace and quiet, no desperate or grieving family members. 'You're here?' she exclaimed, 'Yossef, he's here, it's Ethan! He's here! You didn't tell us you were here! Yossef, did you know Ethan was here? How long have you been in Eretz?' She clapped her hands. 'Why didn't you get in touch, Ethan? Tell me Yossef, did he call you? Doesn't he think it's necessary to visit his family? Does he even care whether we're still alive or not?' But then right away she pinched his cheek and whispered, '*Nu, bubbeleh,* when are you going to visit your Uncle Yossef and Aunt Rachel?' Ethan tried to escape, and with a smile, turned slightly away. Yossef had been a city official in Tel Aviv. Rachel had worked in the Ministry of Immigrant Absorption. She hugged Ethan, each of her movements accompanied with a groan, each gesture a reproach.

Near the window sat Yaffa, one of his mother's distant relations. As an adolescent, Ethan had blushed every time he was near her. She was a blonde-streaked vision with a still-youthful figure and a face that looked too taut. Her cheeks must have been pulled back and fastened behind her ears. She hugged Ethan and pecked him on the cheek, squeaking like a rubber duck. Nimrod, her husband, a giant whose face was a mask of suntanned equanimity, a mummi-fied pretty boy, owner of a large shipping company, nodded at Ethan without smiling and greeted him in a resounding bass, a voice from the depths of an oak barrel.

In the corner, his maternal great-aunt's grandson leaned against the wall. Shmuel, a redhead covered with freckles, had done his military service as a paramedic in the occu-pied territories. There, he had regularly come into conflict with officers by intervening during assaults on Palestinians. After the army, he had spent a year in India, as so many others did. He had wanted to be rid of his fears; some para-phernalia and a few drugs were going to help the process. Now he stood there, as if he hadn't quite arrived, at least mentally.

The room was like a florist's shop. Everyone had brought a bouquet. Nurse Frida found vases and Ethan's father lay on the bed as if on a throne. It was impossible not to see the extent of his pain, but it was just as impossible to miss his efforts to downplay his suffering. He groaned every time he moved. He maintained his composure, but he was stiff and pale. An ambush of so many relatives at once had not been planned. They had all come to the clinic inde-pendently to see him before the weekend began. He didn't send them away and didn't want to show the slightest weakness, because he was Felix Rosen, who was not keen to fight for his own life, but who, for the life of him, would never avoid a fight.

In some countries in Central Europe, Ethan thought, this kind of gathering would be considered an invasion, and even though the detachment and reserve in those countries put Felix off, here he was, squeezed between other members of his *mishpoche,* suffering from their intimacy. No one was concerned about his peace and quiet; his family was a raiding party. The conversation circled around Felix, eluded his silence, hovered over his missing kidney. Nimrod, the shipyard owner, announced that he knew a place where human organs were sold, no questions asked, and it certainly wouldn't cost an arm and a leg. There were enough people who had two of these body parts, that prevented them drowning from the inside out, but nevertheless left them with too little money to keep their heads above water.

Everyone waited a moment to hear what Felix would say to this, but he only breathed a bit more heavily than before. Ethan opened the window to let in some fresh air. 'Naked on the ceiling,' the patient suddenly whispered, 'like *La Ronde.* Contortions. Orgies. A Kamasutra.'

No one knew what to make of this pronouncement until one of the aunts said that she'd seen frescos like that in temples. In India people had a different relationship with the body and with love. There death was just a transition, the individual was merely an incarnation. And even Islamic suicide bombers …

Father is hallucinating, Ethan told them. He sees things.

The others were silent. But Yossef couldn't bear the silence. The rabbis are too strict on the question of transplants and his wife pointed out that each dead bomber was scattering two kidneys in every direction, not counting the bodies of victims.

Yaffa sat down next to Felix and pulled the tray closer. She held the fork out towards him. The others watched, but after a few bites, Felix pushed the plate away. 'Here. It's Dov. You see, Ethan? Dov Zedek!'

'Abba, he's dead. Buried.'

The others looked at each other, horrified, but Felix struggled upright as if his pain had vanished and groaned into the empty air: 'Dov? The corpses have got to go, Dov. Even my father's and yours. I can't help it. Everyone, look, over there in the doorway. The young Adolf Gerechter. A *dybbuk*!'

Even though everyone in the room was convinced the patient was hallucinating, they all turned around, and only then did they notice the stranger. Rudi Klausinger stepped forward and said, 'Felix, it's me. Rudi.'

Fear drained from the sick man's face. He smiled. 'Rudi!'

Rudi pushed forward past the others. Yaffa stood up to make room for him. He bent over Felix, pressed his hand, and Felix pulled Rudi closer and kissed him on the cheek. He patted Rudi's arm.

Felix whispered, 'What do you think about kidneys from India, my son? Should we buy one? Or reject it? Before prices fall …'

Rudi, still holding the old man's hand, did not answer. The others were speechless. Someone hissed, 'Did he say "my son"?'

Nimrod, who as a shipping magnate was immune to surges of feeling, boomed, 'This is not a question of stock prices. No one is dealing in human organs. I was only talking about redress, about damages for personal suffering. A gesture of recognition for those who are willing to donate a kidney.'

Felix held Rudi's hand like the paw of a lap dog and wheezed, exhausted.

Ethan said, 'May I introduce Dr Rudi Klausinger. From Vienna.'

Rudi bowed slightly. The others nodded at him.

Then Felix raised his finger and said offhandedly, 'They're brothers.'

All of a sudden, it seemed that his visitors, rather than Felix himself, were the ones having hallucinations. They stared at the stranger as if he were a ghost. Yaffa's jaw dropped. Her husband shrugged. Uncle Yossef looked even more obtuse than usual. Only Shmuel, the youngest, beamed. Each of his freckles blossomed. He was no longer leaning against the wall, his hands buried in his pockets, but stood up straight. He grew taller. He examined Rudi as if he were one of the marvellous phenomena he must have come across in India, like a yogi who had only drunk water for twenty years, walked backwards and began each day by piercing both of his cheeks three times with an arrow point. Shmuel was enchanted. But one of the aunts stood there, openmouthed and breathing heavily, as if she wanted to fog up a mirror. It took a full minute before she could speak, and even then, she only managed to blurt out one thing, '*Oy vey.*'

Felix gazed at the ceiling, lost in thought, as if none of this had anything to do with him. Ethan didn't know what to say. Wasn't it up to his father or Rudi to open their mouths? But both were silent.

Rudi stared into space. He didn't know anyone here. What was he supposed to say? His mother was dead. They had never been as close to each other as the people in this room obviously were. She had taken him to a foster family in Tyrol when he was still very young and enrolled him in a boarding school. He grew up far from her. His Tyrolean foster parents, rugged mountain folk, had loved him – but like a Martian. They were amazed at how very much one of them he'd become, but in truth, this acknowledgment masked the recognition that he would never really belong. And the extent of his gratitude for their kindness towards him and their acceptance of him simply proved that he was still a stranger. Then he heard Aunt Rachel murmur, 'You know Dina! She's going to kill him. She gave him one of her own kidneys!'

Just then Felix shuddered, and groaned 'Dina!' No one looked in the direction he spoke. They thought he was just reacting to Rachel's comment with another one of his visions, but Dina rushed in. She hugged Yaffa, brushed Nimrod's cheek with her ear, embraced Shmuel, gave Rachel a squeeze and Yossi a peck on his cheek and let Ethan give her a kiss. 'Just look at everyone here!' She looked at Rudi.

Everyone in the room held their breath.

She noticed their hesitation and said, 'How nice to see you, Rudi, dear,' and turned to face the others. She asked the relatives to please go. Right away. Felix needed calm. So many visitors at once was too much for him. She would call them all tomorrow. She promised. And when Rachel tried to object, Dina overruled her. 'Out now, my dears! Understood? Chop-chop. This is a hospital, not a coffee house.'

It was an order. They all crowded out, waving goodbye to Felix.

Only when the door had closed did she turn and look Rudi over, from head to foot. 'You look more alike than I thought. Brothers and no mistake.' She could call him Rudi, couldn't she? And he should call her Ima. A son of Felix's was a son of hers. She went up to him with open arms.

'Thank you,' Rudi managed.

Dina looked up at him. 'What did you expect…' She took a deep breath. 'Felix and I always wanted a second child. In vain. What's important now is to stick together so that Felix will get better.'

Ethan's father gazed up at the ceiling, still, as if the conversation were not about him. He watched the images and the scenes that played out over his head. Dina and Rudi, however, looked at each other fixedly. A twin-pack of determined joy. Ethan, off to one side, watched his own family become strangers to him.

6

OVERNIGHT, FELIX'S PAIN almost disappeared. He still felt a slight ache in his back, but it was a twinge compared to the white-hot pain that had lacerated his lumbar region. The doctors could not explain what had alleviated the pain. There had been no change in his medical condition. He had to continue with the dialysis and would not survive much longer without a transplant.

The hallucinations continued for a while, but the naked people faded into the background. When they did appear, they no longer came as close to him. Before, their feet had almost brushed his bedspread. Now they were well out of reach.

Strangely, Nurse Frida took his fantasies personally. She knew Felix was only seeing things because of the medication. And even though she wasn't completely innocent in the overdose, she felt his visions were an insult. Maybe her guilty conscience was making her worry that Felix, her favorite patient, saw the nurses as whores in disguise and suspected her, small, caring matron that she was, of secretly being the madam in the associated establishment. Did he perhaps think that she had intentionally given him too high a dose of the painkiller? She gave him an offended look and was stubbornly silent.

The attending physician reassured Felix. 'Those are just harmless side-effects. Others become prey to compulsive thoughts. We should be happy that you haven't suffered anything worse. Some patients even develop psychoses after such a mishap.'

Dina feigned surprise. 'I'd never have expected that from you.' And a little later: 'Did you learn anything new?'

Felix did not want to stay in the hospital any longer. He was given a walker, which he was too proud to use very much at home. When he went out on the street for the first time, he fell. Dina screamed. A neighbour ran out to help and tried to help him stand. The doorman in their building wanted to call an ambulance, but Felix refused any assistance. He slowly stood up, looked around and nodded as if to say, 'See here, this is Felix Rosen and he is standing on his own two feet.'

Ethan and Noa visited Ethan's parents every day, bringing food. The entire apartment was filled with clutter. In one corner stood a Biedermeier sidetable with elaborate intarsia, which no one ever saw because it was covered with a piece of the finest Brussels lace, which, in turn, was hidden under a flamboyant 1970s pop style glass vase which shimmered in every imaginable colour and held a large bouquet of bright yellow Gerberas and white roses. In front of the Parisian Art Deco wardrobe stood plastic chairs, and next to it a rustic cupboard. Each room looked like a depot in which various collections were being stored. This is where the Rosens lived, where they'd landed after decades of bustling around the globe, hemmed in by their memories. On the walls works by early Zionist artists hung next to paintings of 19th-century European painters.

The windows were closed tight. The heat was locked out. An air conditioner hummed in each room. Hibernation. Siberian frost. Ethan had warned Noa. They'd brought jackets, carried them through the scorching heat so they could wrap themselves up in them now.

On one of their visits, Felix said to Ethan, 'Between the two of us everything is the same, as it always was. You're not small-minded, after all. He's not taking anything away from you. If it were a question of money, we could easily settle it. We could come to an agreement, keep the inheritance secure. Draw up a will. But he hasn't said a word about that. Neither have you. Odd, actually.'

Dina had also taken Rudi into her heart, so completely, in fact, that Ethan felt his chest tighten at the mere sight of it. Rudi, in turn, revelled in the effusiveness Ethan had always tried to escape in his parents. Rudi felt safe and secure. Accepted.

Ethan should have been pleased. Here was someone who longed for exactly what he himself had wanted to be spared. But he was not happy. He felt he was under constant observation. It seemed to him that every one of his emotions was registered and that inhibited him even more. He began to monitor himself and the thought that he should be open to Rudi just made him more reserved. 'What is it that bothers you so much, Tushtush? I'm your father. I can see you're upset. It's not the adultery, is it? Should I have told Aunt Rachel, Uncle Yossef and Yaffa something like, my dear relatives, our guest here, this stranger, is the late offshoot from one of my errant ejaculations and a wild egg cell? Well, Ethan, what would you have preferred? Not that, surely. I know you.'

Dina was happy to have Felix home again. 'He let himself go in hospital. The hallucinations will stop now that he's home. Around Frida, they wouldn't. She drowns him with attention. I'm not surprised she gave him such a high dose when he asked for it. If he'd stayed there, he'd soon be a complete invalid. He's taken care of here, too, but he's also challenged. It's bad enough that he has to go to the hospital twice a week for dialysis. He wouldn't get better in the clinic. He needs familiar surroundings and his family. His favourite bar. My bridge evenings. Besides, here he can get to know Rudi.

'You didn't know?' She said to Ethan. 'Rudi's moving in with us, into your old room. Do you mind that he'll be sleeping in your bed? Should he leave?' She looked at Ethan sadly, her forehead creased, her cheeks hollow, as if she feared he might give the wrong answer. Ethan shook his head.

Rudi said, 'If you want, I can stay in a hotel. It's not a question of money.'

Rudi couldn't say what he was looking for in Ethan's loft bed, between the teenager's records and the books. 'Just say the word and I'm gone,' Rudi said. Ethan shook his head again.

Noa asked him, 'Are you jealous because he's sleeping in your childhood room? Do you want to trade with Rudi? You can go back to your old bed and he'll join me under the covers. Go on. Tell me what's on your mind, Johann Rossauer.'

Nobody understood why he wasn't happy about his new brother. He had no taste for all the mawkishness. It was too shmalzy, they were laying it on too thick. That weekend, Dina invited them to a family dinner. She wanted to have all the children together, Ethan and Rudi, and Noa as well.

'To family!' Felix toasted.

They switched between Hebrew and German, depending on the topic. A language slalom. Felix started talking about Austria in Hebrew then changed to Viennese dialect to rave about the opera and Rudi picked up the thread. They soon found common enthusiasms. They both named their favorite aria and of course, yes, of course, it was exactly the same. '*Casta Diva*,' Felix said.

And Rudi exclaimed, 'Bellini's *Norma*! But no one can sing it like she could, the one and only.'

'Naturally. She was the best and always will be.' These were two of the faithful, two disciples.

Ethan played along, not out of spite or antipathy, but out of affection for his father. 'But aren't there other divas who can sing just as well? Anderson, Ross, Gruberova … Wasn't it just the times, her talent, her presence? Her marriage to Onassis?'

'What nonsense! That's just mean. She was the *prima donna*, the *diva assoluta,* long before her marriage. She was the very first even to invent that way of singing. She paved the way for others.' Ethan caught Noa's look. He thought he recognised a mixture of censure and pity and he automatically lowered his eyes. No one was under the illusion that they were only talking about music.

Rudi smiled. 'It's just a question of taste.' Yet his tone, the hint of scorn in his voice, contradicted what he said.

Felix and Rudi then raced through the topics, checking

off the most important, and look at that – whether conductor or soloist, actor or director, the names were the same. They were also of one mind on who were the worst. As children, both Felix and Rudi had taken violin lessons. They both disliked cats. They discussed in detail the advantages of various dog breeds and compared their favourite foods until Rudi suddenly revealed that he had a secret passion for rhubarb.

'No! Not rhubarb!' Dina exclaimed.

'Rhubarb!' Felix roared. 'I'd kill for rhubarb!'

'Ethan and I never wanted rhubarb,' Dina explained, 'but Felix insisted we have rhubarb cake, rhubarb sauce, rhubarb crisp and especially rhubarb semolina pudding.'

'Semolina pudding or rhubarb,' Ethan said, 'I don't know which is worse.'

'People hate semolina pudding because it reminds them of scarcity in the post-war years,' Felix shouted, 'but I love them both!'

Rudi seconded him. 'Me too.' Then he added, 'I can't help it. It's congenital!'

Rabbi Berkowitsch sat, lost in thought. He was a small man, whose body could not have been more delicate. His snow-white beard flowed down his chest, narrowing into a long point, its wispy tip tucked under his belt. The rabbi had insisted on meeting in the hospital coffee shop. On the wall hung a certificate that verified, with a rabbinical signature, that all the food and drink served in this establishment was strictly kosher. He lifted his cup and took a sip of milk foam. 'Professor Rosen, do you believe in destiny?

Was it by chance that you were seated next to the devout Jew on the plane that day? By chance that I heard of you?'

Ethan saw that he was facing an obscurant. That peevish smile. The certainty in his tone. This was not faith that had vanquished doubt, but zeal that did not admit any doubt whatsoever. This man seemed impervious to the mundane reality around him, and completely at peace with himself. That said, he couldn't manage to keep his dove-grey silk kaftan clean and had just dribbled coffee down his front. But this indifference to outer appearance seemed sophisticated, as if it were evidence of an elevated spirit rather than sloppiness. And precisely because Rabbi Berkowitsch considered his appearance of absolutely no importance, many were convinced that he was concerned only with the essential, the transcendent. Among the devout, he was widely considered a light of rabbinical wisdom, for the most part because much of what he said was incomprehensible. Furthermore, he was an expert on Talmudic writings. He was a learned man, all agreed about that.

'Chance is nothing other than us getting our due,' the rabbi said. 'All has been written, we just need to decipher it. It is written that one will come and fulfill the prophecy.' Rabbi Berkowitsch had begun speaking in modern Hebrew but recited the saying about the people who live in darkness yet will see a great light that will shine over those who abide in the dark. He then asked abruptly, 'Do you hear? What will come has been set down exactly. Who will sit on King David's throne has been recorded, and his reign will bring peace.' Again he recited the holy verses, spoke of the wolf that will live with the lamb, the leopard that will lie down with the goat, and the calf and the lion that will be led by a little child. The cow will lie with the bear and the lion will eat straw with the ox and the nursing child will play by the cobra's hole. When the old man reached the verse about the infant who sticks his hand into the viper's nest, Ethan was infected by the religious man's enthusiasm even though he didn't believe a single word.

They were destined to meet from the beginning, Rabbi Berkowitsch told him. He, Rabbi Yeshayahu Berkowitsch, had been chosen to track him down, just as Ethan was now called upon to help so that the One, the Anointed, could finally arrive.

'Which Chosen One are you talking about, exactly? About the Messiah, about me or about you?'

'Do not laugh, Professor Rosen.'

'I'm not laughing. I just can't believe what I'm hearing.'

'That's not what this is about.'

Ethan pricked up his ears. Since when was it not about honouring God for these religious men? 'I don't mean to offend, Rabbi, but …'

'Don't worry. You can't offend me.'

'I very much doubt that you are not concerned about my piety and my abiding by the laws.'

The rabbi took another sip of coffee. 'But that's how it is.'

'With all due respect, Rabbi …'

Rabbi Berkowitsch looked at the ceiling then smiled peevishly. 'Respect? Spare me. I know what you think of me. I know you inside and out, Professor Rosen. You see me as a relic, a fossil from the Cretaceous period. I've done my research on you. I've read your articles. Do you think I don't know what goes on inside your head? That I don't notice how you look at me? I make you angry. The devout man in his kaftan makes you break into a sweat. That's how it is. When I breathe, I rob you of air. My get-up makes you feel constrained. My kippah weighs on your head and my sidelocks dangle in front of your eyes. No, I'm not implying that you suffer from Jewish self-hatred. First of all, the hated suffer from hatred, not those who hate. Second, you don't scorn me any more than a monk in his woollen cowl. Third, our heavy garments don't bother you up north, only in Eretz Israel. Your antipathy, your allergy – if I may put it that way – is only active in certain regions. Fourth, I know that you would condemn to hell any German who dared say a word against me. But you know what? I don't need you to defend me, you can stick your respect and your tolerance somewhere else. You accept me? Very well. You admire the strength of my faith? You're impressed by my memory? My knowledge? That may be. You could convince me. But respect? From you? Who are you trying to convince? Me? You think I care about your belief? Am I a Catholic missionary? I only want to know what someone like you does. Why you do or don't do it is another matter altogether. I don't care why, I only care what. What it is you are prepared to do.'

'What can I possibly do to make the Messiah come? Not turn on lights on Saturdays? Tie on leather straps in the morning? Not eat pork? Should I pray, to speed things up?' Ethan leaned forward. 'Consider this, Rabbi: you should be grateful for people like me who don't lay on tefillin and don't observe Shabbat. Grateful! Because of us, the End of Days will not come. You can keep praying and fasting. As soon as the Messiah comes, the whole rigmarole will end, and to top it all, every one of our relatives will rise from the dead. Now, Rabbi, I ask you, who needs this? Do you have room in your apartment for so many visitors?'

The Rabbi smiled pointedly. 'There will be room for all. Even for Jews and Arabs in Eretz Israel. Peace will reign, Professor. Man will no longer be inhumane to man. It will come soon.'

He drank his cup dry, called the waitress over, and ordered a piece of cake. He looked deep into Ethan's eyes and whispered, 'There are secrets behind the letters and between the lines.'

Ethan knew the mystics' number games and their cabbalistic sleights of hand well enough. He enjoyed listening to these devout men just as he would enjoy listening to an African faith healer, a Tyrolean dowser, or a Welsh spiritist. He found such figures fascinating; they were objects of study. He didn't believe in their magic, but he did not doubt the unbelievable powers they wielded, these masters of manipulation and suggestion. They were illusionists.

'Well, Rabbi, are you going to tell me you've already calculated when the Messiah will finally come to this world?' Ethan grinned and tilted his head to the side. He was going to enjoy this to the last moment.

The rabbi took a bite of his cake. 'Don't hold back, Professor. Ridicule me all you like. Yes, just imagine, I have, and I can prove that the time when He will be born is encoded in the holy books. My method was accepted by several authorities up until the moment I announced what I had discovered.'

'How is that?'

The rabbi mimicked him: '"How is that?"' He shook his head. 'Now you want to know what I've discovered, isn't that right?' He whispered, 'I will tell you how. I, Yeshayahu Berkowitsch, with the help of my rabbinic-talmudic knowledge, have established that the Messiah was already conceived a long time ago.'

Ethan shrugged. 'The Christians make the same claim.'

'That was my honourable colleagues' objection as well. They also called me a heretic, a Sabbatai Zevi, an apostate. But I do not claim that the One who will be the Messiah has already come into the world, for the lion and the lamb are not friends and man is enemy to man.'

Ethan grimaced as if he'd bitten into a rotten fruit. 'He was conceived, but not born? That sounds like metaphysical constipation! What good does it do? Should I lay on my tefillin?'

'I have no idea why you keep bring up tefillin. That is not what I'm talking about. We have already discussed that.' Rabbi Berkowitsch took another bite of his cake, letting a drop of cream fall on his shirt, and continued talking. 'What if the Messiah really was conceived decades ago but was never born?'

'What is that supposed to mean?'

'Listen to me, Professor. My records indicated that the anointed One has already been conceived – which shocked my esteemed colleagues deeply enough – and I was also able to determine, by linking together all the open as well as the hidden prophecies, exactly when, where, and by whom. Yes, even which night the man and the woman knew each other in a Galician shtetl. All this I was able to determine beyond any doubt.'

'Beyond any doubt?'

'I admit: it's all a matter of interpretation, Professor! Fine. And yet, it is one possible reading. Moreover, it is the only one that can be accepted by scholars. Still, they are reluctant to think through the consequences. They fear the outcome! The implications! The judgment!' The rabbi did not whisper this last word, but screeched it aloud, and the waitress looked over at their table. He paid her no attention. Ethan looked at the man before him whose rapture seemed to come from another world. Those who had founded religions in earlier centuries must have had this kind of charisma. But Biblical times were over. Weren't those who were bursting with such faith today considered at best fanatics, or even psychotic?

The rabbi continued, feverishly, balling his hands into fists. 'What if, I ask, the Messiah were conceived by two Jews in Poland in the early forties, by a man and a woman whose ancestry and family background, whose lives and fates I could verify? What if all the predictions in the scriptures had come true?' He banged the table to the rhythm of his words. 'Professor, I can show you proof.'

He fished a file of documents, notes and charts out of a bag. 'I've compared historical data, genealogical trees, community registers and court decisions with cryptic signs in various scriptures. It's all documented. We are weighed and measured, Professor, and all of us, whether we're into leather or not, we're all, all of us together, found wanting. We are insignificant, we're nothing. It is written, Professor. A millionfold of nothing. Do you understand?'

For the first time in their conversation, Ethan felt, despite his convictions, that there could well be a compelling idea behind the rabbi's words. A deeper truth. He hadn't yet figured out what the rabbi was getting at, but he could sense the despair that must have driven this devout man in his research and studies.

'The Messiah,' Rabbi Berkowitsch whispered, glancing around, 'was conceived. No one knew about him. No one had seen him yet. But beneath this woman's bosom, an embryo was developing. I can read the signs, I can decode each letter into a number, I can use the methodology of the Righteous to determine the due date on which this child was meant to have seen the light of the world. That descendant of David and Solomon from the House of Judah, who would finally have revealed to us the meaning of all being. But it never came to that. There is no meaning any more, it's all meaningless, absurd. That being never came to be. His mother could not give him life, because she'd already lost her own. It had been taken from her when she was shot. His father would never take the child into his arms because the murderers gassed him. In the winter of 1942, they rounded up everyone in the village and murdered them all within a few days. What can I say? Why recount what occurred in so many thousands of other places as well? They locked men, women and children in a barn and set it on fire. The rest were allowed to watch their relatives scream for help while the smoke billowed and the flames rose, to watch them try to escape the fire, to watch as a few of them jumped out of the windows only to be beaten to death by the SS. The rest watched as many were herded into the forest and made to dig the ditch into which they'd be mown down with bullets. What can I tell you, Professor? … Not one of my words is sufficient. Language fails me. And you would never understand anyway. What can I explain to you? Why the rest were hauled off to the camp?'

Ethan nodded, then asked softly, 'You were there, weren't you, Rabbi Berkowitsch?'

The rabbi turned pale and whispered, 'I can tell you that is what happened, Professor.'

Ethan didn't know where to look. The old man continued, 'I was elsewhere. In the forest.' He cleared his throat. 'We're all survivors, Professor. There weren't supposed to be any of us left. Do you sometimes wonder, Professor, how we religious men explain what happened to us?'

Ethan nodded. 'I know the theories. Some claim that the Holocaust is no different from other catastrophes the Jews have suffered.'

'Nonsense! The planned extermination of an entire people, the industrial production of corpses had never occurred before. Never!'

'Well then, Rabbi, there's also the theory that God was punishing the Jews for their sins.'

'And the million murdered children? Even Satan couldn't come up with a sin that would need to be atoned for by these small ones. Nebbish. There is no explanation. The most idiotic theory is the one that claims the mass murder was necessary for the founding of Israel. Why should God give a country to the Jews, most of whom he'd first allowed to be murdered? That's like saying that fires exist so that firemen can race through the streets in their red trucks with flashing lights and sirens. That's just *mishegoss*. No. Firemen exist because of the flames. The state was founded in reaction to anti-Semitism. All our explanations are worthless because they can't tell us why such a crime had to take place. But what if we can't see the answer because it lies in the future? In front of us. Before our eyes. Right before our noses!'

Ethan was silent. Berkowitsch kept talking. 'You must understand. You're not stupid, after all. Precisely because our explanations don't clarify a thing, we can only turn to God. Do you understand?'

Ethan began to see the monstrosity Berkowitsch was hinting at. 'You surely aren't implying that the extermination was of God's making? The mass murder has no meaning, it is the epitome of meaninglessness!'

The Rabbi waved his hand dismissively. 'The Shoah as a result of blind chance? The atrocity is so evil, so monstrous, it cries out for a central plan. God's existence was never so apparent as at that moment, because He didn't appear, He was absent.'

The thought sent shivers down Ethan's spine. 'Auschwitz as proof of God's existence?'

The rabbi waved his index finger. 'Auschwitz as the devil's work, and if Satan exists, then belief in God becomes a certainty. In the Shoah we recognise the supernatural because there is no explanation for it that our minds can grasp. We are forced to admit that some things lie beyond our under-standing.' And then he shrieked, 'Is it my job to justify the ways of God? He must answer for Himself. Only He can reveal why He permitted it. And the only answer we can accept is immediate and utter salvation. Do you under-stand, Ethan? Nothing less! The end of all suffering. The banishment of evil from this earth. The reign of the Lord with the arrival of the Messiah. Blessed and welcome be the King, the Messiah. *Baruch hu, baruch ha-ba melech ha-maschiach!*' He shouted the last words as if he were the announcer in a Las Vegas boxing ring. An Arab family passing the café just then, on their way to visit a patient, winced as if the yelling were directed at them personally. A nurse admonished him severely, telling him to be quiet, reminding him he was in a clinic where patients needed to rest. But Rabbi Berkowitsch paid no attention to the rebuke or to the neighbouring tables or even to the patients being wheeled past in their wheelchairs. He kept talking, staring fixedly at Ethan all the while and forcing him to ignore the others as well. 'We can accept nothing less. There is nothing else to be found in the books.'

'But Rabbi, you've already said that the Messiah was murdered in His mother's womb.'

'So He was.'

Was it possible that the rabbi did not understand what he himself was saying? Rabbi Berkowitsch opened a folder. The cover pressed the rest of the cake flat and the soft filling squirted out. 'I can see what you're thinking, Professor. I'm fully aware of the contradiction in my claims. This is the paradox we find in the scriptures. On the one hand, we have prophesies that the Messiah will come to deliver the world, and on the other the catastrophe is foretold. We have hidden signs revealing when and where he will be conceived, but we also have evidence that points to a very different conclusion. How can a murdered embryo become ruler of the world? How can the course of history be reversed?'

The rabbi paused, scraped the cake from the cover of his file, and began eating. Ethan looked at him irritably. 'Well, Rabbi, what is the answer?'

The devout man's eyes gleamed. The secular professor's interest had finally been piqued. 'It's up to us, Ethan Rosen. This is the decisive moment, the moment of truth. Our generation has been chosen to accept the challenge.'

'By laying on tefillin?'

'In the name of the Almighty, I am not talking about phylacteries. Are you thick? I'm talking about the Scriptures, about signs. Do you not hear me? I am talking about the secret codes God has hidden deep inside us from the very beginning. They are the beginning and end of our being. I'm talking about an embryo and the text that was written into that being before it came into this world. About God's signature, which it carried within. What is insemination, if not an act of creation? What is at the core of all lives if not the divine insignia, the spiral of genetic information, which biologists have named deoxyribonucleic acid, the ladder of the self? This rotating double helix, as I've told my rabbinical colleagues, is the basic unit of each Torah scroll. It is given to us by God. Do you understand, Professor? We need only be prepared to read it in the light of our knowledge.'

Ethan shook his head. 'I don't think I understand you. You can't possibly mean that ...'

'The rabbinical council understood me immediately, Professor. Why are you being so dense? Pay attention. It has all been written. We know enough about the Messiah once we've deciphered all the signs and codes. Why shouldn't we do what we've done for millennia – the essence of our religion? Reading and learning by heart. We copy faithfully and to the letter. Why not transcribe that which has been given us? Why not use our knowledge to fight against extinction and extermination? The text exists. God's signature lies before us. We know a great deal about the embryo that was killed. We just have to find the closest relatives who survived. Then, using procedures of genetic engineering supported by Talmudic and kabbalistic teaching, and above all with the help of the Almighty, yes, *b'ezrat hashem,* then we can begin our experiment.'

'Rabbi, are you completely *meshugge*? You want to clone the Messiah? Like Dolly the sheep?'

The rabbi crowed with delight. 'You see, you finally understand. However, it's not cloning, because we don't have the original. Not yet! But with the nearest relatives' gametes the child can rise again, the child who was conceived once already and murdered before it came into this world. We might well need thousands of embryos to do this – and God's help.'

Rabbi Berkowitsch's project had been repudiated by the scholars. His reputation had suffered. This man was famous among the ultra-Orthodox in the country. When he was mentioned, the devout Hasidim paid attention.

More than a few were fascinated by his ideas. Many admired his learning and respected his determination. He knew how to perform. He led his own school of thought. His centre was in a small town outside Tel Aviv. There he received men from his community. At night he held audiences, and during the day he worked with his most trusted students and friends. In the early hours those who solicited his arbitration or hoped for his blessing waited for him in the synagogue. They stood in a bare entrance. Neon light bleached the room, and from there a steep stairway led into a tiny office where Rabbi Berkowitsch sat on a sofa behind a table. Against the wall opposite him leaned a young Hasid who assisted the rabbi when he needed something and who summoned the visitors.

Even those who rejected Rabbi Berkowitsch's thinking were not entirely immune to fascination because the logic of his treatises was so convincing, despite the fact that it often led to surprising or scandalous conclusions. His assertion about the Messiah's death *in utero* had elicited a particular indignation, but Berkowitsch defended his theory with every argument at his disposal. He met the opposition with the utmost self-confidence. How was his idea any more outrageous than Theodor Herzl's, who, in Basel more than one hundred years ago, had prophesied the founding of the Jewish state? Had it not been proclaimed that God alone would guide the Jews home? And didn't everyone consider insane those religious factions who had begun to believe that the secular Left could fulfill the divine mission? Hadn't many religious scholars hoped that the Messianic era would begin promptly with

Ben Gurion? Was it reasonable to found settlements in the midst of Arab towns? Or to set up kindergartens that could not exist without the protection of Jewish occupying forces? How was it that these political actions were any more hallowed than the attempt to bring about the birth of the Messiah with the help of secular scientists? Wasn't there a good reason why people said that in this country only realists believed in miracles, expected them and relied on them? He didn't understand Ethan's reservations. After all, there are Hasids who race through this world simply because they believe the Shoah is a sign that the End of Days is nigh and so they expect the imminent arrival of the Messiah. Didn't it then make sense at least to seize the chance to work towards fulfilling an ancient prophecy with modern means? What could be wrong with trying? If the experiment failed, there wouldn't be a Messiah, but some Jewish child or other would be born. Artificial insemination wasn't extraordinary anymore. But what if, through this intervention, the world were saved and created anew? Weren't they obligated to pursue this possibility?

'For months and months, I've been looking for survivors of the family from which the Messiah was to have originated. I found the family line from which the mother of the unborn child came, followed the bloodline and – haven't you guessed yet, Professor Rosen? – you are a distant relation of the embryo that was murdered in Poland. You are one of the family, and young enough to be a sperm donor in the great experiment. You may not lay on tefillin, keep Kosher, or observe the Sabbath and the High Holidays, but you can give us your sperm and sign on to our project. It's about the legacy, the inheritance, about a pledge from the past.'

The rabbi ran his hand through his beard. Ethan stared at the religious man. Why on earth had he agreed to meet him? He was dealing with a *meshuggeneh*, one of those figures from ancient history that swarm through this country by the thousand, pilgrims who suddenly believed they are Christ Himself, for whom an entire clinic had been set up in Jerusalem, one that specialises in this so-called Jerusalem Syndrome: monks who run around as if the crucifixion were not yet past, priests who argue over which level in the Church of the Holy Sepulchre belongs to this congregation or that. For more than one thousand five hundred years, a small, weather-beaten wooden ladder, which someone left there generations earlier, has leant against a windowsill above the sanctuary's main entrance. It cannot be removed because the various religious groups have not decided who should be allowed up there. There are Muftis who preach against any archeological activity in the Old City. These Muslim clerics fulminate that the Jews want to dig up the Dome of the Rock. But the ultra-Orthodox rabbis also rail against any excavation because it would disturb the eternal peace of those who died thousands of years ago. They were only united when it came to preventing a joint Arab and Jewish gay parade in Jerusalem. The press conference held by these godly men in their loose robes, in full regalia or simple black, with their mitres, pointed hoods or ballooning headgear, and adorned with rings, brooches, medallions, amulets, gems, jewels and chains, had looked to Ethan like a drag queen show.

Rabbi Berkowitsch did not stop talking. What did Ethan

have to lose? If the Messiah did appear – this should speak to Ethan – then the suffering of the Palestinians would end and Jews and Arabs would live together in peace. There would be no poor and no rich. All that was asked of Ethan was that he report to this clinic's genetics laboratory, which was working on the rabbi's project. 'Yes, Professor, believe me. Support for my initiative is growing.'

'But Rav Berkowitsch, this has nothing to do with artificial insemination within a marriage. You want to manipulate genes. That is eugenics, not faith in God.'

'Very true. You understand it all very well, Professor. That is exactly why my former friends have lately been treating me like an apostate. But we have no choice. The Shoah forces us to such methods. You cannot stop the train of time. Do bear in mind that this concerns the Messiah.'

He glanced around and whispered, 'I'm finding more and more support. From all over the world. Jews in New York. Protestants in Texas, who believe the messianic child will mean the return of Jesus Christ. Even a Catholic sect.' Rabbi Berkowitsch grimaced. 'Their churches are full of body parts, reliquaries. The organ trade flourished even in the Middle Ages. Vials of blood from Constantinople to Bruges, kidneys from Perugia to London, livers and lungs, locks of hair, bits of skin and brain, fingers and bone fragments were transported throughout Europe. Today cathedrals are still corpse viewing halls. Some saints left behind so many teeth, they must have had the jawbones of crocodiles. From a few martyrs there are so many vertebrae you could assemble necks as long as a giraffe's. My Catholic sympathisers are specialists in the foreskin of the circumcised baby Jesus. They are very keen on it. This Jewish infant's prepuce is their collector's fixation. Their passion! At one point there were many snippets of this foreskin. In one Italian village, Calcata, they still held processions with a piece of it. But this did not please the Vatican and suddenly it disappeared. Stolen. Imagine if we had processions with remains from the Brit Millah! That's all we need. Today, there are only a few specimens of the foreskin left. Before, we could have sewn a parachute from all the scraps. Be that as it may. This Catholic sect calls itself "Cell of the Saviour" because they hope to clone Jesus using reactivated cells from his foreskin. But they're also interested in my project. They hope my Messiah will be the second coming of their Jesus.' Rabbi Berkowitsch leaned back.

He told Ethan that he didn't need to make a decision right away. He should think about what he would like in return for his sperm donation. 'We're prepared to pay a high price. A very high price! But there are other ways to honour your contribution. Think it over. We're happy to grant your wishes.' Rabbi Berkowitsch took a business card from his jacket pocket. Would Ethan please contact him as soon as he reached a decision.

Noa laughed when Ethan told her about Rabbi Berkowitsch. Her favourite part of the story was that Ethan wanted to refuse their offer. After all, nothing less than the coming of the Messiah depended on him.

On the following day, they went to view a flat a university colleague had told Ethan about. In an old Bauhaus building. The owner, an elderly man in a snow-white shirt and anthracite-coloured trousers, opened the door. The flat had a large balcony and the rent was fair. They quickly decided that they'd take it, but didn't want to move in until Nurith returned from America. They still had to take care of Tshuptshik, the red tabby, and the budgies.

That weekend, they visited Ethan's parents. Ethan hugged Dina and Felix. He gave Rudi a nod. The Austrian told Ethan that he'd never felt so at home in Israel before. The day before he'd been to Jerusalem. He could now feel how much it was his city and he wanted to become an Israeli citizen. Noa asked if anyone else could hear a grinding noise. There was tension in the room. While Felix and Dina wore friendly expressions, she could see how much it grated on Ethan.

Rudi told them he'd written a new article on Dov, which would appear in the weekend supplement of the same Austrian newspaper that had published his obituary. This time he'd written a portrait. Felix clapped his hands. Dina nodded with satisfaction. Noa and Ethan asked if they could read it. Rudi handed them the paper. He had intended it as puff piece. Whereas Rudi had formerly hinted at judgement of Dov for his Zionism, he now defended his claim on the Promised Land. He praised Dov for wanting to no longer be a victim, but a free man. Basically, Rudi had once again portrayed Dov as a radical nationalist, but had judged him differently.

Rudi had not yet sent the article to Vienna. He asked if anyone else wanted to read it. He'd like to know what they thought of it. Felix declined. 'I'm not a censor. I'm sure you've done a great job. I trust you completely.'

Noa and Ethan exchanged looks. Rudi said, 'Thank you, Felix.' He ignored their silence. 'Let's not talk about it any more. Please. I regret my earlier version.' He smiled at them all. 'I have a plan.' He'd thought everything over and asked Felix if he would accept him, his son, as an organ donor. It would mean a great deal to him.

Dina looked in dismay at Felix, whose smile had faded. Felix spoke slowly and with distinct friendliness. 'Thank you, but that's out of the question!'

'But why not?' Rudi asked.

'The mere idea of it is perverse. That a son should sacrifice himself for his father?' Felix put his hands to his lower back as if the pain had returned.

'But why not? What does sacrifice even mean in this case? It's an obvious solution. Let me do it. Why do you refuse?'

'You have your whole life in front of you, Rudi. You still need your kidneys. I can't eviscerate you.'

Dina was all aflutter. Felix said that, as his father, he forbade any further discussion of the matter. The idea was completely alien to him.

That was the word that upset Rudi. Alien.

'So I'm alien to you?'

'Not you!'

'So that's how it is!'

Ethan interrupted. 'Listen, I've got a better idea.'

Rudi yelled, 'Naturally you're against it.'

'Why naturally?'

'Because you didn't offer first. That's why you don't want me to do it either.'

Ethan shook his head. 'You are not normal.' He took a deep breath. 'I believe there's an easier way. I recently met with the famous Rabbi Yeshayahu Berkowitsch. You must have read about him. In short, he owes me a favour. If Rabbi Berkowitsch wants to, he can find a man Felix's age or older who can donate a matching organ for Abba. Believe me.'

'And why should he help us of all people?' Rudi asked.

'Because he believes in me,' Ethan said, and promised to explain in more detail another time.

Later, the two of them sat in Ethan's old room and Ethan told Rudi about Rabbi Berkowitsch and his plan to recreate the Messiah. Rudi said, 'But that sounds completely crazy.'

'No doubt, but if it gets us a kidney!'

'And if it doesn't?'

'Then we can decide if one of us should step up for the transplant. Anyhow, perhaps Berkowitsch knows a way out. Sure, it sounds insane. But what's normal? Insanity has been the norm here for a long time.'

Rudi couldn't think of anything to counter Ethan's reasoning.

7

NONSENSE, THE DOCTOR SAID. She was not at all convinced by Rabbi Berkowitsch's idea. She was not at all religious. She did her work whether it would help bring the Messiah into this world or, as she rather expected, just one more squaller. Incidentally, reproductive science was not yet advanced enough to generate the clone of a murdered embryo. The thought of bringing about such an afterbirth of the Shoah was not appealing. 'Nevertheless, I fulfill my duties.'

The doctor – a woman with sparkling blue eyes, ash-black hair shot through with a few ice-grey streaks and a caramel complexion – looked at the two men. A cold smile. As she spoke, she underlined her words with emphatic gestures. She reminded Rudi of a traffic warden. She was the head of the genetics department. Rudi had been surprised by how quiet and empty the hallways were. There were only three others in the waiting room: a woman in an olive green pants suit sitting quietly in the corner, an adolescent boy, a weightlifter in jeans with fidgety legs, and a man in a suit and tie. No obviously sick patients like the ones he had seen in the lift.

The doctor frowned. 'Recreating an individual by hybridising his descendants is an absurd idea. And all that we have are the convoluted calculations and theories of Rav Berkowitsch who wants to conjure up one of God's Anointed.'

'Then why are you doing this? Are you actually working to produce a Jewish superman?' Ethan asked.

Nonsense, she objected again. She was not, she told them, trying to improve genes. Eugenics was out of the question. Berkowitsch wanted just one thing – to reconstruct the embryo that was meant to become the Messiah. 'That's *meschugge* enough. Don't turn this poppycock into something even crazier than it already is.' The rabbi was an extremely intelligent person, a borderline genius, very charismatic, but he'd become obsessed with this absurd idea.

'You admit it and yet you still work with him?'

'It's an interesting scientific project. And well-funded. But the assumptions, the religious theories behind it are completely insane.'

Ethan was outraged. 'Are we in an asylum here? Has this entire country gone round the bend? It's complete madness!'

'Yes. We're not far from the psychiatric department, Professor Rosen. It's on the same floor. In fact, they're involved in the project. Rav Berkowitsch visits them regularly in order, according to the official version, to offer spiritual support to the patients.'

Ethan and Rudi exchanged looks.

The doctor said, 'The truth is that he himself is an object of study, although he doesn't know it. You've met him. He's a phenomenon. Whoever speaks with him is overwhelmed. Haven't you noticed?'

Rudi sighed and looked at Ethan doubtfully, but Ethan asked, 'How can you take part in the project if you're convinced of its absurdity?'

'You're willing to take part because you want a kidney for your father, right? We can use the data from the gene pool to good effect. It has nothing to do with the Messiah. For us, it's about a comprehensive study of a select, manageable group of related human beings who have specific characteristics. We've got human biologists, clinicians, epidemiologists, even psychiatrists, sociologists and historians working together on this project. We want to study when and how certain diseases emerged in this clan. Do you understand?'

This woman, with her hair severely combed back, sounded a bit too insistent. She paused and then said more softly, as if she were revealing the real secret, 'Berkowitsch is not without influence. His authority moulds his community – a tiny one, it's true, but who knows, in a few years he might influence which coalition will sit in the Knesset.'

Rabbi Yeshayahu Berkowitsch did meet with distrust among his own followers, but his theorem that the fundamental unit of the Holy Scriptures was the double helix fascinated men from all camps. In a speech to the Hasidim he had proclaimed, 'Every one of our cells contains the entire Torah.' His theorems were quoted everywhere, either with admiration or complete disdain. He was invited onto talk shows and went. He drew American and European sponsors, wealthy people who didn't know how to prove their Jewishness, who didn't know Pessach from Channukah or matzoh balls from *kreplach*. Millionaires who wanted for nothing but the chance to support a Jewish initiative because their money flowed into all the other Jewish organisations already. Along came Rabbi Berkowitsch and suddenly they were the Messiah's personal patrons. Who was surprised when Israeli institutions then cooperated with Berkowitsch? He found new means of support. First and foremost among the observant. Many of the devout were convinced that Yeshayahu Berkowitsch was insane, but still, he must be a wonder rabbi and a great scholar if the powers of finance, the state and science were united behind him.

The doctor said, 'He's a genius. But to conclude that everyone who is taking part in this project believes in the coming of the Messiah is ridiculous!' The rest was medical routine. She asked, solely for professional purposes, for precise details from both men about their families, until she suddenly remarked to Rudi, 'So you're not a Jew then?'

He did not answer, but Ethan asked, 'I thought you were only interested in genetics and not in the Messiah? Why do you care about his religion? Are you more papist than Rav Berkowitsch?'

'Please stop these accusations, Professor Rosen. Does Berkowitsch know about your parentage, Doctor Klausinger?'

'It's irrelevant,' Ethan interjected. 'The Jewish Messiah's father could be Buddhist, Muslim or Nazi. It depends on the mother.' He banged his fist on the table. 'Since when are you interested in religious law? In this country even lesbians are getting artificially inseminated so they can be *Yiddishe mames* without the need for men.'

'Was that an insinuation, Professor Rosen? Are you implying I'm out of place?'

Rudi intervened. 'He certainly did not intend to. Apologise, Ethan.'

'What for? I'm supposed to apologise because she considers your genes inferior?'

The doctor crossed her arms. 'Calm down. This is a national project. We are researching a specific gene pool. A non-Jew doesn't fit. It's nothing personal, Mr Klausinger.'

'If my brother's semen isn't good enough for you, then you can forget mine as well. Even if it's not eugenics, it is racism!'

Rudi was silent. Had Ethan just called him his brother?

The doctor looked over her glasses at both of them. 'I am following scientific specifications. If you really think that Berkowitsch sees it differently, then let's call him. He can decide.'

'That won't be necessary,' Rudi whispered. He stood up to leave.

Ethan sprang up, too. In the doorway, he turned back once more. 'If you exclude him, then I won't be a part of it either.'

'And the kidney for your father?' the doctor asked. She put the question calmly, as if casually.

All three were silent. Then she gestured to the chairs and asked the men to sit back down. The doctor lifted the receiver, dialled a number, and her face brightened as she said, 'Rav Berkowitsch, this is Tamar. How are you?'

She explained the situation in detail. She even told him about Ethan's threat to quit the project. And surprisingly, the rabbi had no objection to Rudi. Only the ovum was essential. The mother determined the affiliation. He, Berkowitsch, didn't even need any male relatives of the Messiah. When Rudi called out to the doctor that he was planning to convert to Judaism in any case, Berkowitsch shouted loud enough that the two men could hear him, 'Tamar, do your job!'

'As you wish.'

'I don't wish for anything. I am only following the project's guidelines and God's command.'

They waited in the corridor until they were ushered into a room. They had to fill out a form and sign a document. They each got a plastic cup. They were first to urinate into the bowl, stop, turn the stream into the cup, and release the rest into the bowl. Ethan went first. Afterwards, they had to roll up their sleeves to have blood drawn. Ethan looked away as the needle punctured his skin. Rudi smiled encouragingly at the short, thin nurse.

Ethan had from the beginning agreed to take part in the rabbi's project on the condition that he and Rudi were also tested to determine if one of them was a suitable donor. If no other kidney could be found then they would be candidates. Ethan secretly hoped it would come to that. A young resident told them their next appointment would be in a week, and if the analysis revealed no abnormalities, they would then donate their sperm. They should be abstinent for four days prior to the donation. No ejaculation.

Outside, the sun beat down on them. Ethan asked, 'You want to become a Jew? Circumcised and all?'

'Yes, because I feel Jewish.'

'OK then. If you are one anyway, why bother converting? Why do you need the rabbi's blessing? Or do you believe in God?'

'Only if absolutely necessary …'

Ethan smirked. He didn't hide his mistrust. How appealing it was to be a victim without ever having suffered. They loped along, side by side. They left the clinic through the main door.

Rudi suddenly stood still. 'If I were to announce tomorrow that I was going to become Hopi or Sioux, you'd accept it. I imagine that if I were a Celtic druid and put on a helmet with horns, you'd find it picturesque and amusing. And what is a real Hopi? No one runs through the plains with a bow and arrows any more.'

Passersby stared at them. Ethan grabbed Rudi's arm. 'It's alright,' he murmured, and quickly pulled Rudi after him.

Rudi had been a changeling from the first. He wasn't like those children who had read too much Karl May and crept through the park in a feather headdress. He was the Jewish child before he was even born. Ever since the myth of Ahasver, the Wandering Jew, he had roamed through the world. That's how he was seen by those who knew his biological father was a survivor. His father was his black spot. The silhouette with the hooked nose. His mother didn't want to have anything to do with him. He was not a long-desired baby, but an expression of her despair, his birth a defeat. Her lover had chosen his marriage over her long before. A few years later, his mother would most likely have aborted him, under a doctor's care and without legal consequences. But at the time …

Maybe she had tried? Rudi had asked himself this question when he was in high school. But by then she had brought him to his foster parents. She waved goodbye, not without tears in her eyes. Were they for him or for herself?

His foster family had wanted him to feel at home, and he was not to cause trouble for either his mother in Vienna or his mama in the Tyrol. He should settle in. Go to church on Sundays. The priest warned the boy not to take his winky in hand. Those who touched their members went straight to hell, he was told, and for weeks Rudi wasn't sure how he was supposed to get that body part out of his pants to go to the toilet. Nevertheless, no matter how cautiously Rudi took hold of himself, he remained the Jewish child. The world was full of people who wanted to be Jewish, Asian or South Sea Islanders and decked themselves and their houses out exotically. Incense sticks sweetened the air. They set up nomad's tents in their back gardens. They wore berets, grew moustaches and drank café au lait out of bowls in order to feel French. They danced flamenco because home, to them, seemed Spanish. And why not? Why should it be any more ridiculous to wear a sarong at the Wörthersee than lederhosen? Does a kilt look more comical in Paris than it does in Edinburgh?

But he, who had made himself at home in so many countries and so many languages, did not need to wear a costume. In boarding school he was soon considered an expert on all things Jewish. His father, who had never been around, had shaped him through his absence. Rudi had done Jewish Studies and had learnt Yiddish and Hebrew. He knew more about the Torah and the Talmud than many who had grown up in Jewish families. He knew the prayers and the commandments.

His wish to convert was no whim. Others might want a disguise; he wanted a conversion. He wanted to unmask himself. Israelis like Ethan were born in Zion but preferred to live elsewhere, in New York, San Francisco or London, in Paris, Berlin or Rome. Ethan liked the country best when he was far away. In the taxi, Ethan said to Rudi, 'I'm warning you. Judaism is a symptom of old age. All these young people with open faces and fresh views taking the world by storm will eventually grow tired and their faces will melt, their noses will grow longer and their eyes become cloudy until they all think they can see clearly. They'll have become old Jews. And all those who never believed in God, who railed against the coalition and the army, who went to discos and bars every Friday night, who stayed up all night smoking joints, they'll suddenly start lighting Sabbath candles, blessing bread and wine – all because of the children, they'll say – and all at once, they will love their inherited resentments and their deep-rooted fears. Fears no one would have guessed they had. Fears everyone else should be afraid of.'

Rudi shook his head. He felt rejuvenated here. Tel Aviv – when he walked through these streets it seemed that everyone who crossed his path had sprung from books. They spoke Hebrew, Yiddish, French, Russian, English, Polish, German, Italian, Amharic or Arabic. And then there were the undocumented immigrants. They spoke Filipino, Romanian, Mandarin, Yoruba or Igbo.

One day he had been walking on a small side street that ran parallel to the sea front before turning abruptly to the right and opening onto Dizengoff Street, the unflaggingly busy commercial road. In this narrow passage between the old Bauhaus buildings, it was completely quiet. A cat slunk along a wall, birds chirped overhead and suddenly, from a tiny balcony on the second floor, came the unmistakable voice of Lotte Lehmann. It was one of Rudi's favorite songs. *Weyla's Song.* First the gentle waves from the piano, then the opening words: *Du bist Orplid, mein Land!* The hymn to a land of longing, to a place at once near and far. Rudi noticed an old man in a short-sleeved shirt with thick horn-rimmed glasses and snow-white hair, an ancient apparition, sitting on the balcony and staring blankly in front of him. Had he escaped here with the record in his baggage? Was he remembering his former homeland, lost forever? In Tel Aviv in the Thirties and Forties, it was forbidden to speak German on the street and in the cinema. Some German films were advertised as Austrian so as not to offend. *Du bist Orplid, mein Land! / Das ferne leuchtet.* (You are Orplid, my land! Gleaming in the distance). Lehmann's voice grew stronger. The music rose to a crescendo. *Vom Meere dampfet dein besonnter Strand / Den Nebel, so der Götter Wange feuchtet* (From the sea and your sundrenched shore / mists rise and moisten the gods' cheeks). Rudi's shirt stuck to his skin. The midday heat was unbearable. The city stewed. It was far away and yet just around the corner. *Uraltes Wasser steigen / Verjüngt um deine Hüften, Kind!* (Ancient waters rise, / refreshed, around your hips, child!)

Rudi had passed by without being seen by the old man on the balcony. When he left the street, the noise surrounded him again. An Asian woman tottered past on high heels, her jeans slung low around her hips bones. Her thong peeked out at the sides. She rang the doorbell of a store-front that had been turned into a flat. Someone opened a window and she climbed in over the sill. Rudi crossed the street, which was lined with large hotels. On a run-down square near the sea – the ruins of a decrepit discotheque recalled the excitement and rage for sound in the Eighties – he stopped at a stand for a glass of fresh-pressed orange juice. An African man lugged an insulated bag around and sang out the brand of ice cream he sold: 'Artik!'

Near the breakwater, a few metres from the kids' surf-boards and the chassakes, as they called old Levantine flat boats used by the lifeguards here, ran the Yarkon River. If you followed it northwards and veered to the right, you could make out the building Felix and Dina lived in. The view from their living room extended out over the flat rooftops, past the water tanks and thickets of antennas to the minarets and the clock tower in Jaffa. The way to their flat crossed Dizengoff Street, where the bars were over-flowing and waiters ran from one table to the next in the midday heat, and in the midst of all this din, Rudi sat as if he were on the Boulevard Saint-Germain or in Berlin on the Kurfürstendamm.

Du bist Orplid, mein Land. From here, it wasn't far to Jaffa, where the ruins of Arab houses stood next to magnifi-cent new buildings that had risen along the coast. But what was distant? Not Gaza, not Ramallah and not Jerusalem.

Ethan had told him, 'You have no idea. When I was a child, there may have been a few traces left of the original Tel Aviv. In the Sixties, when I was crawling under tables, the adults talked non-stop about politics. Every action was saturated with politics. The talked and sang about it. They laughed and cried over it. Believe me. When I came home from playing with the other kids, the one Israeli television channel rang out from every flat. When the news came on, the volume was turned up in every house, and we, the little ones, trotted home accompanied by reports of the latest events. Back then – even in the Seventies – many people used the public buses, and the drivers had the radio on and turned it up at the top of the hour, and if he didn't, one of the passengers would ask him to because no one wanted to miss a thing, especially not the latest attack or imminent escalation. And even in the Nineties everyone was glued to their televisions whenever there was a newsflash. But today, Rudi, when I see my colleagues, the students in my lectures, my childhood friends, no one wants to talk politics. People don't talk about the government and the parties anymore, they argue about restaurants and bars. Before, they met over a meal to discuss politics, then later they'd get together and talk politics as an excuse to have a another good meal. Today one word about the national situation is enough to ruin their appetite.'

Rudi didn't disagree. He remembered an afternoon the three of them had spent in the old port in a bar directly on the coast. Fighter jets had flown overhead to land at a small airport nearby. A few of Noa's friends had joined them later, as planned. They were all working artists. Six singles and two couples. Kids with skateboards and bicycles.

The conflict was not a topic of conversation in this group either, because everything had already been said.

Why assure each other, yet again, that the situation was hopeless? Why pretend that anything could be expected of the coalition? Or even from the opposition? A few years earlier, Noa's acquaintances would have explained to a foreigner like Rudi what conditions were necessary for peace. Since then, the slogans of the former Leftists had become the majority's empty formulas, had turned into a consensus that seemed nothing more than lip-service. Those who had spent years calling for negotiations were now split into warring factions. One faction believed there was no one to negotiate with on the other side. 'There is no partner', they repeated at every opportunity, and if it was a question of the military, they liked to say '*Ejn brera*', which effectively meant 'We have no choice.' Another faction, however, believed their own leaders and the settlers were to blame for the fact that there was no solution in sight. Some believed it was too late to separate the two nations into their own states. But almost everyone had given up.

Two days later, Rudi and Ethan were sitting in a café. Ethan's many cancellations had been noticed. In the retinue that travelled the globe from one international conference to the next, he was considered a key player. In the last week he'd missed seven different events. Now he was meant to be in Los Angeles, to speak at the Museum of the Holocaust, but Ethan had once again announced he didn't want to go. 'A colleague just asked me if it's true that you're on your deathbed,' Rudi said.

'What did you tell him?'

'I said there was an illness in the family.'

Ethan had asked Rudi to give the lecture for him in Los Angeles. 'You'll be there anyway. Why not read my presentation along with yours? I'll just rework an old paper.'

Two days after that, Rudi flew to the United States. In the plane, he finished his own lecture. The layover was tight. The flight from Tel Aviv was delayed and he was worried he'd miss his connection in Heathrow. He rushed out of the plane and hurried along the hallway with his suitcase and laptop bag.

Heathrow had sunk into chaos yet again. The airport was bursting at the seams. The transit areas were mobbed, nothing moved through security. When it was finally his turn, Rudi threw his keys, wallet, belt, pen and mobile phone in a plastic tray and folded his suit jacket over it. He put his laptop in a second one. He hurried through the security aisle, quickly gathered his things and rushed on. When he'd almost reached the gate, he felt his pocket. His wallet with his cash and credit cards was missing. He ran back to security.

Only after he'd asked the officer a second time in complete despair did his wallet surface. He had long given up any hope of making the connection to Los Angeles. And yet, not only did he board the plane a few minutes later, but the Boeing sat on the tarmac for a full hour until they were given permission to take off.

Too exhausted to sleep, Rudi watched movies on the little screen. In Los Angeles, an assistant picked him up at the airport to drive him to the evening reception in a fancy restaurant. Rudi would have preferred to hole up in the hotel. He wanted to go to the toilet, take a bath and fall into bed, but the other academics, most of whom had arrived much earlier, were already seated for dinner. They were all waiting for him, the assistant explained. It took a long time to get there. The others greeted him effusively. Rudi's last book on museum exhibitions of minorities in Europe had been widely praised. Now that Ethan no longer appeared, Rudi was the new name in their field of study. In contrast to Ethan, who had impressed them with his sarcasm and dark scenarios, Rudi won their enthusiasm with his gentle irony and mild assurance. So it was all the more exciting that Rudi was standing in for Ethan. 'Here he is,' the conference organiser called out to him before turning to the others: 'Rudi Klausinger will not only give his own lecture, he'll also read Rosen's introductory speech. Tell us, is Ethan feeling better? We're all worried about him.'

The dinner was long and Rudi was dead-tired. A new day had dawned in Israel hours before, while in Los Angeles it was still early evening. After midnight he fell into bed, quite drunk. The next morning, his skull felt like it had swollen overnight into a medicine ball. He got up, too late for breakfast. He was the last one in the dining room. Every one else was leaving for the conference. He hurried after them. During the introductions, he took his first look at Ethan's opening speech. He skimmed the text, flipped through the pages, and – there was no doubt – he recognised the contents. It was the article Rudi had quoted in his obituary of Dov.

Ethan had written his provocative thesis in Israel, objected to it in Austria when Rudi had attacked it, and was now having Rudi repeat it in the US. Was Ethan making fun of him? He scanned the sentences and everything they said struck him as false. He couldn't possibly stand behind these words. He had now spent weeks with Felix and Dina, and had learnt a great deal about Dov from them, and on top of that had done research of his own. Not only that, in this museum in Los Angeles, Ethan's theories would only sound crazy. They wouldn't call up the same associations here as they had in Israel or in Austria.

He read it off in the truest sense of the word: he droned one sentence, sighed another, mumbled a third. Still, the audience understood his delivery as a staging and a fitting rendition of Ethan's derisive thoughts. He was congratulated, his presentation singled out for praise, and then he was asked to move along since the first panel was opening with his paper. Rudi was filled with rage. His anger wasn't directed at Ethan, but at his colleagues who did not understand how preposterous everything they had just heard was. So he changed his own lecture accordingly. Rudi addressed the doubts Ethan had raised and stressed the necessity of memory above and beyond all borders and cultures. He contradicted Ethan's theses, but indirectly and without naming him. Enthusiasm for this virtual double act gave rise to bursts of applause, nods and guffaws. One academic from Florida, a stuffed shirt in a suit and tie, whispered 'I love it,' and an English colleague, an extremely tall historian dressed in black with red patent leather shoes, exclaimed in response, 'Hilarious!'

Only after Rudi had finished and the discussion had begun did doubt creep into the audience's minds. But no one dared address him directly and even he had given up.

The discussion he and Ethan had so passionately held in Austria didn't get anyone here worked up.

He didn't speak of the incident after his return. What would have been the point? He only hinted at it to Noa, but she just laughed and told him about a commission she had accepted. Along with her work for a company that made prostheses, she had designed a journal layout for an organisation that supported undocumented immigrants.

Ethan hardly showed any interest in Noa's projects because he was so caught up in his own studies. Rudi, on the other hand, could listen to her endlessly. He didn't know anything about graphic design and marvelled at Noa's versatility. Her work didn't ever seem to be routine. She didn't seem to fit in anywhere, but seemed in tune with everything. She was one of a kind. He watched her surreptitiously, stole glances at her. When she caught him looking at her, she raised an eyebrow. He didn't think she took him seriously. 'Hello, half-brother-in-law,' she'd greet him.

He was suddenly unsure if his affection for the Rosen family had come from his feelings for Noa or if, on the contrary, his delight with his new family was the source of Noa's appeal. It wasn't even clear to him whether he wanted to see her because she was with Ethan or whether he wanted to spend time with his brother because he couldn't stop thinking about her. He feelings about Israel and his plans to stay were just as tangled. He was sure of just one thing: he wanted to become Jewish. He wanted finally to bond with his father through his confession of faith.

8

LIFE IN BLACK AND WHITE. People standing in a circle. The men in jeans and flowered shirts, wearing sandals. The women in shorts or colourful flowing skirts. Everyone is singing. One man stands in the centre with an accordion. '*Layla, layla, ha-ruach goveret*' (Night, night – the wind blows). Dina sits in front of the screen. '*Layla, layla,*' she hums, and *'numi, numi.'* Go to sleep. She sings along but does not fall asleep, does not close her eyes, because at night the memories swarm.

Night after night Dina sits enthroned on the sofa. Go to sleep, go to sleep, only you are still awake, go to sleep, go to sleep. After the late show, they replayed music shows from the Seventies. *Layla, layla.* A black and white show full of life. A group is seated together, young and old. They sing of their dreams, of hardship and the pain of times gone by. They sing of old yearnings and Dina sits there, more than thirty years later, and broods on the songs. They sing: 'We have sowed, but not reaped.' They sing: 'We came to this country to build and be edified.'

This is no gala performance being broadcast. The singers have been squeezed into a bare room. Perhaps the community room in a kibbutz. They sing as if they were listening for their own echo. They look transfigured. Night after night Dina holds out until sleep overcomes her. Tonight, again, she can't tear herself away from the television. Felix lies in the next room, exhausted, done in.

After the dialysis he didn't want to rest, but insisted on going right out. There was a Shostakovich concert in the Felix Rand Mann Auditorium and Ethan's parents had invited him and Noa along. Ethan was almost too late. He had gone to the clinic that afternoon to give his sperm sample. Noa noticed immediately that something was bothering him. He barely said hello to Dina and Felix, but hugged her tighter than usual as he kissed her on the lips. Then he sat next to her and withdrew completely into himself. She could feel that the music was not reaching him. They had moved into the new flat two days earlier and Ethan had begun working again when Felix was discharged from the hospital. In the mornings, he sat down at his desk, answered emails, worked for three hours on his latest book, which he didn't want to tell Noa anything about, and then he spent his afternoons writing shorter pieces – essays, forewords, reviews. He did not allow anything to interrupt his studies. Yet he didn't turn off the phone, left his door open, and now and again read the latest news. Outside influences didn't distract him, but instead seemed constantly to spark new ideas. He couldn't imagine dividing his work and his free time. When he showed up at the concert completely distracted, Noa assumed he was thinking about his work.

In the intermission, Felix brought each of them a glass of champagne. He said, 'I am so happy to be here with you. You have no idea how happy it makes me. It's only a shame that Rudi didn't have time today.' Noa saw Ethan's expression. She was puzzled. Ethan had warmed to his half-brother in the past few days. They had drawn together over Rabbi Berkowitsch and his plan for salvation and they had

mocked several colleagues. When Rudi casually announced
– they were drinking beer in a bar on the beach one night –
that he would not accept the position in Vienna under any
circumstances because he couldn't imagine competing with
his own brother, the spell seemed to have been broken.
Ethan assured him that he wasn't at all concerned with the
position and Rudi nodded. 'I know. I'm not either. It never
was about the position.'

Felix insisted on eating together after the concert. He
suggested driving to a French restaurant in Jaffa that had
just opened up in an old Arab house. Dina clapped her
hands in delight. Noa asked if it wouldn't be too much for
Felix, but he reassured her and tried to reach Rudi who did
not answer his phone. Felix left him a message asking Rudi
to join them.

The restaurant was more Moroccan than French, but the
food tasted all the better. Felix didn't just order for himself
but wanted an enormous appetizer platter and then extra
side dishes for everyone. When Dina pointed out that no
one could eat that much, he said, 'Let me worry about
that.' And he did. He made sure there wasn't a bite left and
acted as if he were not under any dietary restrictions. 'Are
you insane?' Dina cried, but he didn't spare a thought for
his failed kidneys. 'And now for the highlight!' he called
when it was time for dessert. Everyone else declined, but
he ordered a crème caramel.

It started before they even got home. Felix groaned. Noa
had to pull the car in to the side of the road. He climbed out
of the car and vomited up his entire dinner. Then he collapsed, gasping for air. Dina talked to him. Noa unbuttoned

his shirt and fanned him. Ethan stood off to the side, pulled out his mobile phone and called an ambulance. Felix lay there as if the various parts of his body didn't belong together. Noa remembered an ox she had seen butchered during her first summer in the Tyrol, how the animal had snorted in its last minutes and rolled its eyes until only the whites were visible, as if a film had been drawn over the irises.

Noa watched Felix die, saw his eyes grow dull and his gaze blur. He succumbed. Dina clasped her hands over her mouth and bent down to Felix. She covered his hands with kisses, caressed his cheeks and screamed his name again and again. 'Felix!'

Ethan spoke with the dispatcher and told him their location. He circled the car to open the boot. 'Where is the warning triangle, Dina?' She looked at him as if he were from another planet. The ambulance arrived quickly and just as the emergency doctor got out, Felix revived. The doctor said it was just a circulatory collapse. Nothing serious. The EKG didn't show any irregularities. Nonetheless, he wanted to take the patient to the clinic for observation. But Felix grabbed his sleeve and groaned, 'I don't need anything. Just ate too much. Home.'

They tried to convince him. 'Felix!' They implored him to get tested, but he shook his head.

'Father, stop this insanity. You had an attack!'

Felix stood up. On his own. He looked at them all, Dina, Noa, the medic and Ethan, as if they had pushed him down, as if he were rising up against them. Back in the flat, he lay down straight away and fell asleep. Ethan and Noa stayed with Dina. They were too upset to leave.

Layla, layla. Night after night. Dina watched as women just like she had been sang of their youth. She said that in one of the singers she could recognise the teenager who had picked tomatoes in shorts and muddy boots. Noa and Ethan did not understand how she could possibly see herself in this woman. 'I had just fled from Vienna and there I was, standing in the field. We got up before dawn. In the summer we fought the heat, in the winter the mud.'

Haitah tze'irah bakineret asher baGalil. There was a young woman who lived near the Kinneret Sea. In Galilee. Every day she would sing a song of joy. The only song she sang was about a young woman who lived near the Kinneret Sea. In Galilee. *Haitah tze'irah bakineret asher baGalil.* The woman sat in front of the screen and the woman behind it both sang the song, separated by the glass and the years. Noa smiled and warbled along a bit. Ethan said, 'Ima, I have to talk to you.'

Dina turned down the sound. The singing stopped, the lips opened and closed silently, heads swayed side to side. 'What is it?' Dina asked, but Ethan didn't speak. He looked at Noa. She stood up to leave.

'I have no secrets from her,' Dina said. 'Sit down, Noa.'

Ethan went to the bar, took the whiskey decanter and poured a finger's breadth into a crystal glass. After taking a gulp, he sat back down. It was about the kidney donation, he explained. She was aware that he'd spoken with Rav Berkowitsch about Felix. The rabbi was convinced he could clone the Messiah using Rudi and Ethan's sperm.

Dina shrugged. 'There are all kinds of idiots in this country.'

'But I'm talking about Abba's kidney. In any case, they had to run a few genetic tests,' Ethan said and Noa saw Dina's face turn white and her mouth snap shut.

In the clinic, the doctor had called Ethan into her office. 'I know that you are here to donate sperm, Mr Rosen. We need to talk.'

'No problem.'

'We can't use you.'

'According to whom?'

'The test results. Your father is a close relative of the messianic embryo's parents. He seems to be the closest of their kin still alive.'

Although Ethan had never believed in God or salvation, he suddenly had the feeling she was pronouncing him and his family to be of noble lineage. He felt flattered. 'You don't say. Strange.' The thought began to appeal to him. 'Funny! Who would have thought we're related to the Messiah?'

'You, Dr Rosen, are not related to the Messiah at all. There is no genetic match.'

'But you just said …'

'I was talking about Felix Rosen. Not you.'

'I don't understand. What do you mean? Is this about my half-brother being illegitimate again?'

'Mr Rosen, please.' She took a deep breath. 'This is not against you or against Dr Klausinger. We've done the analysis to determine whether or not you are a compatible donor match with Felix Rosen.'

'And?'

'You requested an independent analysis of your family relations.'

'Yes, that's correct. I spoke with the resident about it. Not with you. I also don't want my brother to know about it. I just wanted to know if we really were in the same family.'

'What is a family?'

'If we are related genetically.'

'That I can't tell you without your brother's permission.'

'Fine. Is that it? What does that have to do with the Messiah?'

She looked him directly in the eye. 'We needed confirmation: Felix Rosen is not your father. You are not his biological son. You are not part of the gene pool we are analysing. Do you understand, Ethan? You are not a member of this group. Ethan? Are you listening to me? Do you understand what I'm saying?'

'What do you say to that, Ima?'

Dina looked away and said nothing. On the television they all mutely clapped to the beat and sang noiselessly and full of joy. Noa looked at Ethan's mother. She wanted to take Dina's hand, to hug her. Dina felt Noa's fingers. She twisted her mouth into a tense smile and pulled her hand away.

Ethan asked her, 'Did you know? Is that why you weren't angry with Abba? I didn't understand how you could forgive and forget Father's affair so quickly. I didn't get why you were so calm. But if Felix isn't my father, then it all makes sense. You feel guilty. You've felt guilty for years. For decades. When you learnt about his affair, you were finally even. Does he even know I'm not his son? Did you tell him? Or was I a cuckoo's egg?'

Dina gave a sharp laugh, more of a snort, full of scorn. 'You think it's funny?' Ethan asked.

'What can I say?'

'Is that why you were so happy you could give Felix one of your kidneys? It was a way to make amends, right?'

She still didn't answer and Ethan grew louder. 'Why didn't you ever tell me?'

'Leave her alone,' Noa said.

'I want an answer.'

'It's not always about you,' Noa said.

'And what have you got to do with it?'

'Nothing.'

'Exactly. So please let me and my mother talk.'

She got up to leave. Dina turned to him, 'Have you gone crazy? You're not to send Noa away! Noa, stay. For me.' Then, to Ethan, 'Apologise to her.'

Noa put on her coat and waved. Ethan shouted, 'I want the truth! Who is my father, Ima?'

'What do you want to know?' Felix appeared in the doorway. Pale, with rumpled hair, and in his dressing gown, he leant against the doorframe. His face was puffy with sleep.

'Bravo,' Noa called. 'Now you woke him up.' They all avoided each others' eyes.

Felix looked exhausted. He slumped into a chair near the door and closed his eyes. 'What is it you want to know?'

The old man groaned. Noa went to him. He took her hand, asked her to help him, and stumbled into the kitchen. He turned on the tap and filled a glass with water. He returned to the living room with it and carefully sat down next to Dina on the sofa. He took a sip. Then, after a pause, he began as if he were talking about someone else. 'We've been married for fifty years.' He gently reached for Dina, his hand trembling. 'Look at her.' He faced Ethan. 'And you dare to …'

'He has no idea,' Dina said, but Felix murmured, all the more reason …' Then he bit his lip.

Dina said, 'He got himself tested. For the kidney donation.'

Felix's eyes sprang open and he stared at Ethan. 'What for?' He looked around, noticed the muted television, saw the people on the screen opening and closing their mouths. To Noa, these people from the Seventies looked like colourful fish in an aquarium. She remembered how she had stood in front of the screen as a child and wondered if all these creatures opening and closing their little mouths were trying to tell her something, to warn her perhaps; and now she had the feeling that these men and women from years gone by had appeared on the screen only to warn the country of the present. Maybe these shows should only be shown without sound, she thought, so that the voices wouldn't drown out what lay behind the melancholy melodies.

'Turn it off,' Felix said. Dina grabbed the portable telephone and pressed the red button. She didn't seem to notice her mistake, but kept pressing the button. 'I wonder if you really do have no idea who it is,' Felix said to Ethan. Then he turned to Dina, 'It doesn't matter anymore.'

Somewhere outside an ambulance siren wailed. Felix said, 'It's Dov. Dov Zedek.'

'Are you my papa?' One morning Ethan had climbed into his parents' bed and found a stranger there, and he, the little boy whose father was so rarely at home, had asked in surprise, 'Are you my papa?' Ethan's mother, who had put Dov and his current girlfriend up in her bedroom, told him later, 'That's Abba's best friend. His name is Dov. He's staying with us for two days.'

It took Ethan a few seconds to recover. 'This is a joke, right?'

Felix shook his head. Ethan's father told him he hadn't been able to have children. He tried to smile, but couldn't manage it. It wasn't possible. The camp, he whispered, and swallowed. The noise in his throat was louder than his words. The doctors said that was probably the cause. Or not. 'Who knows?' In any case, he was, and after a pause he finished, sterile. He looked as if he had only that moment realised what he was saying. 'At first we thought we just needed some time. But then …' Dina looked out of the window, and when she turned back, her face was a smiling mask. Ethan was speechless.

He was the one, Felix continued, who sent Dov's cassettes to Vienna after the burial. That was their agreement. 'I was supposed to give them to you if he died.' Felix looked up at the ceiling. 'I don't know how many times I suggested he tell you the whole story. Dov always said that when he became your father he wouldn't be able to remain your friend. He said that that was the deal from the beginning. Not a word to Ethan.'

And Dina said, 'He didn't want any more family. Never again.' Then, 'Felix wanted to but couldn't. Dov could but didn't want to.'

Ethan shook his head. 'I don't understand.'

'Dina never betrayed me.' Felix emphasised each word.

She said, 'It was a different time.'

They noticed that Ethan was looking at them like strangers.

'He'll never understand,' Felix concluded. Dina began, 'We founded a kibbutz,' but Felix interrupted her. 'He won't understand.' To Ethan he said, 'Dov found me in the camp!'

Dina shook her head as if she wanted to contradict him. 'We wanted children. That was the point. Everyone in the kibbutz knew about our difficulty. They kept watch outside our bedroom. Why shouldn't we have asked Dov?'

Felix: 'We believed in the future.'

Dina: 'Most of all we believed in ourselves.'

Noa went into the kitchen and set the kettle on to boil. Dina followed her. She took parmesan, a few radishes, spring onions, tomatoes, tahini and butter from the refrigerator. Noa brought out a few pieces of pita with the tea. She asked who wanted sweetener.

Ethan poured the tea as he asked, 'And Rudi?'

'What about him?'

'Well, when you're impotent …'

'Sterile,' Felix murmured, but Dina said, 'Did you not see right away how alike you are? Dov was a Don Juan. He couldn't stay with any one woman. And this pained him so much that he always immediately turned to the second best to be comforted.' Ethan knew him, after all. It could only have been Dov. Who else? 'Dov met Karen Klausinger in Felix's office by chance. She was his business partner's secretary.'

At that moment, a key turned in the front door. Rudi entered. He didn't say hello, but instead just, 'There they all are, the Rosens.' Suddenly the air was charged. He said, 'I had a test done. A genetic test.'

It was obvious how painful it was for Rudi to speak. His movements were restrained. Noa stood up as if she wanted to hug him. Rudi looked past her and Felix stared wide-eyed at the others. He breathed through his mouth.

Rudi told them he had to admit he was bowled over by the turn of events. He was the one who had placed such importance on being Felix's son. He was the one who saw the letters as proof. But his mother had obviously jumped into bed with other men. He sounded as if he were apologising for Karin Klausinger's sexual adventures.

They hemmed and hawed. It took a while before he understood what they were trying to explain to him. Rudi looked at them in disbelief. He chewed everything over as if he had a tough piece of meat in his mouth. It was Ethan who asked, 'Why the lies? Why the story that Felix betrayed Dina? Why did you claim that Felix was Rudi's father?'

The parents exchanged looks. Had Ethan still not understood? The family secret, Dina said. The resemblance between Ethan and Rudi – but at that moment Noa disagreed and claimed that, looking at them closely now, she could no longer see any resemblance whatsoever. And even Dina admitted that Ethan and Rudi didn't really look that much alike. In any case, Dina continued, she'd been worried that it would come out, that Felix was not Ethan's father.

'That's not the whole story,' Felix whispered. 'I can't recognise Ethan as my son and not also recognise another one of Dov's children.' Felix took a drink of water. 'I only said you two were brothers. No more than that.'

Rudi shook his head. 'All lies.'

Dina said, 'Felix had no bad intentions.'

Rudi simply answered, 'How could you? I've been searching for my father for years.'

'In any case, you belong with us,' Dina said, but he disagreed. No. And furthermore, he wasn't Dov Zedek's son. He was not Ethan's brother.

'The two of us are not brothers. The results are definitive.' He was not related to Ethan and that's why he could not have been conceived by Dov, and therefore it was not possible to count him as a member of the extended Rosen family. He was neither their kin nor an in-law, even if all of Dov's children were counted in with the Rosens and all the descendants of the House of Gerechter – according to the higher system of genetics as practiced by Felix and Dina – were folded into the Rosen *mishpoche*. Even then he still would not be one of them, but a parvenu, a habitual assimilator, in other words, exactly what he'd always been and what he was now known for, and, in fact, how he earnt his living as a social scientist all over the globe because he could turn up anywhere and curry favour.

The sky brightened. Dawn was arriving. There was hardly any traffic on the streets. Rudi stood up. Without a word he went into Ethan's old room. They watched him open the closets and fold his clothes. He packed his bags.

Felix stood. He swayed. The evening's attack had left its mark. He went to Rudi, his back bent. He held his head crookedly. 'Stay here.' Rudi stuck his socks into each other. 'Sleep on it. Where will you find a bed at this hour?' Rudi smoothed the wrinkles from his underwear.

'I need to be alone. At least the new article about Dov hasn't appeared yet.' Rudi sorted his undershirts.

'What does that have to do with this?'

Rudi folded his shirts. 'All lies.'

Felix pressed his hands to his lower back and groaned. He swayed. Noa saw him and stood up, taking a step towards him. He shuffled back to the sofa.

Rudi gathered his books and closed his laptop. Noa stood behind him and put her hands on his shoulders. Rudi turned and she hugged him. Tight. She caressed him. She smiled at him. 'Stay here,' she said.

'Come with me.'

She stared at him. Ethan stood behind her. He saw Noa shake her head. 'Not this way.'

Rudi freed himself from her arms and she noticed that he, who had not been able to take his eyes off her for weeks, had become a stranger to her, too. He hadn't only turned his back on the Rosen family, but on her as well. She looked into his eyes. He turned away and closed his suitcase.

As he put his computer bag over his shoulder, Ethan came up and embraced him. He kissed Rudi on the cheeks and suddenly Rudi's eyes filled with tears. He blinked them away. The two men, who had just learnt that they weren't brothers, seemed more closely related than ever. Rudi nodded and wiped his face, but then stepped back. He smiled at them as if he wanted to end an affair, sheepish and shamefaced, as if trying to keep at distance someone who was becoming too close. He seemed to fear any further contact with the Rosen family. They had hurt him. Rudi, it was clear, was worried he would not be able to say goodbye.

He lugged his bags out to the landing and turned back towards Dina and Felix. 'I can't stay here. The new obituary I wrote just to pretty up your story won't be published.'

'No one forced you.'

'They were lies. Lies for two fathers. Lies for the fathers' country. Lies for the fatherland.'

'That's not how it was.'

'I did my research on Dov.'

'We wanted to turn *luftmenschen* into soldiers, coffee-house Jews into farmers.'

Rudi sneered. 'And you did. Better than expected.'

Dina moved closer to Felix, took his hand and said, 'You want the truth? Are you sure? Are you sure you'll be able to live with it? Your generation – you're perpetual children. What is a father?'

Felix said, 'Stop, Dina. Dov is dead and buried.'

'Let me speak, Felix. He wants to know who Dov Zedek was? I can tell him. We watched children die … Did we lie to hurt you? We believed it was for the best. How could we know Dov didn't sleep with Karin Klausinger? There are worse things than being the son of Felix Rosen. And anyway, who came up with the idea that Felix was your father? Did we run after the gentleman from Austria or did he come to us? You chased Felix down even though he was in hospital. And half-dead, at that!'

'You're exaggerating, Dina. I wasn't dead.'

'One letter after another. The application to the Institute. Dov's obituary! The desperate son. The abandoned child. The lonely brat. He wanted the family legend. He wanted it from us.'

'You still shouldn't have done it,' Ethan said.

'What in God's name was so bad about it? Is Felix not the father of this family? Is there just one truth?' Dina asked.

Rudi put his bag down. His suitcase was in the wardrobe. At that moment, they all thought he wouldn't go. That he wouldn't be able to tear himself away. He would stay with Felix and Dina. Just one night. Than another day. And another after that. Dina asked, 'So we're liars?'

'I didn't say that.'

'But I did. We're liars! So? Were we trying to cover up a murder? We wanted to start a family. A family after Auschwitz.'

Rudi scoffed, 'Always "Never forget" on the tip of the tongue, and then the usual excuses. School trips to Auschwitz to uphold memory, and then falsifying your own past …'

Felix straightened up. He groaned, 'I don't need to justify myself for my memories. I don't need to put up with reproaches. Not for that. Not in my house. I'm not keeping you. Not me!'

As if he'd only been waiting for the word, Rudi ran to the closet. 'I'm already gone.'

He tried to lift his suitcase, but instead tore off the handle. He threw it onto the floor and pulled the heavy case behind him by a strap.

Noa called out, 'Felix, don't let him leave this way.'

Felix, pale and trembling, shouted, 'Reproaching me with my memory!'

Ethan asked, 'Have you all gone insane?'

'Us? He wants to leave!'

'All of you, you're not normal!'

Felix puffed out his cheeks and breathed heavily.

Ethan picked up the suitcase and said, 'Come, Rudi, this is unbearable. Come. Noa.'

She gave the two men a measuring look. 'I'm staying here.'

Later, Ethan would claim that he was not the one who carried the suitcase out and dragged the other man behind him. But Noa clearly saw Ethan take the initiative when Rudi was still hovering uncertainly. She saw the confusion in Rudi's face and years later she would still ask herself what would have happened if Ethan hadn't stormed out so stubbornly.

Dina shook her head. Felix groaned and grabbed his lower back as if the old pain had returned. Noa picked up the glass of whiskey Ethan had left behind and drained it in one gulp.

Felix wheezed. 'All we wanted to do was please him!'

Dina answered, 'That was our mistake. Don't get worked up. It's over and done with. Let it go.' She put down the portable phone and picked up the remote control. She pushed the button and turned up the volume. The voices swelled. *Layla, layla, ha-ruach goveret.*

9

ETHAN THREW THE SUITCASE in the boot of the car. They got into Felix's Audi. Ethan started the engine, pulled out and floored it. The tires squealed on the asphalt in the parking garage. The surface had just been repainted. Grass-green spots separated by bright yellow lines. He pressed the fire-red button on the remote. The door rose and the spikes lowered into the pavement. Ethan waved at the video camera. The doorman in the booth on the ground floor would do his job and recognise him as Felix Rosen's son – but who was he, really?

The vehicle shot up the exit ramp. Ethan was seething. They hadn't understood a thing. That self-righteousness after years of lies! They were happy to let him die in ignorance. They'd kept the truth from him as if he were a little child. And what excuses they'd come up with! They only wanted the best for him. Of course. That's how it had always been. They decided what was best.

Their justification was that they'd founded a family, a state, a world. It was always and everywhere the same. First they denied what happened. Then they said it was better, in any case, not to disturb anything. And then the fuss: when grass has finally grown over a story, some camel comes and eats it away. Then they claim nothing had ever been there in the first place. Nothing but desert. And the tiny house, the yard and field that may possibly have been there, well, they weren't worth mentioning.

Felix had only shaken his head at Ethan's teenage rebellion, 'What can I say: you've got a terrible father!' He'd been fobbed off like a stupid boy, and the worst part was having to admit that he couldn't deal with what he'd learnt a few hours earlier in a calmer, more mature way. He had reacted to the news that he was not his father's son – how absurd, how ridiculous the words alone sounded, that someone was not *his* father's son – like a three-year-old whose teddy bear had been taken away from him. His anger was directed against himself, but his rage was directed against his parents. Weren't they the ones who had made him what he was and didn't want to be?

There was another source of pain. He thought of Noa. She had sided with the others. With his parents. And with the other one. With Rudi. 'Stay here,' she'd said. Or had he also heard 'with me'?

Rudi sat next to him, talking into his mobile phone. He was speaking with the operator, asking for the phone numbers of various hotels. Ethan had just turned in the direction of the seafront. He hadn't thought of heading towards any particular accommodation. He wanted to go through the ranks. There were enough of those showcases along the beach: Carlton, Sheraton, Hilton. Some of the chains were even represented twice. They were all in the typical honeycomb architecture with countless balconies, seaside views. But Ethan heard Rudi asking about a room in Herzliya. As soon as his reservation was confirmed, Rudi called the airline to book a return flight the next day.

Ethan remembered the years when he didn't have a flat in Tel Aviv. They'd landed in a suite in one of those giant tourist hotels. They were living in Chicago at the time. That American metropolis hadn't yet risen. It was a city of neighbourhoods that did not yet form a whole. The frigid winters. The wind that whipped in from the lake. Skyscrapers like he'd never seen before. The IBM building, with its dark glass façade designed by Mies van der Rohe. The Rookery Building, a neo-Romanesque highrise designed by Daniel Burnham. The Sears Tower, that building block edifice. In the summer, they'd travelled to Israel. Back then, they saw the country through the eyes of foreigners. Their friends and relatives had met them in the lobby to catch up over club sandwiches. He had sat by the pool all day. Alone.

He remembered how, when he was in primary school in Vienna, he'd returned to the land of his birth and met up with his friends from kindergarten. They told him he wasn't a real Israeli anymore although his parents claimed the opposite and reassured him with melancholy smiles that he was a true little Sabra. His parents' voices when they said this were very high and thin and it sounded a bit like the sad refrain 'You're already all grown up,' that he constantly heard from his relatives.

The flat in Vienna had enchanted him at first sight. The ceilings were higher than any he'd seen before. The way out seemed strangely long and for a long time strange. He had to go down the endless corridor, past mezzanines and landings and through swinging doors to get to the heavy main portal that didn't move. Smaller doors had been cut into the portal gate, and to open those, you needed a key.

In Tel Aviv, the gates were left open. He and his friends had gone from one building to the next. They'd chased cats through the courtyards. After the Six-Day War, sandbags were left lying in entrances. They'd re-enacted combats, jumped over garden walls, and climbed the sides of buildings. Things were completely different in Austria. On his first day in Vienna, he ran out of his building. Out of curiosity. He had gone looking for other children and was sure he wouldn't have to go far to find them. His parents had told him he wouldn't find anyone to play with on the street, but he had simply snuck out. He had stood there, on the Operngasse in Vienna of the 1960s, puzzled and mute. There wasn't anyone his age as far as the eye could see, only adults. Cars thundered past.

In kindergarten, they all went to the toilet in single file. It made no difference when Ethan told them he didn't need to go. Those who didn't obey got an earful, and Ethan's ears stung. 'Ima, tell them I already went to the toilet at home.' Dina spoke with the teacher and asked her not to force him to take part in the collective defecation. Ethan could not fathom why the other children did not rebel too. Aunt Hedwig saw her authority questioned. As soon as Ethan's mother had gone, she grabbed him by the hair. He howled with rage. She bellowed at him, pulled down his pants, and sat him on the toilet. After a few minutes, she ordered him to wash his hands, then pushed him outside. He stumbled away dazed from crying. In the playroom, he gagged and had to vomit. Now two teachers were screaming at him. Aunt Hedwig berated him in front of the other children. Later she complained to Ethan's father, who had come to fetch the boy. Felix listened to it all without a word. Ethan had withdrawn into himself. He didn't understand what was happening. The grown ups had united against him. They had banded together far above his level. Papa stood motionless as Aunt Hedwig talked at him. Ethan saw his father's rage build as she told him about his son's naughtiness.

First Felix was silent after the teacher had finished speaking, then Ethan's Abba let loose. But to Ethan's amazement, the rage was not directed at him, but at Aunt Hedwig. Who did she think she was to tell his son when he had to go to the toilet. How dare she reproach the child for needing to throw up. And she called herself a teacher. Ethan was not going to stay here one more day. But she should not imagine she was going to get off scot-free. Then Felix stroked Ethan's head and took him home.

'Don't ever let anyone treat you that way,' Abba said later. 'You were in the right. Push back if any one pushes you around. Don't put up with anything. I'm proud of you. I'm glad I'm your father. You hear, Tushtush?' He held Ethan's hand tightly and led him across the street. 'We're no longer going to let any one spit on us and say it's raining. Remember that, Ethan. No more! You're a Sabra. You hear me, Ethan?'

He and his parents were a bastion. Ethan learned to differentiate their public demeanour from their inner truths. They had their own secret language that no one else understood and they mistrusted the sentences of others. Ethan knew the arrogance of both sides. He remembered the times he'd had to justify himself in Israel for his life in

Austria and in Vienna for his life in the land of his birth. In Tel Aviv, an old kindergarten friend said the Rosens were apostates and turncoats, but in Vienna a former school friend claimed the Jewish state in Zion was nothing more than racism. Ethan's entire existence was in disrepute.

The traffic was gradually building on the streets of Tel Aviv. At one traffic light, they waited between a garbage truck on one side and horse-drawn carriage on the other. A young woman, her hair piled high, crossed over the zebra stripes and smiled at Ethan. Rudi nodded back at her.

Ethan glared at him. Here he was, squeezing himself into every crevice of Ethan's existence as if he were Ethan's eternal opponent. Rudi misunderstood Ethan's look. He did not see the accusation, but said, 'They lied to us both.'

Ethan let the words sink into him. They were an echo of his own disapproval, but now they sounded strange. Rage boiled up in him again and this time he didn't know at whom. The light turned green. He stepped on the gas and turned onto the main street.

As the sea came into view, Rudi looked at his arm. 'I forgot my watch.' He slapped his knee and shook his head. But he absolutely didn't want to go back to Felix and Dina's. Never again. Would Ethan mind sending him the heirloom? Rudi didn't even wait for the answer, but kept talking. 'I don't ever want to see them again. Too many lies.' He saw Felix's cassettes in the glove compartment under the dashboard. The songs of Frank Sinatra, Sammy Davis Jr and Barbra Streisand. 'Always talking about the importance of memory, but constantly falsifying their own past,' Rudi said. Two teenagers in swimming trunks and T-shirts headed towards the beach with fishing rods. 'The new piece on Dov hasn't been published yet. Luckily. What rubbish. I only wrote it for Felix.'

Ethan slowly pulled over. He stared straight ahead. 'Only for Felix? Not for Noa too?' He looked at Rudi. Rudi did not answer. In his parents' apartment, Ethan had embraced him affectionately, and now this attack. But just as unexpected as Ethan's accusation was his laughter. Ethan giggled. His chuckles turned into guffaws, then out of the blue, he patted the back of Rudi's head. 'Don't let it go to your head. I'm a bastard, too. We both are.'

Rudi grinned, nonplussed. He wasn't sure what Ethan was up to and eyed him warily. 'You're always going on about ties, about family ties,' said Ethan. 'You don't have to pretend with me. I've seen through you. It was always the same, right from the beginning. Ever since the obituary of Dov. Every one of the ideas seemed familiar. No wonder, right?' Ethan sneered. 'You don't think. You just think your way into things. You don't write for yourself the way others do. No. You write for Felix, for Dina. For Wilhelm Marker, it's the same thing. Always for others. Nothing but lies – you tell lies for yourself alone.' Ethan had talked himself into a rage. 'You reproach Felix for his memory? You resent the survivors of Auschwitz?'

'I never said anything about survivors. Or about Auschwitz.' Rudi shook his head. 'I don't know what movie you're in, but you should stop it now, eject it, and take it back to the video store. I was only looking for my father.'

'They wanted to do what was best for us.'

'It doesn't look that way to me. My mother wanted what was best for me, so she never told me my father's name. My foster mother wanted what was best for me and didn't help me find him. My biological father never intended to marry my mother, but surely only wanted what was best for his family. And Felix? That straw man of a lover, that eternal placeholder, that stopgap, always second best! He knew how important the truth was to me and he lied to my face. And you? Less than an hour ago, you attacked Felix much more directly than I did. Now you're acting like his protector, as if you hadn't attacked him at all. You only recognise the truth by its opposite. And love? Since when does that interest you? You only pay attention to Noa when she starts paying attention to me. If it weren't for me, you'd have forgotten her long ago. If it weren't for me, you still wouldn't know anything about Dov. Or Dina. Or Felix. If it weren't for me, you'd still be in Vienna. With Marker! I didn't tell you any lies, your mother did. So did Felix. And Dov. And your father. Whoever that is. They all lied.'

Ethan could hear himself in Rudi's words and at that moment thought how ridiculous it was to get so worked up. Secrets were at the core of every family. There's no education without fairy tales; no parents' bedroom without the dark; no home without something to hide. He said, 'Yes, they lied to us. But at least they lied for the sake of the truth. You, on the other hand, lie when you tell the truth.'

Rudi laughed scornfully. 'You want to test that theory? Should I write about this in the newspaper? The truth. The true obituary of your father! Of both of them together! Of the biological and the sentimental. That's the article I'm going to write now. How does that sound? I'm going to portray the lot of you in all your ugliness.'

Ethan did not strike out and ram his fist into Rudi's nose. The image flashed in his mind of Rudi bent over with pain. Ethan did not go at him until he tumbled out of the car and lay in the gutter. Nothing like that. He just sat there, frozen. He rolled down his window and looked out at the street. He took a deep breath. The words echoed inside him. 'The true obituary of your father! Of both of them together!' A truck was approaching and suddenly Ethan grabbed Rudi's laptop bag from the back seat and hurled it out onto the road.

'Are you nuts?' Rudi yelled and raised his arm. But even though he was bigger than Ethan, he couldn't find the strength to beat him. When Ethan saw Rudi's raised fist, he finally exploded and hit Rudi, drumming his fists into Rudi's face. Rudi could barely defend himself and tried to duck. The sound of the truck's horn brought them both up short. Rudi wrenched open his door, leapt into the street, grabbed the bag and jumped to the other side of the road as the truck barrelled past, horn blaring.

They looked at each other in open contempt, and Ethan let the car roll as Rudi watched, open-mouthed. He drove a few hundred metres and stopped. He got out and Rudi sprinted after him, trying to catch up. Ethan opened the boot and took out the suitcase, and Rudi screamed, swore, and came up to the car, gasping. He was just a few metres away when Ethan got back in the car unhurriedly and accelerated at the last moment, before braking again and waiting until Rudi had almost reached the car. Ethan drove forward.

Rudi raced after the Audi, as if he could catch up with car on foot. He had simply left his suitcase behind. Once again Ethan stopped and watched Rudi rush after him in the rear-view mirror, and once again he waited only until Rudi was just close enough to think that Ethan would not leave him behind, before stepping on the gas.

When Rudi heard the sound of an engine behind him, he knew what would happen. He spun around and saw a VW Cabrio, full of young men and women. The driver had just slammed on the brakes, the rubber tires drawing skid marks on the asphalt. Now he yanked at the steering wheel to avoid the large suitcase – and hit the pitch-black bag straight on, crushing it flat – a bull's eye, bang on – and with it, Rudi's laptop, his data and documents, his articles and reports, all of which, in the confusion of the last few weeks, he had failed to back up.

Rudi didn't flinch when he heard the impact. Only when they sped past him, did he raise his arms and yell. That gang obviously had no idea what had just happened. They couldn't have guessed what was in the bag. One of them laughed in Rudi's face, another covered his mouth with his hand and quickly turned away as if he'd been caught in a childish prank. Only one of the young women looked back at him, shocked, sobered. Ethan and the mob in the Cabrio; for Rudi they were on the same side, they were accomplices, a band of hypocrites, Pharisees every one last one. Dina and Felix, too, and Noa, who all of a sudden reminded him of the girl in the car who had stared at him with pity. Noa hadn't hugged him until after it was all over. That, he thought, is what is meant by a 'Judas kiss'.

He was exhausted and sweaty. The temperature was rising from one minute to the next. He ran to his suitcase and dragged it to the side of the road. Then he looked for his laptop. The thing had been smashed in three. He swore. He gathered up the pieces. There might still be a chance, he thought. He had heard of a company that could retrieve data from computers that had been burnt, submerged or shattered. He was not completely convinced, but he didn't want to lose hope.

He slowly trudged on, lugging the suitcase and the bag. Then he took out his mobile phone and called a taxi. Why hadn't he ordered one right away when Ethan threw him out of the car? Rudi arrived at the hotel utterly worn out and dishevelled, a complete mess. He tried to put the pieces of his laptop back together. He asked for duct tape. And super glue as well. For his computer! He called a technician in Vienna. If the hard drive was damaged then nothing could be done, he told Rudi.

Rudi flew back to Austria the next day with the tape and glue-covered laptop in his bag. He had tried to fix it himself, although 'with his fists' would be a more accurate term. At three in the morning, he had struck the machine because a specialist had told him years before that sometimes these highly complicated devices needed a good thump. In his desperation, he went at it with a left-right combination straight out of a boxing match. Man vs machine.

He attracted attention at the security check. He looked tense, on edge. The security officer went to get his supervisor. A woman arrived and pushed all the others aside. She obviously specialised in evaluating electronic devices and she asked Rudi to turn on his computer. Fat chance, he answered irritably. Did she not see it was broken? One of the officers laughed when he told them about the car, a Cabrio, to be exact. She shouldn't bend it, Rudi told her, or he would hold her liable for any damage.

She looked at him as if he were completely insane. She gently touched one of the cables. Was he really still worried about this thing? One of the officers looked at Rudi severely and said that there were worse things than a broken computer. They were responsible for human safety, not for his data, the woman said. She would have to inspect the thing right now or he would not be allowed to board. It was a suspicious object. What was the substance oozing out of the case? Who in the world tries to fix electronic devices with super glue? Had he heard of Semtex? You don't need much of such plastic explosives to blow up an airplane.

'Semtex,' called an Israeli waiting behind Rudi and the word multiplied in small detonations. The human queue worked like a fuse. 'You haven't heard of it? An explosive. From the Czechs.' And someone said, 'They found it on him. Now they'll really take him apart.' Everyone stepped back. They looked at him as if he were an idiot terrorists had tricked into carrying a package that would kill everyone in the immediate vicinity. Rudi understood their reaction perfectly well. Of course he had woken their mistrust. His fear for the files he hadn't backed up, his hatred of Ethan and the kids in the car, his fury with Felix and Dina – they could see it all in his face. He looked strange and he knew it.

Any other day, he would not have resented their

suspicion, but now he held everything against them, his broken laptop, his lost data, the theft of his identity, Felix's lies, Noa's rejection, the insinuation that he was carrying explosives. They wanted to know what he was doing here. Who did he know in this country? What did he write about? Did he understand why they had to ask these questions? The security officers looked at him. One of them asked how it was that he, an Austrian, could speak Hebrew so well. Even that did not seem to help Rudi this time. On the contrary.

How easily he could have explained it all the day before. He would have told his stories, about his mother's lover, his absent father who was a Jew. But he didn't say a word. He wasn't even sure himself anymore what he'd wanted here. Who did he really know in this country? Hadn't he been fooled by every single one of them? He noticed that everyone's revulsion for him had infected him as well, though he couldn't explain why. He broke into a sweat. His hands trembled as he tried to open one of the clasps on his bag. Half an hour later, they let him through. The other passengers kept an eye on him and kept their distance.

Rudi had always felt at home in airports before. He thought of calling Wilhelm Marker as soon as he landed. He would put himself back in the running for the position and his chances would be better this time around since the Institute would have given up hope on Ethan and Rudi was no longer an unknown quantity. He looked around. He sat among people of different backgrounds. An Arab family, the grandfather with a *kaffiyeh*, the grandmother with a headscarf, were waiting for the boarding call not far from him. On the plane, a hulk of a man sat next to him. An American. The giant didn't know where to put his legs. Everything was too small for him. He breathed heavily.

They fastened their seatbelts. The man looked at the remains of Rudi's laptop. Rudi saw the horror in his neighbour's eyes and it brought home yet again how strange he must look. Who, in all seriousness, carries a completely destroyed computer from one country to another?

'I have a big problem,' Rudi began, but before he finished his sentence, his neighbour recoiled, looked at him and made a fist. The American pointed at the computer. There are specialists for disasters like that. Sometimes they put the damaged machine in the refrigerator overnight, or on the heater, or they simply leave it alone, depending on what had happened. All just to get the computer to boot up one last time and to back up the data.

He himself was a technician and a troubleshooter. He worked for an international firm and specialised in setting up cellular networks. They called him when there were serious problems with a system. He was originally from Texas, but was always travelling from one country to another. He covered emergency situations. He'd been sent to Tel Aviv because Masada – Herod's old fortress on the mountain plateau in which Jewish rebels, outnumbered fifteen to one by Roman soldiers, had barricaded themselves two thousand years ago – could not be contacted by Israeli mobile phone providers. These heights had initially been conquered by Jewish insurgents. Under the command of Eleazer ben Ya'ir, they had defied the tenth Roman legion for years until committing mass suicide, because to these

Jews, freedom was dearer than life. The heights now lay under Jordanian cell coverage, and anyone who wanted to use his phone on Masada came under foreign rule, at least telephonically. 'They considered this situation a national disaster,' he told Rudi. 'Every day thousands of people climbed up to the fortress, guests of state were ferried up there, troops marched up. Everyone was told: Masada must never fall again, but if you want to call your grandmother in Haifa, Paris or Brooklyn, you've got to call from Jordan.' It was a fiasco.

'I get calls from every continent and country of the world. I go to Australia, Canada, Scandinavia, to Japan, China and Russia. I hardly know these countries, but I know every detail of their cellular networks, and everywhere I go, in almost every language and almost every region, people who need my help talk to me about big problems.'

The man looked angrily at Rudi. He snorted. 'Problem, problemo, problema. Whether I'm in Cameroon or Mongolia, everybody's got a problem. I don't want to hear it any more. It never means the same thing in any two places. It means nothing and everything at the same time.' He had first understood this in a plane, the Texan told Rudi, in a Boeing just like this one, on a British Airways flight. Suddenly, over the Atlantic, in the middle of a flight home, the pilot had announced in that typically nasal Oxbridge accent, 'Ladies and gentlemen, we seem to have a problem.' At that moment, he, the American, panicked. He, who did absolutely nothing in life but solve problems, immediately assumed they were going to crash. And he wasn't the only one. All his countrymen were terrified and began screaming. The woman next to him fainted and he, well, he didn't quite know how to say it, but he went in his pants because he was sure they would drop from an altitude of tens of thousands of feet and hit the ocean surface, an impact no one could survive and even if they did, it would only be to drown in the icy water. The panic was so great that most of the passengers didn't hear what the Brit with the stiff upper lip added. 'I am terribly sorry, but I must tell you that it's raining in New York.' If an American pilot had mentioned a problem, you could count on the end coming soon. With a crash. Certain death. That's the secret code, he said. US pilots speak a jargon of controlled cool. They would say, 'Houston we have a problem here,' before the connection failed, the aircraft exploded and the dot on the radar vanished.

The Englishman in the cockpit back then was terribly sorry about the weather, but surely had no idea what effect his words would have. His faux pas was not mentioned later because everyone's attention was directed at the woman who had fainted. She gasped for breath and moaned heavily. The flight attendants called for a doctor and two passengers came forward. In the general commotion, no one criticised him for soiling himself. Since that incident on the way from Heathrow to Kennedy, when anyone called him, the troubleshooter, with a problem, he always remembered the panic that had come over him and the stink of fear. Because it means everything and nothing when someone, somewhere, says they have a problem, and when occasionally, in certain countries, someone says 'no problem', *nema problema*, or, as in Israel, *ejn beaja*, then you can be sure that the situation is hopeless and that everyone has given up. That was why, although he wished Rudi lots of luck in saving his hard drive, he had to warn him. He stared at Rudi and discreetly squeezed his thighs together. He, the American, didn't want to hear another word about a problem for the rest of the flight.

Rudi respected his request and was silent. He now had time to think over all that had happened, and when he landed in Vienna, showed his Austrian passport at border control and the official crossly waved him through, Rudi decided to make good on his threat against Ethan and write a third, definitive obituary of Dov.

Ethan had not looked back. He had just driven away. Not a glance. Just gone. It wasn't *schadenfreude*, but he was happy to have left Rudi behind. He wanted to get away from Rudi, did not want to be in same car as this 'wannabe' brother, who had insulted his father, no, both his fathers – yes, both, since he did have two, after all. He wanted to shake off this hanger-on from Vienna. He had wanted to for a long time, from the very beginning, actually.

Nonetheless, his conscience was uneasy. Felix would ask him where he had left Rudi in a prosecutorial tone. Ethan could picture Dina shaking her head, and Noa would fix him with a look, stare him down and then say he must have been out of his mind to throw Rudi out of the car far from a bus station or a café. Ethan tried to reassure himself. Where had the others been? Why hadn't Felix, Dina or Noa done anything when Rudi left? No, he would spurn their reproaches.

Ethan briefly considered driving back and picking Rudi up after all. Years later, he would wonder what would have happened if he had gone back. They probably would have returned to Dina and Felix's apartment in silence, cooled down, or at least sobered. Maybe everything would have turned out differently. They would have embraced Felix, appeased him.

But Ethan did not turn back. Instead he turned on the air conditioner and felt around for his mobile phone. As he drove along the Ayalon highway into the city he dialed Yael Steiner's number despite the early hour.

'It looks bad.'

'What's that supposed to mean? You were happy to have me back.'

'No one doubts your qualifications. It's about the money. Your contract.'

'So, no raise?'

'Worse.'

The longer he listened, the stronger his suspicions grew. Were they punishing him for having left? He did not say a word. In fact, he feigned understanding. Under no circumstances would he beg. No. The only adequate response was icy sarcasm.

'Look, Yael, what can I say … I can't claim I'm disappointed. It's more like I've been proven right.'

'Come on, don't make this personal. Things are tight here.'

'Yes, you have no idea how tight.'

She envied him his cosmopolitanism. She resented Ethan for demanding a raise for his return. As long as he was gone, she'd tempted him with promises of mutual solidarity, of duties to each other and to the country.

Yael said, 'I'm sorry. Believe me, it's nothing against you. We're all affected.'

'Nowhere else do I feel as foreign as I do here.'

'Why is that surprising, Ethan? Home is where you feel more like a stranger than anywhere else.'

She asked him to please inform her of his decision in the next few days. He hung up without saying goodbye and stepped on the gas. He wanted to get back to his parents quickly, because he suddenly felt like they were the only ones who had never betrayed him. This thought and a childish need for attention were eating into him. They blended in with his exhaustion and hunger, of which he was suddenly aware.

He was sorry now that he had fought so fiercely with Felix, that he had attacked Felix so mercilessly. Not just the night before, but in all the years since his childhood. Always on the lookout for a flaw. He let his parents know how much their love and their expectations weighed on him. But since his father had been so ill, their relationship had changed. With death so close at hand, didn't Felix seem calmer and more accepting than he ever had been before?

Ethan listened to his voicemail. Rabbi Berkowitsch had left him a message. Ethan wanted to hang up, but once again couldn't resist the penetrating voice. 'I need to speak with you, Mr Rosen. I understand if you're furious with me. I'm very sorry. You are not the one we thought you were and you, yourself, believed you were. Your mother disgraced. Your father exposed. Your family torn apart. I'm very sorry.'

That's the way it is, Ethan thought and kept listening to the rabbi.

Berkowitsch said, 'Mr Rosen, I'm calling you about the kidney for Felix. On that front, nothing has changed. *Nebbish* that I am, I'm in your debt. I need Felix Rosen. He is the last surviving close relative of the messianic family. I need him and he needs me. Please call me. With God's help we will find a kidney.'

Ethan had to stop at a red light. A beggar limped between the cars. An Arab family hurried along the street, the grandmother in a colourful robe, the granddaughter in jeans.

Ethan turned onto his parents' street. He heard a siren. It grew louder and louder and then wailed right next to him. An ambulance. The speeding vehicle overtook him and raced on straight ahead.

Noa did not understand what she was doing there and years later would wonder why she had stayed with the elderly Rosens that night. Dina had encouraged her several times that night to go home, but Noa had stayed.

'Go. What are you waiting for?'

Felix, that much was clear, could have used the reconciliation. His son had disappeared without saying goodbye. No solace. Noa had recognised the extent to which Felix had collapsed internally. His eyes became vacant when Ethan and Rudi stormed out of the apartment. Maybe that was the reason she was not able to leave the older couple.

She hoped her presence would distract Felix and Dina somewhat from the argument with the two men.

Dina said, 'You can't help anyone here. It would be good if we all went to bed.' But Noa stayed. Dina sat on the sofa, watching television, but her head swayed like a poplar in the wind. Sleep overcame her time and again, but her agitation soon woke her. On the screen the figures from times long gone still sang and swayed from side to side.

Noa was infected by this dance of the spirits and she, too, had trouble staying awake. She was just about to pull herself together and go when Felix tumbled into the room. He looked so transparent that for a moment she thought she was looking at a ghost, at one of the undead. Felix fell more than walked. He stumbled from one step to the next. With his final ounce of strength, he made it to the rug and fell face forward onto the sofa. It seemed like a milky sheet of glass was covering his gaze; his eyes were wide open and he struggled to breathe, fighting off anxiety, the fear of death. Felix gasped, panted, wheezed and Noa heard him trying to form words, but she could not understand the sounds he made, more animal noises than human speech and perhaps not even expressed consciously. It seemed to Noa that Felix could no longer hear anything, neither Noa's questions, nor Dina's screams – 'Felix, what's wrong! Felix, say something! … Felix!' – and that Felix did not understand what was happening. Noa rushed to the phone and called an ambulance. She screamed the address and 'Hurry! He can't breathe. No, he's not conscious,' and then leapt back to his side, pushed Dina away, stroked his forehead and kissed his limp hand, moving quickly to shift the unconscious man onto his side and pull in his knees. But his body rolled halfway onto his stomach. She pushed against him with all her strength, then she forced open his mouth with her hands and tore open his shirt while Dina wailed, 'Felix! Sweetie! Be strong.' Noa straightened up and rubbed the man's back. She grabbed her mobile phone and dialled Ethan's number. He answered, 'Hello?'

Noa screamed, 'Your father!'

He asked, 'What is it?'

All she said was, 'Hurry. The ambulance is already here.'

She ran to open the door for the doctor and the paramedics. They shouted at Felix, but he no longer answered. They put an oxygen mask over his face. They tried to find a pulse. They examined him. Noa watched them use a defibrillator. They laid the body on its back, took out a hypodermic needle and a syringe, and rammed the needle into the chest. The sofa and floor were soon littered with packing material, hoses and plastic tubing. Dina just stood there. She ran her hands through her hair. She bit her lip. She shook her head. She looked at Noa. Noa nodded very slowly as if to say, 'This is it.' She looked at Dina as if asking her, 'Is it?' But Dina was silent.

Felix's face was swollen. His skin grew ever more sallow. His breath whistled. He fought for air. An eternity passed before the doctor and paramedics finally lifted the bulky figure onto the stretcher. They tried to get a hold of him, but he went rigid. He fought against their grip. It was as if each of his limbs was resisting all help. He made himself heavy and the paramedics carried him like a wet sack. Ethan came in before they had reached the door.

He nodded at Noa and embraced Dina. His mother sobbed loudly into his shoulder. Noa cried. He asked the doctor where they were taking his father. The doctor named the hospital. It wasn't far. On television, the black and white shadows from earlier times still sang. One woman struck up a Yiddish song. An Itzik Manger ballad about a boy who wants to keep a tree company as it has been abandoned by all the birds in winter, but the coat his mother has made him wear to keep him from freezing makes his wings too heavy. The tree stands bare and alone.

They pushed the stretcher out of the doorway and into the lift. Dina was to accompany him in the ambulance. Ethan and Noa called the next lift. They descended to the basement and ran through the garage to the car. Ethan sped off. In the distance they saw the ambulance and its spinning blue light. They couldn't stop near the emergency entrance but had to go via the hospital parking lot.

It took Ethan some time to find a spot. They ran to the ward. Dina stood there. Alone. In the neon light, she looked even paler than usual. Father's heartbeat stopped. He's in the surgery. They're trying to revive him. They'd told her they'd do everything they could.

They waited.

They were shown into another room. The chief surgeon came towards her. He shook his head. Dina sobbed. She put her hands to her head, beat her fists against her temples, again and again, and Noa put her arms around her, held her. The two women stood, overcome by the same trembling. Ethan, immobile, stared into space. He did not come to until the doctor who had treated Felix during the past months came up to him and put his arm around him. Ethan caught a glimpse of his face in the mirror and saw that it was dislocated, distorted with pain, and all he could think was, 'This is it, then.'

Better to be dead
and turn into a tree
with birds as guests
now that'd be something
to look forward to.

Elfriede Gerstl
1932 (Vienna) to 2009 (Vienna)

10

ETHAN HAD NOT EXPECTED THIS. Even when the doctor plunged the needle into his father's chest, even when the medics pushed the stretcher out of the apartment, and when they said that his heart had stopped, Ethan was convinced that Felix Rosen would not die. Even after the chief surgeon said the words, Ethan still did not understand what had happened.

Ethan's face in the mirror – his own and yet a stranger's – when the doctor put an arm around him. There, in the glass, another stood and grieved, whereas the news of Felix's death had not yet reached him. Or rather, Ethan understood that his father was dead, but not that he wouldn't be able to discuss it with Felix. He understood that Felix was no longer be able to speak, but not that he could never again contradict his Abba. Essentially, Ethan had believed that the old man would survive everything, even death.

Yet he lay there. If they wished, they could say their goodbyes to Felix. They stood at the side of his bed. Felix's face was waxen. His body was covered, but his feet were exposed. Ethan stood, motionless, next to the corpse. He touched his father's shoulder gingerly, as if afraid he might wake him. Dina felt for Felix's hand under the sheet. She covered it with kisses. Noa gently stroked Felix's forehead.

They still could not comprehend what had happened, even after the doctor explained it several times. Ethan felt the lassitude that prevented him from understanding what he was being told. He listened and heard the words, but could not figure out what they meant. His intellect was intact, but something inside him was dead, had withered away and would not recover.

There was nothing more to do in the hospital. They returned to the apartment with Dina. Ethan's mother went from room to room as if she were floating. Ethan came up against Felix everywhere. His smell hung in the air. His clothes hung in the closet. Medicine bottles stood on the kitchen table. The worst was the chaos around the couch. Leftover bits of plastic. The packaging from the injections. Tubing. Vomit. Abba had lain here. He packed up the throw that covered the couch for the dry cleaners.

His mother wanted to be alone. She waved them away. She turned her face to the wall. She had to pull herself together. But above all, she needed to rest. No, she didn't need anyone near her. No, she didn't want to go to Ethan and Noa's. No.

'We'll come back this evening,' Ethan said. Out on the landing, after they had pushed the call button and were waiting for the lift, Noa hugged him.

They drove to their apartment, threw their clothes on the floor and fell into bed. Noa fell asleep immediately. Ethan lay awake. The light seemed brighter and more glittering than usual. His mobile phone rang. He slipped out of the bedroom so that he wouldn't wake Noa. It was Rabbi Berkowitsch.

He started spluttering, 'Ethan, this is very unpleasant for me.'

'It's not important anymore, Rav Berkowitsch.'

'Ethan. Listen to me. I'd certainly understand if you didn't want to have anything more to do with me.'

'Felix Rosen …' Ethan began, but the rabbi interrupted him: '… is our last chance. Felix Rosen is the last one. The very last one. He is the only survivor who can help us. We need him.'

'Too late, Rav Berkowitsch.'

'Why? I'll find a kidney for him!'

'It won't work.'

'That statement means nothing to me. No one will stop me – not the murderers, not my colleagues, not the state laws. No one. Do you hear me? Otherwise it will all have been meaningless. I believe! Do you even understand what that means? Do you have the slightest sense of that? Belief! It's not an assumption, not hope, not certainty. It's my lot. My watchword. My life! I won't give up. Today we can create new life from an old man's cells. There are ways to make Felix Rosen fertile again. I will find a kidney for him. I've got through situations that seemed far more hopeless!' He took a deep breath. 'Why aren't you saying anything?'

'He's dead, Rav Berkowitsch. Felix Rosen has passed away.'

There was silence. Then: 'That can't be. That's terrible. We're lost! It's a crime!'

'It was a heart attack.'

'What a misfortune. A catastrophe!' The rabbi seemed desperate. 'Maybe there's hope. Perhaps we can save a few of his cells. You say it happened just now. The body doesn't die immediately. That's the principle of transplanting after all. The brain gives no sign of life, but the kidneys, the liver, the heart still function. Why shouldn't that be the case for semen or other cells? The salvation of the world depends on it.'

'Rav Berkowitsch, he's been dead for hours. Do you want to plunder his corpse? This is my father, a human being. Have you forgotten?'

The rabbi stopped. A sigh passed through the wire. 'You're right. Salvation will not come this way. It's all over. Done.'

'Life goes on, Rav Berkowitsch.'

'No. It's all over. It's no use. They were all murdered for no reason … All of them. Before my eyes. We are lost.'

At that moment, Ethan choked up. He swallowed the bile that rose, then whispered, 'I beg your pardon, but my Abba is dead. He died. Today. Here. Not there. Not then. This is not about your father, but mine. Do you under-stand, Rav?'

The connection went dead. Yesheyahu Berkowitsch, a religious authority in Israel, the spiritual leader of a Hasidic community, had simply hung up on him.

Ethan went into the kitchen. There was no question of sleep now. He made himself an espresso; his movements were hectic. He cut himself a slice of bread, and from the refrigerator he took the spicy spread, a blend of aubergine, paprika, garlic, chili peppers and olive oil. He got a plate and a knife from the drawer. Every noise sounded sharper than usual. He sat at the table and made a few notes as he ate. It was time to plan the funeral. Friends and rela-tives had to be notified, an announcement placed in the newspaper, the burial organised. The most important thing was to be alert. What if Berkowitsch and his troops really did want to tamper with the corpse? Would he have to protect his dead father from a madman?

The doorbell rang. He was not expecting anyone. He went to the door and looked through the peephole. Outside stood the rabbi. Ethan did not remember giving the religious man his new address and he called through the door, 'What do you want?'

'To apologise. I don't know what came over me.' Ethan opened the door. Berkowitsch looked him in the eye. 'I was in the wrong. I forgot myself.'

'No problem.'

The rabbi nodded and remained standing in the doorway. Ethan finally asked, 'Would you like to come in?'

'Don't worry – I just wanted to offer you my condolences and offer my help. If you need me. For the burial.'

What a black-robed vulture, Ethan thought to himself. He could feel the rabbi gaining power over him. He was easy prey. Berkowitsch knew exactly what went on inside the recently bereaved, no matter how secular they were. Where the sociologists could find no answers, the rabbis were specialists. That was their field and they were more effective than a placebo because even those who did not believe in ceremonies found them helpful at the graveside.

Ethan thanked Berkowitsch and politely explained that he would discuss it with his family. When the rabbi was gone, Ethan picked up his mobile and thought over whom he could ask about whether Berkowitsch would be right for the task. Ethan scrolled through the names and numbers in his contacts and came upon the entry *Papa mobile phone,* and it suddenly hit him. He would never again be able to ask his father for advice. Very soon he would be praying for Felix Abraham Rosen, he would be saying *Kaddish* for his father.

That evening, Ethan and Noa drove to Dina's. She had covered all the mirrors in the apartment with black cloth. Ethan asked her guardedly whether she would want to accept the rabbi's offer. Dina's succinct response was 'Why not?'

'What if he starts talking about the Messiah again?' Ethan countered. 'Berkowitsch is a fundamentalist, a Jewish Mullah. If Felix weren't already dead, he'd die of rage.'

Funeral rites had never been important to Felix. His Austrian business partner had asked him years before where he wanted to be buried. In his native city, Vienna, in Chicago or in Tel Aviv? Or maybe Jerusalem? Felix answered that he didn't care, but he didn't even want to live in Jerusalem, much less be buried there. Dov had been a Jerusalemite. He had even bought a cemetery plot there and hadn't asked Katharina, but instead Dina and Felix, if he should reserve adjacent plots for them. Felix had answered, 'I'd much rather have a parking spot in front of your house than a grave next to yours.'

The news of Felix's death spread like wildfire. While Ethan dialled one number after another on his mobile phone, informed family and friends and left messages on answering machines, those who had heard the news third-hand called the landline. Ethan reached acquaintances in Vienna, Paris and Chicago and business partners in Moscow and Singapore. Some told him about deaths in their own families. Ethan answered them with, 'I have to make more calls. You know, the preparations.'

Nimrod Karni, the shipping magnate who had advised Felix to go after a kidney from India, suggested, 'Maybe it was better for him this way. He suffered so much from his illness. You know how he was. He never wanted to show weakness. He was a man!' Ethan quickly said goodbye, but many others remarked that Felix had never wanted to be a burden.

Were they right? When Ethan's father had broken his leg, he had refused to use a cane. And later they could not convince him to wear glasses with a stronger prescription even though his myopia had got worse. Felix had driven until the end and always very fast. He was a speeder, as if he could outrun danger that way. His driving was legendary. He yanked at the steering wheel, slammed on the brakes only to floor the accelerator again. He always drove, regardless of the weather, through storms and blizzards. Even so, in the worst visibility, when no one could see much of anything, he could see almost as well as those with ordinary vision. Still, in normal conditions, darkness was the worst. Felix, effectively night-blind, only perceived shapes and dim lights. His only guidance was the other cars' tail lights. Felix had driven Ethan in the Audi once. An old pickup truck was parked in the middle of the seafront boulevard. The truck stood there, in the dark, as Felix drove down the boulevard, straining to see anything through the windshield. Only at the very last moment did Ethan realise that his father was going to crash into the parked vehicle. He shouted, 'Right there, Abba! There's a truck.' Felix yanked the steering wheel to the left. The tyres squealed like a car chase in an action movie – but his father remained calm. He smiled as if nothing had happened, as if he had not heard the tyres.

Never again would Ethan sit in a car with Abba, with his father, who had lived his life at full gallop, always rabble-rousing. Instead, Ethan sat there and recounted the circumstances of Felix Rosen's death, of his last few weeks, his last days, his last hours. He did not say anything about the argument. Nor did he talk about Rudi, even though a few people asked about the unknown relative. The rumour had long since done the rounds. Uncle Yossef, who had met the Austrian in the hospital room, asked about the illegitimate son, as did Yaffa, the shipping magnate's wife. Others had heard of the social scientist from Vienna who had written an obituary for, no, against Dov Zedek. One of them asked, 'So, what's with his Nazi son?'

'He's not a Nazi,' Ethan replied.

'But you yourself wrote that he's an anti-Semite.'

'He's not an anti-Semite.'

At that an Iraqi Jew, a family acquaintance, said, 'They're all anti-Semites, Ethan. They absorb it with their mother's milk. If not before.'

Uncle Yossef said, 'But Felix did introduce him as his son, after all.' And Yaffa wanted to know, 'Do you find it unpleasant?' Ethan could not tell them the truth. They would not have believed him in any case. A new family legend arose from these few conversations. Ethan explained that Rudi, his half-brother, had unfortunately had to leave Israel shortly after their father's death. There was nothing he could do. Yossef added, 'It's almost as if Felix held on just long enough to be with his family and his two sons.'

'You think?' Ethan asked. 'I don't know if Rudi will be able to come to the burial.' He assured him, 'We have nothing against it.' And added, 'We hope he will.'

Dina also stuck to that version of the family legend, though she had not conferred with Ethan, and when Ethan handed her the receiver, Dina assured her brother Yossef that they would naturally ask Rudi to return to Israel for the burial. But the boy must be very busy. He had spent weeks in Israel so he could get to know his father and had neglected his work and his career. He surely had duties waiting for him in Vienna.

Naturally, it wasn't simple, Yossef agreed, but then Yaffa called Dina. There are several flights a day to Tel Aviv. Rudi could most certainly find time to attend his father's burial. She had just talked with Moishe and Udi and also with Eli, Felix's barber for so many years, and they all agreed with her. If Felix had recognised the boy, then Dina should not stand in the way, even if the situation was difficult for her. The boy is part of the *mishpoche*. Rudi had gone to so much trouble for his father. And anyway, Dina was Felix's great love, his wife, Yaffa told her. He'd always stayed with her, with Dina. That's the only thing that counts and now it was important to rise above jealousy and be magnanimous.

There was no avoiding the topic. But revealing that neither Ethan nor Rudi were the dead man's biological sons was unthinkable. What could Ethan say? After all, he had only known about his real parentage since yesterday. Furthermore, speaking about those entanglements now would have seemed to him like a betrayal. And if he were keeping his own secret for himself, did he have the right to bare Rudi's? Rudi himself should explain who Felix was for him. Rudi could decide if he wanted to be a brother, a son, one of the Rosens.

Ethan had an aversion to these family busybodies, their interference and intrusiveness. In other families, the relatives would have waited, would have kept themselves in check, only to gossip that much more avidly behind the others' backs. But they would at least have kept up appearances. Not here. Here they all kept sticking their noses in each other's asses, only to commiserate that they didn't exactly smell like rosewater. Ethan was unspeakably annoyed. At the same time, the feeling that Felix would have wanted him to call Rudi and inform him kept getting stronger.

'I have to tell him. He has the right to know what happened. He should decide if he wants to come to the burial and if he wants to present himself as a son.'

Dina disagreed: 'He didn't want to be a Rosen any more. Remember? He said it just yesterday.'

'Ima, yesterday I still had a father.'

Rudi Klausinger sat at his desk, a new laptop in front of him. The technician in the computer store had thrown the old one away immediately. At best, the thing might be interesting as a specimen of controlled waste, he had said. The article was written and submitted. The editor had responded enthusiastically when Rudi told him he wanted to send in a kind of reportage about his search for his Jewish father, an article centered on the question of what history actually is.

'That sounds interesting. It will be a balanced presentation of a topic that is usually only treated dogmatically. It could show what results from personally engaging with historical facts. Do I need to know where I've come from to understand where I'm going?'

Rudi let his editor talk. He promised to send the piece in the very next day. Then he sat down and worked through the night. His thoughts became clearer as he wrote. He recounted his search for the Rosens. He described the sense of Jewishness that came over him, so much so that he had even considered converting. He mentioned Rabbi Berkowitsch and his plans to recreate the Messiah in a test tube. And had he himself not wanted to be reborn as Hebrew? What if he had been Felix Rosen's genetic son? Would that have made him an anti-Nazi from birth? More Jewish? What if he found out now that his father was the commandant of a concentration camp?

In his article, Rudi asked if identifying with the victims might be counterproductive. In Israel, in Germany and in Austria. Was the constant evocation of the mass murder inspiring today's youth with the idea of dressing up as new Nazis? Was the memory of the Second World War not stoking hatred on all sides, especially in the Middle East? Were we in danger of poisoning the present with the past?

At the conclusion, he returned briefly to his personal situation. Nothing bound him to Felix Rosen any longer. Nor did anything bind him to the stranger, whoever he was, who, with Rudi's mother, conceived him. Rudi did not know him. He did not miss him. Not any more. He was cured of that for good.

The article, Rudi was perfectly aware, was too harsh and much too long. He sent it in anyway. The editor could decide. The editor could tell him if he was violating a taboo that should not be broached. Not in Austria. Possibly in Israel, but not here. Rudi felt the need to direct his anger at someone. He wanted to be brought to his senses, but could not resist playing with fire and secretly hoped his article would be published uncut.

He tried to turn his mind to other things and phoned Wilhelm Marker, the head of the Institute.

Marker sounded convivial. 'Doctor Klausinger? I've been trying to reach you for weeks.'

'I just wanted to enquire. About my candidacy.'

'That's exactly why I called, Professor Klausinger.'

'But I called you, Professor Marker.'

'The position is still vacant. Rosen is in Israel.'

'I was with him, Professor Marker.'

'What? With him?'

'Well, actually, with his parents.'

'How's that? As a friend?' Wilhelm Marker asked.

'No,' Rudi answered, 'as a son.'

The head of the Institute was speechless. He needed some time before he could speak again. Still, he did not inquire further but suggested to Rudi a few times when they could meet and negotiate his terms of employment.

As soon as he hung up, Rudi's mobile phone rang. He was certain it was the call he had been expecting from his editor and answered without looking at the display. 'This is Klausinger.'

'Hello, Rudi. It's Ethan.'

Silence. He considered cutting off the connection straight away.

'Don't hang up. Listen to me.'

'Why should I?'

'It's about Father.'

'What have I got to do with him?'

Ethan was about to answer, but Rudi talked over him. As the former whispered, 'Felix is dead,' the latter roared, 'Felix is dead for me.'

'No, not because of you. It's not your fault,' Ethan said.

'What's not my fault?'

'That he's dead.'

'What?'

'Yes.'

'What do you mean, yes?'

'Father passed away.'

'No!' Rudi fell back in his chair and his 'No!' rang out again and again.

Then they both fell silent.

'How did it happen?'

'Heart failure. On the night you left.'

'No!'

Rudi stood up. He paced the room. Ethan could hear his steps. Rudi talked to himself. He could not believe it. Felix had been so indestructible. After all, just recently he had …

Ethan said, 'He'll be buried tomorrow. But we want to give those coming from abroad time to fly in.'

'Of course.'

'It would be nice …'

'Yeah …'

'It would have meant a lot to him.'

Rudi remembered the article.

Ethan said, 'You were like a son to him.'

Rudi sighed, 'Yes, well …'

Ethan started in on him. 'Cut the nonsense.' And then, 'I'd like to list your name in the death notice. In the newspaper. Is that ok?'

'Of course.'

'This is not about heredity. Don't you want to sit shiva for him?' Rudi would have to decide soon, Ethan told him. He told Rudi when the ceremony would be. There was still time to book a flight.

Rudi sat at his desk for several minutes, completely wrung out. Should he go to Tel Aviv or not? Suddenly he remembered the article. On no account could it appear now. Not after Felix Rosen's death. He ran to the telephone and dialled the editor's number.

'It's about my article. Something terrible has happened.'

'Great piece. You nailed it. Especially in connection with the death notice. My condolences, by the way.'

'Which death notice?'

'I thought you knew. Your name is on it. Ethan Rosen called it in earlier. The notice for his father.'

'In your paper?'

'Yes, tomorrow. Don't worry, it'll appear. Good idea, that, to put the notice in the local paper in the town where he was born and then expelled from and where he returned to live later. – And thank you for your article. Really, a great piece. I can't wait to see the reaction.'

'But my text is in blatant contradiction with the death notice. He's dead. Do you understand?'

'I saw the connection. I can read. Very subtle. That ambivalence. Who hasn't felt it?'

'But don't you have to cut it – make it sharper?'

'Without his death, I'd never have published your article. It's not topical. And way too long. But now – great piece!'

'My text can not be published.'

'What? Are you nuts?'

'It's not OK. I rescind it.'

'Too late. It's already in production.'

'I forbid you to publish it under my name.'

'Under whose name, then?'

'You have to stop the machines!'

'Not possible. In a few hours, the edition will be for sale on the street. There's nothing we can do at this point.'

'But the later editions?'

'I can't have a two-page spread just disappear. How do you think that would work? Should we black it all out? Are we playing Metternich?'

'It's still my commentary. Mine!'

'That's right. And it's announced as such on the front page and will appear in the paper. Don't worry. Your name is in bold face,' the editor said. Rudi realised it was hopeless. He could not take it back. He sighed, and at that moment, maybe the editor, Fred Sammler, felt sorry for him, because he said, 'If you'd like, we could take the death notice out of the morning edition. Would that suit you? If the contradiction bothers you so much then we'll get rid of it. For the readers to make the connection between the Felix Rosen in your article and the one in the notice, they'll have to read your essay to the end. But at the moment your name is in bold under the headline and in the notice. That stands out, of course. What do you think?'

Rudi was silent. Should he slip out of the death notice and not commemorate Felix at all? 'No,' he answered decisively.

Perhaps he didn't book his flight to Israel despite his article, but because of it. He wanted to go to the cemetery and then sit shiva. But what if it came to a confrontation at the funeral? What if one of the guests brought up his article? He hoped the Rosens would not have seen the article then.

A few hours later, Rudi knew: his wish that his article might be overlooked had been naïve. It was the personal side of the story that interested everyone most. His declaration that he did not miss Felix Rosen and wanted nothing more to do with him alongside his simultaneous announcement that he would never forget Felix caused a scandal.

He looked at the article online. A heated debate about his article raged. The comments seethed. Rudi was denounced, insulted and mocked. Some saw him as a secret anti-Semite, others as a pseudo-Jew. For some he seemed too Jewish, for many others he wasn't Jewish enough. Some objected that he was making a case for whitewashing history, others praised him for exactly that – he didn't know which was worse.

The articles getting the most comments were featured on the newspaper's homepage. His climbed quickly to the top. Someone who identified himself as *Mario Nette* attacked him personally. He knew Rudi from their time at university. Rudi Klausinger had always been a denunciator. At the Institute he had smelt fascists all around him. Rudi read along as one defamation brought another. In the meantime, some claimed he came from a family of Nazis and had previously attracted attention for his frequent anti-Jewish attacks, whereas others held him up as a paradigm of Jewish self-hatred. An agreement between the two sides was already in sight – at his expense – when he decided to go out and buy the print edition.

A two-page spread was devoted to Felix and him. Rosen's picture was on the left, and his on the right. The old man looked friendly. His picture, however, had been taken during an academic seminar just as he was whispering a sneering comment to one of his neighbours. He looked as if he found Felix revolting.

Rudi's phone rang. An old friend asked if he was doing well, but even the question seemed like a reproof, as if he had doubts about Rudi's sanity. 'Are you actually still doing well?' And just when Rudi began to think his friend had not called about the article after all, the latter brought it up. Tentative. Cautious. Concerned. He murmured, 'My condolences, if I can put it that way.' And then, 'I have to say, you are very …' He hesitated, searching for the right word; '… audacious.'

Early the next morning, the editor of the culture section in a respected German paper telephoned. 'Dear Mr Klausinger, I wanted to ask if you'd be willing to sharpen the article you published in Austria yesterday for us.'

'It wasn't sharp enough?'

The editor suggested he follow up on a few points and clarify a few others. But Rudi declined. He was mourning Felix Rosen. He had nothing more to say. He wished the whole affair could just be forgotten.

'I'm afraid it's too late for that, Mr Klausinger.' The article had been linked to German media sites. Bloggers in all the German-language spheres and in Israel had taken positions. He shouldn't forget that Felix Rosen was the father of Ethan Rosen, the famous sociologist, whose books were very well received and whose theories were sensational. And Felix Rosen was a survivor, that was important, too. Rudi had landed in the focal point of a new debate. 'Congratulations, Mr Klausinger. That's quite something!'

Another German and an Austrian newspaper called, requesting interviews, and a commercial broadcaster was planning a talk show with the title: 'Is Auschwitz dying? What will be left of the memory when the survivors are gone?'

Rudi stopped listening. He caught only the last sentence the television producer dropped in almost casually. 'I've already spoken to Ethan Rosen.' Ethan had agreed. He would take part in the discussion if Rudi signed on as well. On a satellite channel. She said, 'I sent him your article.'

No, Rudi told her, he wouldn't speak. He couldn't. He hung up and turned his computer off. If he wanted to go to Israel, he'd have to leave now, but he sat in his room, ready to go, but unable to pick up the phone and call a taxi. He'd stay in Vienna. The others would accuse him of having betrayed Felix; they'd be right. He had denounced

Felix, exposed him, had trumpeted the fact that Felix was neither Ethan's nor his own father. Still, maybe the truth was not clear enough for the readers? All the same, the text contradicted the death notice.

Rudi sat next to his packed suitcase, ticket in trembling hand. He was bleary-eyed from lack of sleep. He decided to put his shoes on and get his coat. He went to the wardrobe. He slowly tied his shoelaces as if it were a task that required the utmost concentration. He acted like an explosives expert defusing a mine. When Rudi was done tying his shoes, he sat back on the couch. He looked at his watch. If he wanted to go to Israel, he had to be at the airport at least two hours before his flight. It was half an hour by taxi to Schwechat. If he didn't order one now, the plane would take off without him. He sat there and reached for the phone. The head of the Institute answered, 'This is Marker.'

'Hello, Professor. This is Klausinger. I wanted to let you know that I can't come in before next week.'

'I read your article today.'

'Yes?'

'Fascinating. Almost unsettling. Especially with the death notice. The contradiction.'

'There is no contradiction. The one has nothing to do with the other.'

'Is that so? In any case, fascinating.' There was hesitation in Marker's voice. 'The way you deal with questions of identity and your own origins is interesting.' How strange. Apparently, his very provocation had made him an expert in the eyes of the famous professor. Marker asked, 'No doubt you want to go to the burial?' He didn't even wait for Rudi's answer before he said, 'I completely forgot to express my condolences.'

Rudi burst into sobs and was unable to answer Marker, and couldn't even thank him for his expression of sympathy. Something overpowered him; he didn't know what more to say and stammered a goodbye. After Marker hung up, Rudi wept uncontrollably for the man he had a loved for a few days as his father and had hated in the end because he wasn't. Rudi suddenly realised that he was grieving for his father. Rudi's father had died with Felix Rosen; with the latter's death Rudi's search was over, whoever Felix Rosen or his biological father may have been.

They met in the entrance. They embraced. The whole family had gathered. Uncle Yossef and Aunt Rachel hugged Rudi tightly. Nimrod Karni, the shipyard owner, nodded at everyone from above. Yaffa, his wife, fell on the necks of family and friends all the more effusively. She wept louder than Dina. Ethan looked more sunburnt than usual. He managed to look red and pale at the same time. He held Noa close as she leant against him. With Felix's death, the playfulness between them had ended. She would never call him Johannes Rossauer again. They stood at a slight distance from the body, which lay under a black cloth on the bier. They propped each other up. Dina was the only one who kept her composure and her countenance.

Even the discharged soldier Shmuel, who had spent time in India, was there. His parents stood next to him and his sister, who had come with her husband and an infant a few weeks old to pay Felix their last respects. This led some to remark that that branch of the family was a bit over-represented. The newborn hung in a sling over the mother's belly. Only the crown of his head poked out, like the top of a feather duster.

The baby was called Noam. Yossef nodded to the young parents and said, 'When he's grown, he won't have to serve in the army.' This was his standard comment, which he had been making for decades, since the founding of Israel, over the crib of every newborn, and Yossef was glad to be able to use it today. 'Yes, when this little one's older, he'll be spared the army.'

'Of course he won't have to do his military service,' Shmuel said, 'because by that time, there won't be a state of Israel any more.' Someone murmured something about self-hatred. Ethan had to smile and Noa was glad to be distracted from her grief by this little skirmish.

Across the room stood a man in Orthodox garb, surrounded by his ten sons, all of them with sidelocks. They had come with Efrat, a distant relative of Felix's, who was lingering with the women. She was the only one there in a wig, a heavy skirt and tights. Much too warm for the weather. When they were children, Efrat and Ethan had played doctor for the first time together, and they had shown each other what it looked like down there so they could then play mother and father. They had lain on the couch and pretended they were begetting children. Later, as a seventeen-year-old, Efrat, blonde and thin, was always in a mini skirt. She was interested in art and theatre, studied interpretive dance and acting and was soon the rising young star of a modern theatre company. She supplemented her earnings as a model on the catwalk. Those were hot summers. When she ran into Ethan, she gushed about how open and multifaceted a country Israel was. Why did he have to gad about abroad when everything he could want was right here in this country? What was he looking for elsewhere?

A few years later she had fallen in love with an elite pilot in the army, a young wild man with long hair and leftist views, who ran around in torn jeans and played in a rock band. Only after their wedding did it come out that he had fallen under the influence of a rabbi, who had told him, the pilot, that there was a way he could avoid falling from the heavens even if his plane were to crash. When, soon after, he showed up for his regular training in the flight simulator in religious dress, complete with *peyot* and kaftan, the guard on duty opened the door only briefly to say, 'I'm sorry, we don't give!' For this ambitious young man, who had actually wanted to rise very high, that was the end of his career. He stood there now in his caftan, a thin man with a sad full beard, surrounded by his ten children and in eye contact with Efrat, who had grown very fat.

People had come from other continents – business partners from the United States, Europe and even the Far East – to attend the funeral. Half of the hospital ward was there: the doctors, but also the nurses who had taken care of Felix, Nurse Frida among them. A large crowd had gathered. Katharina retreated to a corner. Ethan, who had been standing rigidly and accepting condolences with a bitter expression, saw her. He went over to her, Dov's last lover, and hugged her. 'We haven't been meeting in the best places, lately,' he whispered in her ear, and she rested her head on his shoulder. Before returning to his spot, he asked her to join them at his parents' place afterwards to sit shiva with the family.

Everyone had taken their places. Rabbi Yeshayahu Berkowitsch stepped forward. Behind him stood the heavy-set Hasid from the airplane, who would have liked to bind Ethan to tradition with leather prayer straps as if in sado-masochistic love play. Berkowitsch, standing behind a lectern, cleared his throat. He hesitantly placed one word after another as his assistant rocked back and forth, as if he were chomping at the bit to perform a dance that was his own particular specialty. Berkowitsch talked about grief, of the pain suffered by those left behind, of the comfort that would now come to them. 'For dust thou art, and unto dust shalt thou return.' Felix Rosen had experienced the way death comes over men, Berkowitsch said, and pointed out, in his forceful way, how ephemeral all matter is, and how insignificant man is. He called out, 'What is man? Lord, I am as nothing before you. I am nothing, a nothing come from nothing.' And with this, the Hasidic satellite of this religious lodestar was overcome with enthusiasm and a sentence escaped him. 'Yes, he is nothing, less than nothing!'

Berkowitsch, however, did not let himself be deterred. He praised the dead man's deeds, recounted his life. 'It is our duty, as has been written, to speak only good of the dead, but it is impossible for me to pass over the horrors that were inflicted upon him.' Berkowitsch spoke about the extermination, and his remarks culminated in the phrase, 'All of us, whether born then or now, whether Felix Rosen or this infant among us today, were meant to have been exterminated, and we are all, we Jews, survivors!'

The rabbi now had everyone's attention, and even Noam, the baby who had just been declared a victim of the persecution, started screaming, as if he wanted to raise his voice against all the Nazis in the world. Tears welled in the eyes of more than a few guests. Ethan stared at Dina. He whispered, 'Where is he going with this?'

Berkowitsch spoke of the enemies who, even today, still wanted to murder all Jews, including the newborns. He spoke of the new Nazis, of Amalek's children and his children's children, who must be fought. The cemetery hall turned into a bunker. 'No pity for the murderers!' Berkowitsch exclaimed, as if Felix Rosen had been killed in a war against the Arabs.

This was not the same Berkowitsch Ethan had met just a few days earlier. He had abandoned his hope of messianic genetic manipulation, of a test-tube fertilisation that would redeem the world, and was focused instead on the Apocalypse, on the Extermination, on the Catastrophe. Berkowitsch glowed. Sweat poured off him. He waved his arms. In the face of death, we must arm ourselves with commandments and prayer. The Jewish state must be defended, not just militarily, but spiritually. 'With prayer, not just rockets.' For what, otherwise, did the martyrs die; those who do not want the Nazis to be the ultimate victors must return to the scriptures. He spoke the next sentences forcefully and with great fervour, while his disciple in the crowd behind him flailed and nodded so violently that a sidelock hit Uncle Yossef in the eye. 'Felix Rosen is not dead. If we wish it, he will live on in us. In our belief. We owe it to him.'

When Berkowitsch finished, the Hasid stopped his rocking. Efrat and her husband smiled dreamily, but the rest of the mourners looked a bit piqued.

Yossef came forward to make a speech. Dina and Ethan looked at each other. Noa sighed. Embarrassed, Yossef ran his hand through his hair. He pulled a sheaf of papers from his breast pocket and began to speak of Felix, of his goodness and readiness to help others, of Felix as a husband and a father. Yossef said, 'No one else was as unconditionally devoted to his son.' At this sentence, Yossef faltered. He looked around as if searching for his audience. He turned to Dina, looked her in the eye and tried to put his speech back in his jacket pocket, but missed, and the pages fluttered onto the ground and sailed under the bier on which the body lay. Yossef stared at his speech as if he now regretted having thrown it away. He looked at everyone around him. They all held their breath. Ethan shook his head. Dina rolled her eyes. They were both worried that Yossef would start talking about Rudi, but instead he announced, 'Felix was an atheist.'

Muttering spread through the crowd. But Yossef did not relent. 'It's the truth!' Uncertainty made his voice cutting, his tone sharp. Felix Rosen had come here precisely because he didn't want to live in a ghetto, a Polish shtetl in Hebron. He wanted to be Hebrew. Several friends and family members started nodding. Yossef said, 'That's what he was fighting for. To his last drop of blood.' At this point something tipped inside Yossef. His voice swelled and he was caught up in enthusiasm for his own rhetoric.

It was as if Felix had not succumbed to a disease, but had died in battle. If Felix were here now, Yossef proclaimed, he would declare that it was worth sacrificing his life to this battle. 'He had a very low opinion of Orthodox rabbis,' Yossef told them. 'For Felix, you and your settlers were racists, fascists, Khomeinis.'

Before Yossef could say another sentence, the heavy-set Hasid shouted, 'Heretic!' Rabbi Berkowitsch muttered, 'Moishe, are you *meshugge*? Be quiet!' But his Hasid elbowed his way through the mourners and pushed Yossef away from the lectern. Uncle Yossef shrank back, and someone said, 'Just look at that swollen matzoh dumpling, a rampant teratoma.'

'Anti-Semite!' the Hasid bellowed, and Uncle Yossef shouted back, 'Mutant! Degenerate!'

'Jewish Nazi,' Efrat chimed in, but Shmuel, her cousin, countered, 'You all call us Nazis, but you still expect us to protect you and your settlements.'

'Go have one of your smokes, it'll calm you down,' she told Shmuel.

Some tried to appease the quarrellers, but that only made things worse. 'Enough. We don't need to put up with this!' Efrat's husband shouted to the Hasid, Moishe, while Nimrod said to Uncle Yossef, 'What do you expect? They're straight from the Middle Ages.' Someone advised the Hasid, 'Don't let him provoke you, he's not even a heretic, just an ignorant nebbish.'

The businessmen who had come from abroad did not understand a word, especially since the argument was in Hebrew. They had come to pay their last respects to Felix Rosen. They had prepared themselves to take part in a Jewish funeral. They had studied the rituals. But not a single handbook or manual mentioned such a hue and cry around the body. One of them asked Katharina, 'Is that branch of the family arguing over the inheritance?' She glared at him as if he had made an anti-Semitic remark.

In the middle of the bickering and uproar, a voice suddenly rang out. Someone had gone up to the lectern and raised his voice over the quarrelling. 'Felix is dead. Do you hear? He's lying right here. Here. He is among us. Felix. He is dead.' Suddenly he was there, someone nobody had noticed earlier; they'd missed him and now everybody was looking at him and paying attention.

Rudi stood before them, and everyone was silent, shocked, surprised, revolted. 'Felix is dead! You hear? I only met him a short time ago. Still, Felix was like a father to me, granted, only because I was looking for one. He did not go the synagogue. He didn't live only in Israel. He had business ventures on every continent and worked with men from many countries. His Jerusalem was always elsewhere and everywhere at once. He was at home in interval spaces, where one human being meets another.'

With each word the gathering in the hall calmed down, and even the rabbi, Yeshayahu Berkowitsch, nodded at each new thought; his Hasid listened with his head cocked. Only Ethan was distracted from the words that seemed to be consoling the others. He was thinking of Dov's cassettes instead, the message from beyond that Felix had sent him after his friend's death. 'But how does a second voice sound when the first has been silenced? How, when we are no longer? It will happen soon enough. All dead.'

Rudi said, 'Felix is dead. You hear? Felix is dead. But for me, he lives on and I love him.' The cantor immediately began to sing. A lamentation that filled the room. Notes in the twilight. Sounds of dusk. *El male rachamim.*

And when Ethan said Kaddish afterwards with the rabbi and the others, when he followed the body, when he tore his collar as a sign of mourning, when all the others filed past to comfort him after throwing a shovelful of dirt into the grave, when he then, together with Rudi, with Shmuel, with Nimrod and with Moishe, the Hasid, grabbed the spade and filled the grave, he thought of Dov, whose burial he had taken part in only weeks before, but this time, unlike then, tears filled his eyes. He looked over at Noa, who was watching him, standing close to Ethan's mother, who stared stonily into space and held herself upright.